CW01395348

BERLIN
SHUFFLE

ULRICH ALEXANDER BOSCHWITZ was born in Berlin in 1915. He left Germany in 1935 for Oslo, Norway, studied at the Sorbonne in Paris, and wrote two novels, including *The Passenger*. Boschwitz eventually settled in England in 1939, although he was interned as a German "enemy alien" after war broke out—despite his Jewish background—and subsequently shipped to Australia. In 1942, Boschwitz was allowed to return to England, but his ship was torpedoed by a German submarine and he was killed along with all 362 passengers. He was twenty-seven years old.

PHILIP BOEHM has translated over thirty novels and plays by German and Polish writers, including Herta Müller, Franz Kafka and Hanna Krall.

BERLIN SHUFFLE

ULRICH ALEXANDER BOSCHWITZ

TRANSLATED FROM THE GERMAN
BY PHILIP BOEHM

PUSHKIN PRESS

Pushkin Press
Somerset House, Strand
London WC2R 1LA

Berlin Shuffle was originally published in Swedish translation
in 1937; it was first published in Germany as *Menschen neben
dem Leben* in Stuttgart, 2019 by Klett-Cotta Verlag

First published by Pushkin Press in 2026

Hardback ISBN 13: 978-1-78227-914-3
Trade Paperback ISBN: HB ISBN 13: 978-1-80568-051-2

A CIP catalogue record for this title is available from the British Library

The authorised representative in the EEA is eucomply OÜ,
Pärnu mnt. 139b-14, 11317, Tallinn, Estonia,
hello@eucompliancepartner.com, +33757690241

Offset by Tetragon, London
Printed and bound in the United Kingdom by Clays Ltd, Elcograf S.p.A.

Pushkin Press is committed to a sustainable future for our
business, our readers and our planet. This book is made from
paper from forests that support responsible forestry.

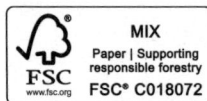

MIX
Paper | Supporting
responsible forestry
FSC
www.fsc.org   FSC® C018072

www.pushkinpress.com

1 3 5 7 9 8 6 4 2

PREFACE

Philip Boehm

Berlin in the late 1920s was home not only to the flourishing nightlife we know from *Cabaret*—it was also a leading center of science, architecture, technology, and the fine arts. While Brecht and Weill's *Threepenny Opera* was breaking box office records, Albert Einstein was presenting his paper on unified field theory to the Prussian Academy of Sciences. The most industrialized city on the continent boasted a new airport at Tempelhof, subsidized housing projects, and the impressive Berliner Funkturm tower, which would soon broadcast the world's first television program.

But the Golden Twenties turned out to be not so gilded for the hundreds of thousands who lost their jobs in the wake of the world economic crisis of 1929, sending the unemployment rate to over 30 percent by 1932. Evictions soared, and prostitution, which was already widespread, surged—as did organized crime. Beggars and vagrants were a common sight.

It is these destitute and down-and-out Berliners who are shuffling through the streets of Ulrich Alexander Boschwitz's early novel, slowly making their way to the Jolly Huntsman pub, where some come to drink, some to listen to the music, some to dance. There's the world-weary Fundholz hoping his begging will earn him enough for a little schnapps, and Tönnchen, forever fixated on food. Frau Fliebusch has come convinced she'll find her husband who never returned from the Great War, while Handsome Wilhelm is attending a meeting of criminal *Ringverein*. Fritz Grissmann has plans to snag a woman: He starts waltzing with the wife of the embittered blind veteran Sonnenberg . . . and disaster ensues.

But the disaster on the mind of the twenty-two-year-old author is larger than a barroom brawl. His scenes of conflict between characters "caught under the wheels of life" invite the narrator's tragically prescient reflection:

"To date, the World War and the Inquisition have achieved the greatest success when it comes to large-scale eradication of humanity. It is to be expected that in the coming years we will experience entirely new episodes of annihilation."

This authorial debut displays the same sharply drawn portraits that characterize Boschwitz's later novel *The Passenger*. The rediscovery of that work, as well as this one, is in large part due to the efforts of the German editor and publisher Peter Graf, who learned of the book from Boschwitz's niece. Graf located the original manuscript of *The Passenger*, revised it in accordance with the author's written wishes, and published it to international acclaim. The rediscovered novel is now available in more than twenty languages, roughly eighty years after the author's death.

Following that success, Graf turned to this book—the author's first novel, which had appeared in Swedish translation in 1937 under the title *Människor utanför* ("People outside"), earning the author comparisons to Hemingway. In 2019, Graf published the first original German edition, keeping Boschwitz's German title *Menschen neben dem Leben* ("People alongside life"). This translation follows that publication, with some slight additional editing.

Here, as in *The Passenger*, the author's cinematic structure

displays carefully calibrated shifts of perspective, as close-ups
revealing the inner thoughts of the protagonists give way to long
shots that vividly evoke the vibrant and often violent city that
was Berlin. We hear the din of the city: the rumble of buses and
honking of cars whose drivers surge impatiently ahead, heedless
of pedestrians. To escape the hubbub, or to snag a little shut-eye,
people turn to the parks. But even there we encounter characters full of aggression and resentment—the festering disaffection
that would feed the Nazi storm. "It's all the fault of the Freemasons and the Jews," rants one out-of-work locksmith.

Ulrich Alexander Boschwitz was born in 1915 to a Jewish father
and a Protestant mother. His father, who had converted to
Christianity, was drafted at the beginning of World War I and
died of a brain tumor just weeks after the birth of his son.
In 1935, in the wake of the Nuremberg Laws, Ulrich's sister
moved to Palestine, while he and his mother escaped to Scan-
dinavia. Other moves followed: France, Luxembourg, Belgium,
and finally England. When the war broke out, he and thousands
of other German and Austrian refugees were deemed "enemy
aliens" by England and were interned on the Isle of Man. Later
he was deported to Australia aboard the *Dunera* alongside
hundreds of other refugees—including a grandson of Sigmund
Freud, who had been similarly classified. The men were subjected to various abuses by their captors, such as theft and
beatings, and many personal effects were tossed overboard.
Boschwitz himself lost a manuscript he had been working on. In
Australia, the deportees were placed in an internment camp in
New South Wales. Finally, in 1942, the British authorities reclas-
sified the refugees as "friendly aliens," and Boschwitz was freed.
He decided to return to England aboard the MV *Abosso*, but on
October 29, 1942, that ship was sunk by a German submarine,
and Boschwitz perished, at the age of twenty-seven, along with
361 other passengers. With him sank the manuscript of a new

novel he had written during his internment, which he had titled *Traumtage* ("Dream days").

On July 13, 2019, a *Stolperstein*, or "stumbling stone," was laid in Berlin at Hohenzollerndamm 81 to memorialize Boschwitz, his mother Martha, and his sister Clarissa, whose daughter Reuella Shachaf was present. In her speech she noted, "It hurts to think how many books were lost by his death."

The two books we do have only amplify that sense of loss. Like *The Passenger*, *Berlin Shuffle* is a testament both to a remarkable talent and to a turbulent time—a message in a bottle finally retrieved, and startlingly relevant.

BERLIN SHUFFLE

ONE

Walter Schreiber was a good-natured man. His entire being radiated affability and understanding. He was living his life, and he didn't claim that he alone had the right to do so. He conceded that others, too, were entitled to exist—as long as they didn't deal in vegetables.

His shop in the basement was doing well despite being located in a decidedly poor part of town. The nearby tenements were crammed with people who earned very little, because times were tough. Many were on the dole, forced to live off the state, while others received no support and couldn't find work. Nevertheless they managed to scrounge up enough to buy potatoes and cheap vegetables from Walter Schreiber. Even in the toughest times, people couldn't break their habit of eating.

Walter Schreiber didn't rack his brains figuring out how they did it. He stood downstairs in his shop, selling produce with a friendly smile across his broad, benevolent face. His prices weren't higher than anyone else's, and he categorically refused to grant credit—for him, this was a question of fairness.

"What's good for the goose is good for the gander," he liked to say. "Since I can't possibly let two hundred people buy on credit, I don't let anyone. After all, what I give to one person I can't deny to the next, and these days everybody's strapped, including me."

But now and then he did give things away. Mostly when they could no longer be sold. The concept of quality had reached even his neighborhood, and although his clients weren't particularly choosy, in autumn they still refused to buy potatoes that had been harvested the previous year and had since sprouted quite profusely. And so, when even rock-bottom prices no longer tempted any buyers, he was able to part from the goods in question and simply gave them away.

A set of stairs led down from the street into Schreiber's shop, which was quite spacious—almost too big for his purposes. He had outfitted the main room to look as professional as possible. It was well lit and nicely lined with wallpaper. The vegetables, fruit, and baskets of potatoes were attractively arranged.

The previous tenant—a coal merchant—had also utilized the small side room, which was connected to the main room by a door and a few steps. But since it was a whole meter lower and so damp that it was completely unsuited for keeping produce, Schreiber only used it to store baskets for vegetables and crates for dried fruit.

Every time he had to enter that room, it struck him as nothing but a nuisance. A single window opened onto the street, and the cracked, murky glass let in an ugly light. The air was so stuffy and unhealthy, he always had to cough when he went in to fetch something. He would have preferred to take the room, which his landlord had thrown in practically for free, and wall it off from his shop. Every morning he had to spend time airing out the mustiness that had seeped into the main room.

Schreiber stood tallying figures at his small desk, of which he was very proud, since it lent the whole shop the air of a serious commercial enterprise. It was two in the afternoon, and for a brief period there was nothing to do; the shop was quiet. Then he heard someone climbing down the stairs. He left his desk and went to meet the presumed customer, busily rubbing his hands together.

An old man stepped inside, and Schreiber eyed him with

amazement. His clients weren't exactly the most elegant—he was used to that—but this man was not so much dressed as draped. A jacket that was far too big hung loosely from his shoulders. A pair of trousers, which once upon a time had been tailored in the American fashion, was now a colorless oversize mass of cloth that covered his legs like sacks. Their former owner must have been a tall, corpulent man; otherwise there was no explaining the difference between the wearer and the worn. This man was short, and when he walked, he gave the appearance of wearing a skirt instead of trousers. The crotch came down to his knees, and the pant legs, which once were clearly too long, had been cut off, leaving a fringe of loose threads. On top of this, he wore a hat that fit him quite well and only accentuated his ridiculous, scarecrow-like appearance. His face was yellow and bony. He looked around the room with lusterless eyes.

Schreiber wondered what the man would ask for—at most a couple pounds of potatoes or carrots, he thought.

The old man walked up to him. "Guten Tag," he greeted. His voice sounded unclear and exceptionally indifferent. "I heard you have a basement room available. I might want to take it."

For a moment Schreiber didn't answer, just went on observing the man closely. An odd duck to be sure. And a stranger to the neighborhood as well. Schreiber knew the locals, and he'd never seen this man before.

"Who told you that?" he asked, eager to find out.

"I can't remember. Somebody in the shelter, I think. Were they wrong?" The man looked at Schreiber expectantly.

Schreiber nodded. "No, they weren't wrong. There is a room. But you won't be able to move in. It's fine for a basement business, but not as a place to live."

"I see." The man took a step closer. Schreiber caught a strong whiff of cheap schnapps. "Well, I'd like to have a look. I don't want to live there. Just sleep. But it has to be real cheap."

Schreiber thought a moment. God, if I could make a couple extra pennies . . . why not? Hopefully the man was honest and wouldn't break into his stock. But there were ways to make sure that didn't happen.

He nodded energetically at these last thoughts. Then he said, "Follow me. I'll show it to you." He headed to the side room, and the old man—Schreiber guessed he was between sixty-five and seventy—trudged behind him.

Schreiber stopped in front of the large, dirty door that was held together with metal strips, fished in his pockets for a key, and turned it twice in the lock. As he did so he said, by way of warning, "The air in there's a little bad."

The old man did not react. At this hour—around midday—a sallow daylight filled the room. As the two men climbed down the steps, they were struck by the dank, musty air. Baskets and wicker panniers lay piled up in a corner.

The man inspected the space. He walked alongside the walls, touching them here and there, squeezed past the baskets, and studied everything very thoroughly. Schreiber grew impatient. He went halfway back up the stairs to peek into his shop, but there were no customers.

"Well, how do you like it?" Schreiber asked.

Instead of answering, the man held out his hands, which were moist from the walls.

"Yes, I know," Schreiber said regretfully. "It's a bit clammy."

"How much are you asking?"

Schreiber wrinkled his forehead as though pondering. Finally he said, with a generous smile and a condescending tone, "I'll let you have the place for one mark fifty a week—any cheaper I'd be giving it away."

The old man agreed to the price. He rummaged in his pants for a handful of coins—each smaller than the next—and counted them out.

While Schreiber scrupulously checked the amount, he asked the old man, "When are you coming?" The latter took off his hat, lowered his shiny bald head as though in greeting, and answered, "My name is Fundholz. Emil Fundholz. I'll come this evening, together with Tönnchen and possibly with Grissmann."

When he heard that the man was planning to bring two others, Schreiber was taken aback.

"If three of you are planning to live here, it will cost more than one mark fifty."

Schreiber had never rented out a living space. But somehow he divined what landlords said in such cases.

The old man shook his head vigorously. "Only Tönnchen and I will stay here. Grissmann is just a visitor," he explained.

Schreiber took that in and noted the names. "Ah, so Grissmann is just a visitor. But for Tönnchen or whatever his name is, it will cost one mark extra."

The old man held out his open hand. "In that case give me back my money," he said calmly.

Schreiber heard a customer entering his shop. "I don't have any more time," he said, now very busy. "But I'll give you a break. So let's just leave things as they are. But no more than two people can sleep here, otherwise it will cost more. Let's say that you come every evening at seven, and I'll lock you in the basement. In the morning I'll come from the market hall at half past five and let you out."

This solution had just occurred to him, and he thought it was excellent. This way he could rent out the room without being afraid that his shop might get robbed empty in the night.

Fundholz followed him up, protesting vaguely, but Walter Schreiber was already very cheerfully attending to a working-class wife who was asking for potatoes, carrots, and bouillon cubes. Fundholz stood waiting off to the side.

The woman stared at the old man in amazement. "Nice weather today," she said.

Fundholz said nothing and just gazed blankly past her.

Walter Schreiber jumped in with a confirmation. "Very nice indeed!" he said, with a friendly laugh, as he gave the lady a sly wink.

Fundholz didn't seem to notice. Then he proceeded to take an enormous blue-and-green-striped cotton handkerchief from his pocket and blow his nose with a mighty snort. The woman laughed as she paid and left, while Walter Schreiber scowled angrily at Fundholz. Why was he sticking around? This roving ragbag was going to wind up scaring off the clientele.

"So, this business about locking us up at seven o'clock, that's not going to work!" Fundholz was speaking more firmly and resolutely than before. "You can shut us in at eleven, but not at seven!"

Schreiber realized that grown men couldn't be put to bed at seven in the evening, so he agreed. "Fine. I'll come here every evening at ten and let you in. But if you're not on time, you'll have to sleep in the Tiergarten. I've got to get going early in the morning and can't play doorman for a bunch of late-night carousers."

The old man bleated out a laugh. "Late-night carousers— that's a good one. Really good." Still laughing, he climbed up the stairs. Once he reached the street, he turned back around. "So, I'll see you at ten this evening."

Then he put his hat back on and vanished from sight.

TWO

Walter Schreiber lived in a two-room apartment just a few houses away from his vegetable shop. If it wasn't very cold or raining, he would stand on the street in front of his door and smoke. He was quick to feel confined. He had three children, the oldest of whom was seven, and they made a terrible racket in the small apartment.

But because he was a good-natured person and also proud to have such lively children, it didn't cross his mind to stop them from running wild. Only when he wanted to sleep did he require absolute peace and quiet.

His wife had been sick for a long time. Tuberculous nodules, according to the doctors. Walter Schreiber didn't believe in doctors, and he didn't believe in homeopaths. Rather he trusted his own good common sense and remedies of his own devising. According to his diagnosis, the reason his wife was wasting away to the point of coughing up blood was that she didn't eat enough. And so every day he forced her to devour a large serving of meat: After all, meat gives strength!

But it was strange. Instead of growing stronger, she grew weaker and weaker, and she always ran a fever as soon as she had eaten. Over time she developed a genuine loathing for meat and fat, to the point where every beefsteak sparked a row so severe, it was as though she wanted to murder him. Nevertheless

Walter Schreiber consistently prevailed upon his wife to consume what he considered to be the best cure.

Still, he couldn't understand how his wife could be so foolish as to not want to eat meat, considering how expensive it was, especially given his insistence on buying the very best cuts for her. After all, meat was a luxury he seldom afforded himself. He subsisted mostly on vegetables, which he could set aside for his private use at cost, in other words very cheaply. No, his wife didn't know what was good for her. She kept on demanding to see a doctor. And yet for what it would cost to see a doctor, he could buy ten beefsteaks, Schreiber calculated as he stood outside the door, deep in thought.

Somehow his pipe didn't taste right today. His draws were too irregular—no doubt in part because of the constant annoyance he was subjected to. People just don't have any idea what's good for them, he thought indignantly.

A pair of lovers was standing in the corridor, pressed tightly together. Schreiber disapproved. When he was young, people were better behaved. Besides, he knew the girl. It was Hilde Schultze from the fifth floor. He used to like her, but she'd been sassy to him once when he tried to give her an encouraging pinch on the cheek. Now there she was with some fellow. You could tell where that was going to lead. His kind gesture of affection had been rejected, and now some scoundrel out of nowhere who . . .

But it was already ten. He had to open up for the two vagrants. What kind of fellows were they anyway? He would definitely have to find out. One mark fifty was practically a giveaway. If someone really could sleep there, then the basement room was worth more than that.

He strolled over to his shop. Even from a distance he could see three figures standing in front. One was enormously fat. He looked like a big barrel of beer. So he must be the one the old man had called Tönnchen, or Little Barrel. Schreiber approached the group, and the fat man laughed as he came close. He wasn't just stout—he was swollen, distended, downright bloated. His jacket fabric was stretched so tight over his tubby arms, they looked like two sausages. His hands were small and flabby.

In the light of the streetlamp, the man's laugh struck Schreiber as utterly sinister. He was a sensible person and didn't believe in ghosts or apparitions, but now he felt a cold shiver run down his spine. The steady laughter seemed to have notched the fat man's face; his lifeless eyes were sunken behind pads of fat, and the man's entire head had a greasy gleam, which made his features appear even more vague and indistinct.

Tönnchen held out his hand. Walter Schreiber shook it, but the moist, fleshy hand automatically slid out of his grip. Schreiber wiped his hand on his pants while Tönnchen went on smiling. Finally it dawned on Schreiber: The man was feeble-minded. And now that he'd found an explanation for what he hadn't been able to comprehend, his mood improved.

Old Fundholz leaned against the wall and disinterestedly observed the goings-on. He hadn't introduced Tönnchen, or given any other sign of life, but Schreiber was reassured. An idiot and a harmless one at that—well that was all okay. Now he wanted to have a closer look at this fellow Grissmann, who was standing a few meters away and gave no indication of coming any closer.

Walter Schreiber opened the basement. I'm curious, he thought, if that third man will want to live here as well. He switched on the light. "After you." He invited the men inside, and Tönnchen went ahead, grinning, while Fundholz turned to Grissmann: "You coming?"

"I don't want to," Grissmann answered, and without saying another word he walked away.

Odd customers to be sure, thought Walter Schreiber. All three were clearly a little screwy. That "I don't want to" sounded practically whiny, like a pigheaded child refusing to eat, and yet this Grissmann was a fully grown, decent-looking man.

Fundholz followed Tönnchen, and after a moment Schreiber heard a giggle coming from the basement, followed by a smacking sound. He hurried in after the others. Tönnchen had taken an apple out of a basket and bitten into it. Now Fundholz was holding it up to Schreiber. "He's crazy, but crazy in a harmless way," he said in a serious voice.

Schreiber looked at the apple. "That's a Gravenstein, forty-five pfennig a pound. That apple costs fifteen pfennig!"

Fundholz rummaged through his bag. "Here." He handed Schreiber the money and restrained Tönnchen's arm with his free hand.

Schreiber thanked him. He made a habit of keeping track even of small amounts. And for the future he intended to take note of what had just happened and learn from it. From now on he would always enter the basement before the vagrants, as he still called them in his mind. He sized them up mistrustfully. But they didn't seem to have pocketed anything. At least Schreiber had the impression that their pockets didn't look fuller than before. In a gesture of generosity, he reached into the basket of dried fruit and gave Tönnchen a handful of prunes. Then he unlocked the door. "Careful," he warned.

Fundholz climbed down first. Tönnchen trotted behind, grinning despite having evidently just been slapped.

"Give me back the apple," he said in a high voice well suited to his overall appearance, before he shoved the prunes into his mouth.

Without a word, the old man handed him the Gravenstein.

"Good night," Schreiber said politely as he took his leave. Then he carefully set about the cumbersome task of locking the side room.

The two men could still hear him going back and forth in the shop, moving baskets around and finally bolting the upstairs door.

Fundholz lit a match and looked around. A shimmer of light fell on Tönnchen's grinning face, but Fundholz wasn't annoyed by the man's permanent grin. He was long over feelings such as annoyance and well on his way to complete indifference. His past lay behind him like a dream, and his future was foggy, uncertain, and rather uninteresting.

There had been a time—it was so far back he sometimes thought he was imagining it—when he had given money to beggars. He had earned money then, had had a home and a wife. Thousands of days had passed since then, days in which he had begged for money himself, and thousands of nights when he had had to sleep in shelters, on benches, or in basements. His life—his genuine, civilized human life—lay more than ten years behind him, and he would have to keep begging for the rest of his days.

Tönnchen took a few baskets from the pile and tried sitting down on them. They cracked and broke under his weight. Startled, he jumped up.

Fundholz didn't pay him any attention. He took off his jacket, spread out the newspaper he had brought, and constructed a bed by carefully laying the pages next to and on top of one another in one of the basement's driest spots, but the dampness immediately soaked through the paper. He left it where it lay, then took down some baskets and began placing one inside the other, turning them upside down so the bottom was on top.

Having determined that three or four nested together would hold quite well, he took a dozen panniers and secured them between the basement wall on one side and a row of crates on the other. Then he lay down and carefully distributed his weight. Because he was a calm sleeper, he had no need to fear that the structure beneath him might collapse.

Tönnchen looked at him uncomprehendingly, and when Fundholz had blown out the last match, he spoke.

"Tönnchen wants to sleep, too," he explained.

Fundholz cursed and lit another match. "I'll get hold of some blankets tomorrow," he said. "Now just lie down somehow. I want my peace and quiet."

Tönnchen obeyed. He lay down on the floor, then jumped right back up. "Cold and wet!" he announced.

Fundholz climbed down from his crates. "Don't make such a racket!" He lit another match and grumbled as he constructed a similar, albeit more stable, bedstead.

Without a word of thanks, Tönnchen lay down, and soon both fell asleep.

Tönnchen started whimpering in his sleep, probably tormented by some fearful vision, and his wheezing and snoring woke Fundholz up.

He had run into Tönnchen one day in a courtyard and befriended him. Dirty, stinking, and wrapped in tattered scraps of clothing that made Fundholz's rags look sumptuous, the colossus of fat had stood there smiling as he poked around in a garbage bin. Fundholz had never seen anything as squalid in his life. Then the man had said to him, "I'm Tönnchen! Do you have something to eat?" and for some reason this seemed to remind Fundholz of home, so he gave the man a few bits of bread, which he had just obtained somewhere.

The fat man greedily wolfed them down. And ever since he'd been traipsing after Fundholz like a dog behind his master and was good for absolutely nothing. He couldn't even beg properly. People would open the door, but as soon as they caught sight of his imbecilic grin, they would slam it right away in horror. It took Fundholz a few punches to get Tönnchen to wait for him in some other place. And since Fundholz couldn't shake him off— not that he'd seriously tried—Fundholz had kept him fed and cadged a few articles of clothing for him.

When it came to begging—or fencing, as it was known in the profession—Fundholz was far more successful. He wasn't exactly a joy to look at either, but that was offset by his age and the hangdog look he took on when asking for a small handout. Fundholz was aware that Tönnchen belonged in an asylum, and from his companion's confused chattering, he gathered that the man had earlier been in Herzberge—Berlin's largest asylum for the insane. But he couldn't bring himself to abandon Tönnchen or even to hand him over to the police.

Fundholz himself was in a perpetual small-scale war with the authorities. Not without reason, he suspected it was their intent to lock him up in the workhouse or otherwise detain him. He had already been jailed several times for vagrancy and other transgressions of the law. But Fundholz was a man who despite everything preferred his freedom to being detained. Of course at times that meant going for days eating nothing but dry bread, but he still preferred this meager fare to the food served in jail, although the latter had been quite delicious. In jail he could never resist giving in to a feeling of melancholy. He missed his freedom of movement, since over the past ten years his roaming across town had become a way of life. He'd passed through every district of the city. There was nowhere he hadn't begged, nowhere he hadn't slept. And he clung to this independence, this freedom of movement, with a dogged tenacity.

Just as he couldn't live without his freedom, he understood that the last thing in the world Tönnchen wanted was to return to Herzberge. While he didn't value Tönnchen's company, Fundholz realized that it wouldn't be right to break away from him, even if Tönnchen was a freeloader, and one with an enormous appetite. Despite the fact that Fundholz gave him the lion's share of what he collected, he kept catching the fat man rummaging through garbage bins. Fundholz never did that. He still had the remnants of certain inhibitions from his better days. He didn't steal, and he didn't eat garbage. Those were the last vestiges of his former worldview. And since he had met Grissmann, his situation had actually improved.

Recently the man had come up to him and asked if he wanted to earn three marks. Fundholz had stared at him in amazement, because for him three marks was a fortune.

Grissmann, too, was poorly dressed. He appeared to be about thirty years old, wore a flat cap, and had a gray, haggard face, but compared to Fundholz he looked positively splendid. Fundholz had had the impression that Grissmann was exceptionally jittery and fearful. At their first encounter his eyes had darted restlessly this way and that, then he had stared briefly at Fundholz, and right afterward he had begun anxiously scanning the street. Nonetheless Fundholz had immediately declared his willingness to earn the three marks, whereupon Grissmann had handed him a sizable package.

"Inside there's a suit. Take it over there to the secondhand clothes dealer and sell it. I'll wait here. Then bring the money to me, and I'll give you the three marks as promised."

Without any further questions, Fundholz had taken the suit to the shop.

After the proprietor of the establishment had examined the article of clothing, while holding forth on the worthlessness of used clothes in general and this suit in particular, he asked Fundholz gently, "So how much are you asking?" Fundholz, who had never dealt with used clothing and had no idea what the suit might be worth, simply shrugged his shoulders awkwardly, whereupon the dealer patronizingly handed him five marks.

That had seemed a lot to Fundholz. Five marks was still five marks. Grissmann, however, didn't share that view and gave him two marks instead of three, which would have been too much, as Fundholz had also realized.

Finally, after completing their business, they had shared a glass of beer. Naturally Tönnchen drank two, but since Grissmann paid for them, Fundholz didn't care. After they had introduced themselves and warmed up to one another a little, Fundholz learned that Grissmann was unemployed, that he had a place to sleep somewhere, and that he, just like Tönnchen and himself, spent all day roaming about the city.

Unlike most men of his age, Grissmann didn't seem to have any acquaintances, and Fundholz sensed that Grissmann wanted to team up with him. The old man was opposed to the idea. It pained him to have to speak. Speaking meant thinking, and he didn't want to think. He had given up thinking and ruminating over his problems. He lived very primitively. Food, money for schnapps, a place to sleep. That was all he cared about.

He spoke only when he was asking for alms, and even then very little. His attire was eloquent enough.

To be sure there were those who suspected that every beggar was really a rich man in disguise, and as a matter of policy refused to give anything or else came up with this theory as an excuse not to give. In general, however, poor people were more understanding, and the old man had never had to starve.

Fortunately it turned out that Grissmann also didn't talk much. In fact to some degree he resembled Tönnchen, even if he wasn't as childish, but rather timid and fearful.

Fundholz rolled around restlessly on his bedstead. He couldn't fall back asleep. The air was stuffy and stale, and the fat man whimpered in his sleep as though someone was trying to murder him.

Fundholz fished in his pocket for something he could smoke. He found a cigar butt, a beautiful cigar butt, almost as long as a finger, and began smoking. After a few minutes he felt his tiredness coming back. He stubbed out the cigar and put it back in his pocket. Soon he fell back asleep.

THREE

Grissmann would gladly have taken a look at the basement. But in the end he had changed his mind. With a basement like that there really wasn't much to see, and there was bound to be another opportunity. Besides, at the moment it wasn't important.

Instead Grissmann roamed restlessly through the city.

He had been unemployed for a long time. At one time he had worked as a streetcar conductor, but they'd fired him after a routine check showed that twenty marks were missing. He hadn't been able to give a satisfactory account as to the money's whereabouts, and his own defense had been so pathetic and disjointed that no one doubted that he had pocketed it himself.

For twenty marks you don't ruin a man's entire life, which was why the company had declined to report him. But they did let him go, and without notice, after generously paying out what he would have earned had he been dismissed under normal circumstances—though they had not been obligated to do so.

The fact is that Grissmann had simply lost the twenty marks. He wasn't a very attentive person. Maybe he gave someone too much change, or perhaps someone had cheated him. He really didn't know.

He lost his job at the worst possible time.

New ideas from America had arrived in Europe, ingenious systems designed to reduce human labor to the minimum and replace it with machines wherever possible. This was known as rationalization.

Machines clearly possess certain advantages. Unlike humans, they have no will of their own, not a spark of individuality. They don't go on strike, at least not as a collective, the way workers do when they want to put pressure on the factory owner to raise wages or at least not lower them. Machines strike only as single units and then simply because of defects that can be eliminated.

Humans, on the other hand, expect more from life. When the owner makes money, they want to share in the earnings. They hold political views, which they also champion. And these views are very frequently at odds with those of their employers.

So the owners purchased machines. Where ten clerks had previously been employed, there were now two accounting machines, which needed just two or three people to operate them. Where hundreds of laborers had once been kept busy, now only some forty were required. Machines made all problems seem splendidly solvable. The only thing missing was a mechanical human, but as soon as that was invented, all future production could proceed entirely without workers.

Conveyor belts determined the speed of work in the larger factories, which could now discard the nasty system of foremen pushing and prodding the workers. It was enough to speed up the conveyor belt, so that each person had to work a little faster. Whoever couldn't keep pace was let go.

Meanwhile, by their sheer existence, the unemployed kept their working colleagues in constant fear of losing their jobs. Who in that position wished to go on strike? Who still wanted to make demands?

Everyone knew: If I don't want to put up with it all, someone else will. So in the end everybody was willing to do whatever it took.

A golden moment seemed to have finally arrived. According to the laws of free competition, demand determines supply. The demand for labor was low, but the supply was very high, and therefore wages could be lowered.

Meanwhile those who did have work were forced to pay for their colleagues who didn't. The deductions to support the unemployed rose, and paychecks shrank once again. The ability of the workers to strike was quashed, as was their will to do so. So far so good: It all added up.

But it turned out there'd been a miscalculation. The workers replaced by machines could no longer buy anything—neither suits nor dresses. Their purchasing power shrank to the point where they couldn't afford the smallest luxury. Though their needs stayed the same, they lacked the means to satisfy them.

Moreover the machines didn't have enough needs to replace the human buyers. To be sure they did fall apart. New industries arose to produce machines and to produce machines for the production of machines. And these factories, too, were constructed according to the most modern tenets of rationalization.

The textile manufacturer, who had grinned as he let go a third of his personnel and—thanks to the new machines—had been able to produce twice as many wares with those he'd kept on, was suddenly shocked to realize how much demand had dwindled. True, the need was still there, but the money was lacking. Everyone was unemployed.

Grissmann had no idea about all these connections. He blamed his misfortune on the matter of the twenty marks, and the fact that he couldn't find work was undoubtedly due to his own inadequacy, for he had long been convinced of his own inferiority.

His father had instilled this in him. A tall, burly man with a puffed-up face, he had started drinking in his early youth, and had first worked as a hauler, then later as a cabman. Disinclined to drink beer and other more innocuous beverages, he only drank brandy, and beyond doubt more than was good for him.

In those days, *hauler* referred to someone who handled household moves. Then as now these people were extraordinarily strong and had a great attachment to beer. By the time they finished their hard work, their throats were burning. Usually the men received a tip, which they immediately spent on drink, and they seldom stopped with just one.

But old man Grissmann didn't drink only to quench his thirst; he drank to make himself thirst for more. And once beer was no longer able to put him in a state of intoxication, he guzzled brandy. And after the brandy undermined his health and strength, he had to change professions and took up driving a hackney cab.

Nevertheless he still had enough strength to beat his wife and his son, Fritz, whenever he was in a good mood.

Fritz was short and dwarfish, which was why old Grissmann tried beating the weakness out of the boy, but to no avail: The boy stayed weak and fearful. Then his wife died, and a little later Grissmann senior landed in jail on account of a brawl.

Fritz wound up in an orphanage. He was tormented by his lack of courage. In the orphanage he initially tried to prove himself through acts of cruelty. He tore the legs off flies one by one and thrashed the smaller boys, but that didn't make him any braver. And because everyone in the orphanage sided against him and his cruel acts usually ended with a whipping, which he had to accept, he only became more fearful.

He now suffered from insomnia. He didn't work during the day, and at night he wasn't tired and couldn't fall asleep. He actually had a room with a bed, but he shared it with two other young men. They snored when they slept and mocked him when they were awake.

They, too, were unemployed. But they had immediately intuited that here was a person who was even worse off than they were. A person hobbled by inner weakness. Grissmann was afraid of them, and they had happily registered his fear.

Both were younger than Grissmann, but they felt far superior.

Life had been tough on them, and in return they were tough on everyone else: Their jokes were brutal and seldom funny.

As he continued his roaming, Grissmann couldn't make up his mind as to what to do. He didn't want to go home. But he also didn't have much desire to go to a pub. He didn't enjoy being around people. And crowded places in particular always tended to unsettle him.

When he reached Friedrichstrasse, he slowed his stride and walked down the busy street, sticking close to the buildings. He passed by the S-Bahn arches. Here there was less activity, but then people came streaming out of a cinema. He again picked up his pace. Beyond the cinema were nothing but taverns and smaller places of entertainment, and music spilled through the open doors onto the street. Grissmann kept going. The subway station with the luminous U was already behind him.

He slowed his gait. What did he want out here anyway? Even he had no idea.

Two streetwalkers strolled past him with swaying steps. Neither was still young. Their cheeks were caked with makeup and their short skirts revealed their thighs. They wore shoes with very high heels and pale, flesh-toned stockings. Their voices wafted back to him. They were talking about apartment furnishings. "I saw a cheaper bedroom set at Wertheim's," he heard one say.

Both were swinging their purses and intently scanning the surroundings for clientele.

Grissmann followed them.

They heard his steps behind them and simultaneously turned their heads. But the sight of a shabby man clothed in an old suit didn't promise much in the way of business opportunity.

Out of habit both had smiled obligingly when they looked back, but when they caught sight of Grissmann their smiles disappeared.

He felt his cheeks go red. Even these two, he thought, consider themselves his betters.

He overtook the women. As he passed them he was suddenly gripped by a completely senseless hatred. Someone ought to put a knife in their backs, he said to himself. With a certain joy, he repeated the thought two or three times. Then his mind turned to something else, and he went on traipsing aimlessly through the city.

It was almost one in the morning when he arrived at his place. He crept quietly into the room, took off his clothes with hardly a sound, and climbed into bed.

He jumped up in a fright: He was lying on something soft. He reached out his hand and picked up a dead gray animal. It was a rat.

With an incoherent cry of rage he flung himself on the person lying next to him. As he yelled he kept swinging the rat at the man's face.

The man woke up and defended himself, but he was no match for Grissmann. Seldom had Grissmann felt such strength. In a mad frenzy he slammed his fist in the man's face. Then he again grabbed the rat and tried pressing its head into the man's mouth.

At that point the third man jumped in to help his friend, and together they managed to overpower Grissmann. They beat him until he was unconscious, then dumped him on his bed.

"It was just a joke!" one of them said scowling.

They lay back down. But both knew that they would never provoke Grissmann again.

"That fellow's perfectly capable of slitting a man's throat," said the younger of the two before falling asleep, not without a certain respect.

FOUR

⸺

Walter Schreiber unlocked his basement.

I'm curious how the two tramps spent the night, he thought. Phew—I wouldn't spend a night in that hole for the world.

He opened the door wide to let in fresh air. He sniffed. Had they been smoking? Then he opened the smaller room. Both men were still asleep, and they'd been so brazen as to use his baskets as sleeping pads.

Fundholz woke up first. He made a grumpy face, clambered down from his encampment, and stretched, still drowsy. Then he jostled Tönnchen.

The younger man blinked and said, "No rutabagas! I won't eat them!"

Tönnchen had dreamed about Herzberge. In the asylum they had again been trying to force him to eat rutabagas. That was the only food he despised, and he hated it with all his heart. He often had such dreams. People were always trying to get him to eat rutabagas—to the point of actually stuffing them into his mouth. Whole mountains of rutabagas!

He looked around, distraught. But there was only Fundholz, who said, "Get moving! We have to go."

Tönnchen stood up.

Fundholz turned to Walter Schreiber. "Can we leave the

baskets the way they are? It's impossible to sleep on the floor, it's much too wet."

Schreiber refused. "No, that won't work! The baskets will break. Besides, this isn't a furnished room. It's a basement! I didn't include the baskets in the rent. You'll have to get hold of some straw!"

Walter Schreiber was in a very bad mood today. At the market hall he had discovered that the price of apples had fallen sharply. And apples were exactly what he had in abundant supply.

The pair passed him by without a word. Where in the world do they wash up? he wondered. They probably don't.

He wasn't wrong. Fundholz very rarely washed himself. On the one hand, washing was one of the problems Fundholz didn't take seriously, and on the other, he seldom had the opportunity to do so. Of course he could wash up in the shelter, but he preferred to sleep apart, without so many others nearby. Besides, as amazing as it might seem, there were people in the shelter who were even worse off than Fundholz and who tried to remedy this disparity by stealing.

Walter Schreiber watched them leave, shaking his head in disapproval. These are genuine derelicts, he thought. Not just a couple of fellows fallen on hard times.

The two walked side by side, tired and with stiff legs. They headed to a park, where they sat on a bench and went on sleeping. Tönnchen started snoring right away. Fundholz stood up and moved a few benches farther off, where he could barely hear the snoring. He soon dozed off, but the sun bothered him. And so to his dismay he would occasionally wake up, then fall back asleep.

FIVE

Grissmann arose around ten in the morning and felt his body aching all over. Puzzled, he glanced at the mirror and then remembered.

After washing up he took another look at his face. The beating had left it bloodied in places and covered with brown and blue bruises.

In fact it's strange that I blacked out again yesterday, he thought. Whenever he flew into a rage he would lose consciousness, and he asked himself why that might be. Once, in the orphanage, he had gone after a supervisor with a spade, after the other children had spent all day harassing him and the supervisor had snapped at him because of some petty thing. But then, in the middle of the fracas, Grissmann had suddenly keeled over. They told him later that he'd also been yelling. Did he yell yesterday?

The landlady entered the room without knocking. Grissmann was still half naked, but neither took any offense. "You'll have to move out of the room by this time next week. I'm not running some psychiatric clinic here. And I'm kicking the other two out as well!"

She walked out and shut the door.

Grissmann stood there a moment, dumbfounded, then thought, What do I care?

He got dressed and went to the park to speak with Fundholz. He felt strangely drawn to the old man. Fundholz and Tönnchen had really hit rock bottom. They were literally crawling in the dirt. Compared to them he was something better. And old Fundholz had never made fun of him. That man didn't make fun of anything anymore.

Grissmann had a plan. He'd long wanted to undertake something that would help shake off the pressure that weighed on him. What had thus far stopped him from doing so was not some moral inhibition: The only thing that restrained him was fear. Without that he would have become a burglar long ago. He had fantasized a hundred times about coming into money by pulling off some bold stroke, even if it was unlawful.

He hoped this would accomplish two things at once. First, he wanted to improve his situation, which meant procuring money, and second, he wanted to prove to himself beyond all doubt that he was not a coward.

He had only stolen once: It was on the very day—not that long ago—that he'd used up his welfare money. He'd spent it too quickly and didn't know what he was supposed to live off for the next few days. The opportunity presented itself in the form of a pushcart that belonged to a laundry. Grissmann had snatched it when the fourteen- or fifteen-year-old delivery boy had gone inside an apartment building and left the cart unguarded for a moment. After first nervously checking around to see that no one was watching, Grissmann grabbed the shaft as though he were simply playing with it. Then all of a sudden he took off, his knees shaking with fear, first at a quick walk, then soon after at a run. He raced through dozens of streets before allowing himself to catch his breath.

The operation had gone well. Grissmann had been able to empty the cart without incident and safely stash away his loot. He had then sold the suits and dresses, partly through Fundholz.

Fundholz hadn't asked where the items had come from, so Grissmann wanted to discuss his new plan with him.

He came across Tönnchen first. Instead of waking him up, Grissmann just kept walking. Then he saw Fundholz sitting a few benches farther on, staring blankly into space. Grissmann sat down next to him. "Good morning," he said.

Fundholz returned the greeting and was taken aback when he noticed the blotches on Grissmann's face. But he didn't say anything and just went on gazing at nothing.

Grissmann started off with a stammer. "Fundholz, how would you like to earn a hundred marks all at once?"

Fundholz smirked. He didn't believe in miracles. Besides, it was almost time to go. He always set off on his daily tour around eleven. Any earlier didn't make sense, since so many people were in a bad mood early in the morning. Some because they had to go back to work, and others because they had no work to go back to but still had to get up.

To set off before eleven was completely pointless. He knew from experience that one door after the other would be shut in his face: Over the past ten years he'd learned the trade from the bottom up. Begging was no simple matter. You practically had to be a psychologist. Fundholz didn't know what psychology was, but unconsciously he understood quite a bit of it nonetheless.

He could tell from a person's particular facial expressions what to say and what to expect. Some people were optimists. They opened the door wide and smiled. They seemed glad about anything that came their way—including the beggar Fundholz. Unfortunately these people were in the minority, but if you encountered them, they usually gave, and gave generously. All you had to do was smile at them humbly, so they wouldn't feel offended.

Others opened the door with a degree of wariness, because they were expecting collectors or court officials. Fundholz encountered this species more often. For the most part they were pleasantly surprised to find a beggar instead of the dreaded unpaid bill, and they often gave something. To these people Fundholz showed his everyday face, with a hint of sadness in place of a smile.

Then there were people who slammed the door the minute they saw him. Here it was important to differentiate between outright rejection and a possible handout. From his brief glimpse of a resident's face, Fundholz had to determine whether the person would give something or not.

It could be that a few minutes later the door would be opened again, and he would be handed a coin. But it could also be that the resident would fling the door open just to yell, "Are you still there?"

And then there were the choleric types, who were riled up about something or other and vented their rage on the first person they encountered. For these people Fundholz appeared as if on cue. They blurted out wild threats or even notified the police, whereby the ones who threatened were nicer than the ones who decided to act.

When he'd first started begging, Fundholz had frequently been taken in by a feigned friendliness, but he now moved to a different district as soon as he encountered this strained cordiality. It was extremely suspect, and the police were always interested in beggars like him.

On the other hand, there were cases—very seldom, and Fundholz always remembered them fondly—when he chanced on people who had just run into some luck or at least believed they had. Very young married couples, successful businessmen, or people who had just fallen in love often radiated an abundance of joy and a need to have even the tramp at the door share in their newfound happiness. Such encounters brought Fundholz large sums, enough to let him take the rest of the day off.

Grissmann kept on speaking, but Fundholz wasn't listening. He had to get going soon; it was bound to be eleven already.

One hundred marks. No one earned sums like that. A hundred marks was more than a wishful dream. It was as unreal as wishing for an automobile. There was no point in getting involved.

Grissmann listed all the things a person could buy with a hundred marks. Fundholz almost burst out laughing. He knew perfectly well himself what he could get for a hundred marks! My God, Grissmann must think he was as stupid as Tönnchen.

A man with a stoop walked past their bench, wearing blue spectacles and the dotted armband of the blind. His face was unshaven and full of stubble. A woman was walking beside him.

Fundholz watched them pass. The man looked familiar. It was Sonnenberg! Loath to get involved, Fundholz waved Grissmann away.

The latter had meanwhile gone silent, having realized that it was hopeless trying to recruit the old man for another venture. Fundholz was too much at peace with his situation to take any more risks.

Fundholz stood up. Slowly he walked toward the blind man, whom he'd recognized from the way he walked. "Sonnenberg!" he cried out.

The man turned around. His left arm was loosely hanging onto the woman's right. He was now facing Fundholz, his mouth slightly open.

Well, he can't exactly see me, thought Fundholz. "Sonnenberg!" he called out again.

"Yes," answered the blind man. His voice sounded deep and firm.

Fundholz went up to him. "Hey, Sonnenberg, it's Fundholz, can't you tell from my voice?"

"Ach, Fundholz," the man answered, his tone verging on disdainful.

The old man approached and held out his hand.

Sonnenberg found it and squeezed. His grip was very firm. "My wife," he said, by way of introduction.

Fundholz then offered his hand to the woman, who looked

to be about thirty years old. She had ash-blond hair and a plump face, with practically no chin and an ugly, saggy mouth. She was wearing a dark wool dress that was far too big for her. She looked at Fundholz with wide-open, astonished eyes, but didn't say anything.

"Well?" Fundholz asked the blind man.

Sonnenberg laughed. "Closemouthed as ever I see. How are you? Still scrounging around town?"

Fundholz nodded, and when he realized the blind man couldn't see that, he said, "Yes."

Sonnenberg nudged his wife. "Isn't there a bench here? Why are we just standing around like this? I have to stand enough as it is. The whole day at Wittenbergplatz." Then he explained to Fundholz, "That's where I sell matches."

The woman looked for a bench. Finally she and Fundholz led him to the one where Fundholz had been sitting and where Grissmann was still waiting for the older man.

Fundholz made introductions. "This is my friend Sonnenberg, and that's Grissmann."

"You in the same business?" Sonnenberg asked.

Grissmann said he wasn't.

"What do you live off then?"

"Unemployment assistance," Grissmann stated. The interrogation bored him.

"Right."

They sat together for a few minutes without saying much to one another.

At last Fundholz stood up. "I have to go. Be well, Sonnenberg. Where can you be found these days?"

Sonnenberg groped for his hand and ultimately caught it. "Spare me a mark, Fundholz," he said. "Seeing as you always have money."

Fundholz tried to free himself, but the blind man kept his hand firmly in his grasp.

"I don't have any money. But here!" With his left hand, he

took the cigar butt from the previous day out of his pocket and handed it to Sonnenberg.

Sonnenberg let go of his hand, took the stub, and stuck it in his mouth.

"Well then, I'll be seeing you. Maybe soon at the Jolly Huntsman? You can find me there almost every evening, playing my accordion."

The woman fetched some matches from her jacket pocket and gave him a light.

Sonnenberg again held his hand out for Fundholz.

But Fundholz didn't take it, fearing another shakedown. "Goodbye," he said. Then he went to the bench where Tönnchen was still snoring and nudged him.

Tönnchen looked up at him, smiling.

"Wait here. I'll be back in two hours."

Tönnchen wanted to get up and join him.

"Just sit tight," ordered Fundholz.

Tönnchen obeyed. His grin faded into a whine, but Fundholz ignored that. He walked off without looking back.

Sonnenberg heard Fundholz talking. "Who is he talking to?" he asked Grissmann.

"That's Tönnchen. He's somewhat of a half-wit. Fundholz drags him along."

Sonnenberg thought for a moment. "Tönnchen—no, I don't know him. Does he also go begging door to door?"

"No, he's too stupid even for that."

Sonnenberg smoked. Then he said, "Fundholz is also stupid."

Meanwhile his wife leaned over and smiled at Grissmann.

Grissmann's face turned red. He didn't have much experience with women. Back when he was still earning money, he'd had a girlfriend. But that was years ago. In recent years he'd been with a streetwalker now and then, but that was it. Lately he didn't have enough money even for that. He was embarrassed. He looked away, then stole a glance at the woman.

She was definitely not beautiful. She had an ungainly figure, and the missing chin made her face somewhat birdlike. But he found her appealing because she was smiling at him.

The blind man was going on about what a stupid dog Fundholz was. He boasted that whenever he wanted he could relieve Fundholz of everything he had on him without the old man putting up any serious resistance. "That's how stupid he is," he concluded.

Grissmann applauded with an approving laugh. But his laughter was meant more for the woman than for the blind man. The woman also laughed.

Sonnenberg seemed to enjoy the expression of approval. "Yes," he assured Grissmann, "I used to be an entirely different person. You should have seen me back then. Before they shot out my eyes. That was 1915. We were posted to a small village not far from . . ." He began recounting his war adventures.

The woman smiled at Grissmann. She already knew all the war stories. She had long since grown weary of the blind man. He was a real brute, and whenever his misfortune got to him, he would beat her. He also drank a lot, although he couldn't hold his liquor.

He had never seen his wife. One day—he was already blind—he had run into her somewhere. His service dog had died a little earlier, and he hadn't yet received a new one from the Society for the Blind.

Back then she was in a very bad way. After being dismissed from her job as a housemaid, she was unemployed and had to work the streets. But she didn't earn much. Men didn't find her attractive, and she also wasn't sufficiently aggressive to catch their attention. "With looks like yours," one of the girls once told her, "you have to practically holler at the men up and down the street." That was more than she could manage, so she was glad when she met the blind man. He had married her right away.

She was severely disappointed. While he did receive welfare payments from the state, he spent it all on drink, so they had to live off whatever he earned selling matches and occasionally playing the accordion.

She wanted to get away from him. While she didn't have great aspirations in life, she'd had enough of this raging blind man chasing her around the room every other day. She smiled at Grissmann.

"That's the way it is all right," said Sonnenberg. "You set off in the morning with two eyes, and come evening they drag you back like a blind chicken. You have no idea what it's like! No idea!" he finished.

A deep rage showed in his face, which was gray and grimy and full of stubble. That's how it always went: He started off calmly telling his stories, and then his anguish and fury got the better of him.

He gave his wife a brutal shove. "Let's go! Move! You stupid cow, what are you waiting for?"

She stood up and smiled at Grissmann, practically pleading.

The younger man scratched his head, at a loss. He didn't know what to do. Uncertain, he stood up.

"Where are you headed?"

"I'm taking my husband to Wittenbergplatz," the woman answered, again hopeful.

"That's right," Sonnenberg chimed in. "And then you're sticking by my side! Understood? Do you suppose I want to spend another whole day standing there without being able to say a word? What are you thinking anyway? Doesn't earn a single mark, eats up my last coins, and then expects me just to sit there by myself! Come on, let's go! Tell that dimwit Fundholz I said hello," he said in parting to Grissmann, who was even more discombobulated by Sonnenberg's ranting.

The blind man was likely getting suspicious, and Grissmann felt scared. "I'll do that," he said.

The two set off. The woman looked back several times. She mouthed the words *Jolly Huntsman* without letting a sound pass her lips.

She's crazy, too, Grissmann thought, not understanding what she meant. He looked at her blankly and nodded.

Then he saw how Sonnenberg gave her a sharp poke with his elbow. She turned back around and spoke with the blind man. Then he heard her laugh. "Maxie, let's go to the Jolly Huntsman tonight. You can have some more peppermint schnapps, and that will put you in a better mood."

Grissmann heard the blind man mutter something. Aha, he thought, she'll be at the Jolly Huntsman this evening. I'll show up there, too. I wonder where it is. He decided to ask Tönnchen.

He went to the bench where Tönnchen was still sleeping. Grissmann nudged him and sat down next to him. "Where is the Jolly Huntsman?" he asked.

Tönnchen woke up and spat. "Where is Fundholz?"

Grissmann explained that Fundholz would be back soon and repeated his question. But he was unable to get anything out of Tönnchen. I'll find out from Fundholz, he decided.

SIX

———

Fundholz hesitated in front of a door with the nameplate *Charlotte von Trasse*. He had managed to gain entrance into an elegant apartment house. The doorman had left the front door open and was probably sitting in a pub somewhere.

Fundholz had spent a long time debating whether he should enter the fancy residence. The broad marble staircase had exerted an irresistible attraction. But combined with the bronze railing and the red velvet runner, it also made the building somewhat intimidating.

In the end he'd given himself a push and climbed right up to the top floor. He intended to start there and work his way down.

"Charlotte von Trasse," he read again. He rang the bell tentatively, not without first checking to see if some forerunner had left a mark on the wall that would indicate this lady's generosity.

What a fine old custom, he thought, this communicating to future beggars. You drew a couple lines on the wall or cut a notch in the door with your pocketknife to inform future mendicants. Unfortunately many people wiped away the signs or got rid of them by some other means. They had to be constantly renewed.

The door opened and an elderly lady peered out. Fundholz was struck by the fact she was dressed completely in silk.

"Would you happen to have some leftover bread? I haven't

eaten in a long time," he asked in a meek and muted voice. As he spoke he cast his gaze humbly at the floor. Only after delivering his request did he look up.

The lady looked him over in astonishment. She had a narrow, pale face, with a very pointed nose and a narrow mouth. "Wait here," she commanded. She shut the door, leaving Fundholz unsure of her intentions.

Her tone had sounded elegant and patronizing. Apparently she's in a good mood, he thought hopefully.

The day hadn't brought him much luck. Everywhere he'd gone, people had been in bad moods, or at least ungiving moods. The entire morning had yielded a mere thirty pfennig. That was the only reason he had dared venture into the better neighborhood.

The door was opened again, this time by a servant girl. "Come in," she said, curling her lips in disdain.

Fundholz obeyed, but he was scared. What would this turn into? What good could come of inviting this beggar Fundholz into such a luxurious apartment? Best I should get out right away, he thought. Who knows, perhaps the pointy-nosed lady is fetching the police.

They came to a broad hallway that was laid out with beautiful rugs.

"So," the girl said, picking up a rolled-up rug that was lying at her feet. "Give this a good beating downstairs. I'm coming to keep an eye on you."

Fundholz took the rug in both arms. It was very heavy, but the old man was glad. Surely there'd be some money in it, if they were having him work.

They went down the front stairs, the girl following a few steps behind. She didn't want to be seen next to such riffraff.

As soon as they were downstairs the girl said, "Turn left."

He obeyed, and they arrived at the rear entrance.

Once again the girl let him go first. She was afraid of the ragged old man. The newspapers were full of stories. These were the kind to pounce on young girls and violate them. Not that the girl could be considered very straitlaced, but old Fundholz was hardly her type.

At last they came to the courtyard. "Listen," the girl said assertively. "Next time you'll take the back stairs!"

Fundholz nodded. With great effort, he managed to toss the rug over the carpet hanger bar. The girl handed him the beater and looked at him sternly. Fundholz started beating the rug, but the girl was dissatisfied with his performance. "You have to hit harder," she said in a tone of authority.

Fundholz tried. But he wasn't strong enough. After only a few firm beatings, his arm started hurting. He took off his jacket and laid it next to him on the ground.

The girl started laughing when she saw him standing there in his oversize trousers and dirty, tattered flannel shirt. But Fundholz didn't pay her any attention. He went on beating. The blood rushed to his head from the exertion. Once again he had to pause.

"What's that?" asked the girl. "You think you're finished?"

Before Fundholz could answer, she took the beater and showed him the proper way to use it, laying into the rug with a savage enthusiasm. Perhaps she was imagining that the rug was Frau von Trasse or some unfaithful fiancé. In any case the dust billowed up in thick clouds. Then she suddenly stopped. "This is how you beat a rug!" she said and pressed the beater once again into his hand.

Fundholz resumed the work, but his attempts ended as feebly as before. Because he had no strength, he was incapable of striking more forcefully.

The girl gave a scornful laugh. She'd been afraid of this. It was ridiculous. "Leave it be," she said. "There's no point. You're too weak for beating rugs."

Fundholz didn't contradict her. He was more concerned about a handout than about proving his strength. But for now he had to wait, while the girl again started beating the rug. He watched her with a certain reverence as she went at it.

Soon the girl was finished. She took down the rug, rolled it up, and went to the back stairs. Fundholz followed timidly.

Once again they climbed four flights of stairs. Then the girl opened the door, while Fundholz stayed meekly outside.

"Wait here," the girl commanded, then closed the door behind her.

Minutes passed. Soon she returned and handed him a bundle. Fundholz thanked her. On the stairs, he opened what he had been given. There were three buttered slices of bread, neatly wrapped, next to a piece of dried-out cheese. Fundholz was furious. First they made him beat rugs, and then they gave him some dried-out cheese and three slices of bread. And these people were clearly millionaires! He would have liked to mash the bread onto the wall, the way beggars sometimes did when the handout was not in line with their expectations. But then he reconsidered and pocketed the slices for Tönnchen.

Today was decidedly a bad luck day, Fundholz thought, and went on cursing. Having reached the ground floor, he rang another doorbell. The nameplate said *Schnickard*.

An old woman answered. When she saw Fundholz, she immediately shut the door in horror. She had been reading a crime novel, and the sight of him had a devastating effect on her agitated imagination. Fundholz heard her hastily locking the door behind him and very loudly sliding the latch.

He went on his way. This was familiar. He'd often had such bad luck days when he only managed a few pfennig. It probably didn't make any sense to keep trying. Evidently there wasn't much to be had today.

On the way back, he made some calculations. He only had seventy pfennig left: forty from yesterday, thirty from today. But he'd manage somehow. Good thing he'd taken the bread.

He scanned the street for constables but didn't see any. On days like this it could easily happen that he'd be dragged into the station, and the endless questioning would start all over again. "Where are you from? What do you live off? Where do you live? Are you registered? If not, why not? Are you married? Previous convictions? How many?" The interrogations would go on interminably. They would frequently detain him while they pored over mug shots or sifted through profiles. And usually it took a very long time before they released him—after all, a tramp couldn't just go roaming about unpunished—and each time it was unclear if they'd release him at all.

Today he was having a streak of bad luck. So today he had to be especially careful. Because you never knew when a streak like that would break. It could end in a flash, but it could also last a painfully long time. And what would become of Tönnchen if he were detained?

Fundholz had a long way back, and the neighborhoods became more and more ordinary with every step. The apartment houses with the broad entryways gradually gave way to old, squalid workers' barracks. Now and then he spotted a constable coming down the street and carefully ducked into a side alley.

Finally, after a long trek, he reached the park. He looked around for Tönnchen, but he couldn't find him anywhere. Nor did he see Grissmann. Fundholz suspected that the two had gone off together.

He was tired and sat down on a bench. They'll show up eventually, he thought, and fell asleep.

SEVEN

Grissmann couldn't stand being around Tönnchen for long because of his incessant grinning, which had no outward cause.

How in the world does he do it? Grissmann wondered. Constantly grinning like that must hurt a person's face. He asked Tönnchen gruffly, "Why are you snickering all the time?"

Tönnchen gave what seemed to Grissmann a sad look but didn't answer.

Grissmann stood up. "I'm getting something to eat. I'll be back at three. Please tell Fundholz he should wait for me."

He spoke to Tönnchen using the formal "Sie," as he didn't want to put himself on the same level—the man was simply too harebrained.

Tönnchen also stood up. "Food," he said, smacking his lips. "Tönnchen hasn't eaten anything today. Tönnchen is hungry!"

Grissmann gave him twenty pfennig. "Go buy some buns. You should get eight for twenty pfennig. Or ten old ones. That will keep you full until Fundholz comes back."

Tönnchen took the money and ran off without thanking Grissmann.

Grissmann was already annoyed at himself for giving him the money. Now once again I'll have twenty pfennig less to eat, he thought bitterly. Too damned soft in the head as always. And yet Fundholz actually keeps the idiot fed.

Tönnchen and Fundholz always waited until two or three in the afternoon to eat. Fundholz's stomach was small and trained to eat little food, and Tönnchen had to follow his master's lead. They ate only twice a day, but then Tönnchen devoured his food like a beast.

Grissmann slowly left the park. Today I'll go to the Jolly Huntsman, he decided. He wanted to have a woman again. He wasn't particular about her looks—besides, they're all alike, he thought.

He sauntered across the street and saw Tönnchen coming back from the bakery. The saleslady was watching him, clearly appalled.

Grissmann plucked up his courage and gave her a glance, but she turned away with a sneer, and Grissmann went on his way, chagrined. Then he thought about the conversation with Fundholz. He'd realized right away the old beggar wasn't the right man for his plan. He was already too far gone.

Nevertheless, Grissmann wanted to go ahead with the break-in. He knew a small cigar stand where an old woman ran the counter by herself. His plan was to hold up the shop in two days, which would be the thirtieth of the month. He suspected that then he would make off not only with the day's takings but also with the rent money. Because surely the woman has to pay her rent on the thirtieth, he thought.

His plan was to enter the shop a little before seven o'clock, together with Fundholz. The woman didn't know him. In fact he'd peeked through the window several times to determine that no one else worked there, but he was certain she hadn't noticed him. Fundholz was supposed to suddenly feel ill and ask the woman for a glass of water. Grissmann would then follow her into her living quarters behind the shop and hold her there, while the old man cleaned out the cash register. Grissmann would then search the woman for additional money. Old women like that always had money on them; Grissmann was sure of it.

He was proud of his plan, which struck him as promising. He was certain that in two minutes, everything would be over and done with. They just had to show up a little before seven and things would take their course. But this Fundholz couldn't be counted on for anything that made sense. He was mentally lazy to the point of stupidity. And Tönnchen was even more useless. Pity that Sonnenberg was blind. He would definitely be good for something like this.

But now nothing would come of his beautiful plan, and Grissmann was very disheartened. He cursed his bad luck. For once he'd managed to find a decent target that was sure to pay off, and then it didn't work out. Maybe the old woman kept whole heaps of money—who knew?

In a sullen mood, he entered the local pub where he often went for a midday meal. The tureen of pea soup with bacon cost forty pfennig. Bread came with that for no charge. He didn't have much appetite. He ate his food languidly. I have to find work again, he thought, so I can earn money, and so I can spend it. What kind of life could he have with just a few marks a week? His suits were going to seed. Pretty soon he'd look exactly like Fundholz.

He had a sour taste in his mouth. Beer cost fifteen pfennig. If he hadn't given that idiot twenty pfennig, he could be drinking a beer right now.

A few haulers were sitting at the next table. They were talking loudly and swigging their beer. One of them was eating a pork chop. He was smacking his lips appreciatively, now and then taking a swallow from the large glass in front of him. When it was empty, he ordered another.

Grissmann watched him with envy. It must be nice to have enough money to eat and drink whatever you want.

The hauler took a large swallow. "That sure hits the spot," he proclaimed contentedly.

Grissmann turned away. Then he heard the man say, "Well, Karl, what do you say to my woman?"

Grissmann turned back and saw the man handing a photo across the table.

"A real dish," the other man praised.

Grissmann stood up, went to the counter, and paid. As he did, he heard the first man say, "Everything in life is chance, my boy, pure chance. You know how I met her? It was at the zoo." The hauler laughed happily.

As Grissmann opened the door to leave, he bumped into a man coming in. His cap was crooked, and he was slurring a drinking song, "Trink'n wir noch ein Tröpfchen." As he sang, he spread out his arms.

Grissmann bent over. Everything in life is chance, he thought. He had found a coin, a whole mark—probably the drunken man had lost it. Grissmann walked away, his mood much improved.

EIGHT

Minchen Lindner had an apartment near the Kurfürstendamm. It wasn't very big—three rooms with a kitchen and bath—but the place was nicely fitted out.

Runners lined the narrow corridor, which led to a large, modern dining room with elegant furniture. Beyond that was a charming little parlor. At least Minchen Lindner found it charming. The entire parlor was lined with pink silk fabric, and all the furniture was in the same color. The small chairs and armchairs even featured the same pattern as the wall covering. Pink curtains hung at the windows, with yellow sheers that also had a pink shimmer—probably because they were embarrassed. The carpet was a single color, and it goes without saying that that color was bright red. Minchen Lindner would have liked most of all to hang pink pictures on the walls. But since that was out of the question, she decided on two sunrises, which nonetheless contained a goodly amount of pink.

Minchen Lindner also claimed as her own a sumptuous bedroom with a broad double bed. This room, too, was quite handsomely furnished, or, in the parlance of Minchen and her girlfriends, it was "cute." But she didn't like it as much as she liked her pink parlor. And even the saucy pictures that hung next to a larger-than-life painting of an angel could not change that. She liked the bedroom all right, but despite everything she preferred her parlor.

She felt much like those businessmen who have great grand offices but prefer to stay in their private homes. Workrooms are never as beautiful as private rooms. Private rooms belong to you alone.

The bedroom did not belong solely to Minchen Lindner. The large boudoir was to some extent her office.

The director of an important factory, an older, elegant gentleman, had one day literally picked Minchen Lindner off the street. She was a pretty young girl, and the older gentleman had decided she was too good for that life and shouldn't be left to go to ruin so quickly.

He set her up in the apartment with the pink parlor, every month gave her three hundred marks in addition to the rent, and asked only to visit her two or three times each week.

And so the bedroom did not belong solely to Minchen. Even when Herr von Sulm—that was the older gentleman's name—wasn't there, Minchen had visitors. Herr von Sulm couldn't know about that, though. Not that he was jealous, although perhaps he was, but Herr von Sulm was worried about his health.

Minchen Lindner had no regard for that. Herr von Sulm was a punctual, proper man. He arrived punctually in his office, and he also arrived punctually at Minchen's apartment, after having first telephoned. He never showed up for an appointment without announcing himself. He was a man of tact and good breeding. Even to visit his mistress, he would not have presumed to show up without calling first.

Minchen knew that. Which was why she had clients besides Herr von Sulm. Not that she couldn't get by on the three hundred marks; she was even able to save some of that. But she was afraid that Herr von Sulm might die one day or pick a different young girl off the street.

For this reason, Minchen made provisions for such regrettable but thoroughly conceivable circumstances and maintained a standing business relationship with various other older gentlemen. Berlin had no shortage of lonely older men of means. They sought companionship but could not do so openly. They were probably a little ashamed of their gray hair or bald heads. They placed little value on spiritual kinship—they were already beyond that. Nor were they looking for intellect and wit—that they could find in the articles and editorials of their newspapers. They simply wanted more youthful sensuality. And that was what Minchen Lindner offered them.

Long, firm legs supported a supple body. She had regular features, with a little button nose, and there was nothing dissolute about her person. She wasn't the vamp type—more the sweet little innocent thing.

She had previously worked as a salesgirl in a shop that sold soaps and perfumes. When the shop went bankrupt, following the trend of the times, Minchen had had to look around for something else. But there was no position to be found. Her aspirations, however, were higher than the twelve marks she received in unemployment assistance, so she soon started earning extra money on the side.

Then Herr von Sulm entered her life, and her situation fundamentally changed.

Now she sat every day in her pink parlor, listened to the radio, and was bored. She had no financial worries—on the contrary, she had more money than she needed, as she was neither wasteful nor extravagant—but she was terribly bored.

Right now it was especially bad. She was bored at night when the older gentlemen were there, and she was bored during the day when she had to wait for the night and the older gentlemen. She owned dresses and hats and very pretty undergarments, she had everything she needed, and despite all that she was not content.

To be sure, she was far better off now than she had been before she met Herr von Sulm, but back then she had been free. She had had a boyfriend—Heinz, who was a mason—and they would go out in the evening for a few marks. It had been exciting and interesting to see a movie or occasionally an operetta. Now and then she'd brought him up to her place. That had been an experience—quietly sneaking into her furnished room. Then her boyfriend had left her, after making a wild angry scene because he'd found out she was still running around at night. She had managed to get over the breakup after she realized, looking back, that Heinz had been a very crude fellow. Herr von Sulm was much more polite. Still it had been nicer to have one boyfriend than to be the girlfriend of half a dozen older gentlemen.

The phone rang and she answered.

"Who is it? . . . Oh, Father." Minchen Lindner wasn't particularly pleased.

"What do you want? Money? Yes you can have some." She stamped her foot. "No, don't come here. If you come here, I won't give you a thing. Tell me where I should bring it!"

For a moment there was silence on the other end of the line. Finally the old man said, "Come to the Jolly Huntsman this evening."

Minchen Lindner took a nicer tone. "Where is that, Father?" She jotted down the address. Then she said goodbye and hung up.

"Be there at ten o'clock," her father had managed to call out.

Minchen Lindner sighed. Her father was another dark side of her life.

Old man Lindner had previously worked as a bailiff, an office he had held for a long time. With his briefcase under his arm and his mustache curled upward, he had been a very familiar sight in the Steglitz district, which was his jurisdiction. Everyone who knew him greeted him with respect. His particular clientele were people of little means, to whom he appeared powerful and important.

He was almost more powerful than the entire government. Because the German foreign minister, for example, could not determine if the bed and the chair or the armoire and the dresser should be auctioned off. Only Bailiff Lindner could do that.

Lindner embodied the power of the state, which he carried over into everyday life. Like an executioner taking the heads of those condemned, Lindner, by virtue of his office, would take the furniture of those in default, place it on the auction block, and then send an official report, from which they learned that they also needed to pay Herr Lindner for his trouble in seizing their things.

Yes, Herr Lindner had been an important person. But he had committed the same mistake as many important people. His own power and standing had gone to his head. He had forgotten that he was merely the enforcer of policy and had begun to think independently and on his own authority.

Every so often he neglected to register certain objects, saving them from the auction block so they could remain with their owner, for which the owner would reward him. At first it had been kindheartedness that had prompted this. Later it was greed.

This scheme had worked well, as long as only little things were involved. But then one time he was ordered to impound the belongings of a man who had owned a well-furnished six-room apartment, and that had been his undoing. Herr Lindner was paid fifty marks, and in return he impounded items valued at a mere three hundred marks, when he ought to have seized six thousand marks' worth of the man's possessions.

The creditor, though, was familiar with the debtor's financial circumstances and knew that the man had things in his apartment worth at least ten thousand marks. He informed the court, and Bailiff Lindner was dethroned.

Other irregularities were also uncovered. Eight hundred marks had been missing from the settlement, so Lindner wound up in jail for a year. When they let him out, he was unrecognizable.

The jailers had removed his powerful mustache, and a humiliating bare spot now stood in place of his former bristling whiskers: This outward aspect had wrought an inward change as well. Lindner no longer felt powerful in his person. He left jail a broken man.

He began to drink, engaged in petty thievery, and sank from being a symbol of the state and civil order to becoming a bona fide bum.

Minchen supported him. But she didn't want him to come to her apartment. In the first place, she was ashamed to receive someone so far gone, and in the second place, she was afraid that his demands would skyrocket once he saw her setup.

Today she wasn't expecting any company. She was looking forward to the evening, as it had been a long time since she'd been to a decent pub. She found the establishments in the well-to-do western part of the city boring and stiff. The minute you had a good laugh at something the snooty pack would look at you askance. Once a woman had called Minchen's laugh a "servant girl's giggle." The stupid people fancied themselves better than their domestic staff.

Minchen let out a scornful breath. When it came to the men of the upper class, she felt she knew them well enough. And the women were probably no better, she concluded.

She rang a bell, and a tall girl stepped into the parlor. Minchen, too, paid a maid to do housework during the day.

"Come and sit with me," said Minchen. "Let's play cards."

The girl fetched some playing cards, and they launched into a game of bezique.

NINE

All the day-old buns were gone, so Tönnchen used the money to buy eight fresh ones, which he started stuffing into his mouth the minute he left the store. But eight buns at once was evidently a little too much. Especially when they were devoured so quickly with nothing to wash them down.

Tönnchen had a stomachache, as though something were pinching him inside. He rubbed where he thought it hurt, but that didn't help. He didn't feel any better.

Tönnchen felt scared. He looked around helplessly. More than anything else he would have liked to take off his pants and see what was pinching him. But that wasn't allowed. Once when he was in Herzberge they'd given him a terrible beating because he had started undressing in front of the others.

Tönnchen's power of recall was very limited. But some things had left such a deep impression that they broke through the fog clouding his brain—rutabagas was one example, and he was also aware that acting on certain desires had wound up causing him pain. So now he instinctively felt that he shouldn't yield to the urge to take off his pants. No matter how natural it seemed, he couldn't do it. Somehow he just couldn't. Unfortunately.

He stopped in front of a sausage shop and peered longingly through the windowpanes. He still had a stomachache, but the sausages whetted his appetite. Eating was the only thing that brought him any joy. He didn't eat merely to satiate himself, but rather out of love for the act of eating itself.

Tönnchen consumed everything that came his way. He picked things to eat off the street the same way he rummaged through the garbage bins. Because at one time he had been close to starvation. That was long ago, but now and then he still felt that overpowering sensation, coupled with an intense fear of not having anything to eat. Whenever this hunger reappeared, this feeling that he knew from before, he would start howling. And he wouldn't stop howling until he spotted something to eat.

Once upon a time even Tönnchen had been normal, although no one who knew him in his current condition would believe it. It wasn't until he was twelve years old that he lost his wits.

His father, who worked as an agent for a firm in Berlin, had owned a house in the country. A little summerhouse, as was all the rage at the time. The Christmas holidays were a serious business, and Ernst, as Tönnchen was called back then—a chubby, good-natured schoolboy—rode out to the country with his father to make sure the place was in order.

Every month Herr Seidel visited his cottage in the country. This house had always been the pinnacle of his desires, and once it was in his hands, he didn't restrict its use to summer but visited it throughout the year, at every opportunity, under the pretext of making sure everything was as it should be. In truth, though, he simply wanted to enjoy his possession.

Ernst was an only child. His mother had died young, and so he and his father lived together in a small two-room apartment. Herr Seidel managed the household himself, as he didn't earn quite enough to afford both a maid and a summerhouse. Besides, he had to pay for his son's tuition, schoolbooks, and other items.

The country Christmas celebration had gotten off to a merry start. The old man was happy to see his summerhouse again, and his son was happy because of the wonderful presents, the time off from school, and his father's good mood.

Together the two of them had gone through the cottage. Seidel had checked everything and found it all in good order. That's when the misfortune occurred. Ernst became too boisterous, started playing with a large vase that had been part of his mother's dowry, and accidentally dropped it.

His father had often scolded him on account of his bad behavior. Herr Seidel had always been strict, both with others and with himself. He had worked his way up and was more than a little proud of that. He had intended for his son to study at the university, but unfortunately he was forced to recognize that the boy was not particularly talented.

Seidel was beside himself with rage and gave Ernst a few hefty slaps, then locked him in the cellar to stew for three or four hours. But instead of three hours, Ernst wound up spending nearly a whole week locked away.

After the incident with his son, Seidel went to a nearby pub, where he drank some coffee and a few shots of brandy. But as he was leaving an hour later to let Ernst out—his attitude toward his son having mellowed in the meantime—he was run over by a beer wagon while crossing the street and died on the spot.

The wagon and horses had so disfigured Seidel's body that it took days to identify the corpse. Only when his Berlin acquaintances learned of the accident did they begin to worry about the child and alert the police. On the same day his father was buried, they went to the cellar and fetched Ernst, now a howling idiot. He spent months in the hospital, but all the doctors' efforts to cure his mind were unsuccessful. Little by little, Ernst turned into Tönnchen. He grew fatter and fatter, because the five days of starvation had transformed him from a human being into an animal that ate as much as it could and could never get enough.

Tönnchen was still standing in front of the sausage shop, staring longingly, but his stomach was feeling better. Suddenly he thought "Fundholz" and ran back to the park.

He saw the old man sitting on a bench and poked him.

Fundholz woke up feeling hungry. He fished the bread out of

his pocket, handed a slice to Tönnchen, and then took one for himself. Tönnchen instantly finished off the one slice and had Fundholz give him another.

Afterwards Fundholz stood up and went to the bakery, where he bought buns for fifteen pfennig and some old cake for twenty. He shared this with his fat companion, though he kept more of the cake for himself. To his surprise, Tönnchen didn't seem to be all that hungry. All he ate was his share of the cake. The buns he stuffed in his pocket.

Fundholz wondered if he should go to a pub. He liked to drink schnapps. Schnapps perked him up on the inside and made him feel nice and warm. Every day he drank at least two shots. He usually drank both in the evening, before going to bed, but today he felt the craving somewhat earlier, as was often the case.

Tönnchen trotted after him. Fundholz had no intention of giving him anything to drink. He believed that crazy people had no need to imbibe, since they seemed drunk enough as it was.

A while back Grissmann had bought Tönnchen two glasses of beer, and afterward the man could barely stand on his own two feet. He had tried propping himself on Fundholz, and the old man had almost collapsed at the attempt. No, there would be no schnapps for Tönnchen.

Fundholz told him to wait outside the pub. Then the old man stepped up to the counter and ordered a shot of peppermint schnapps, which he drank slowly, savoring every drop. By the time he paid his tab, his eyes were brighter, and he seemed younger and livelier. "Let's go," he said to Tönnchen, and together they returned to the park.

Thanks to the schnapps, Fundholz felt a surge of fresh vitality and initiative. He resolved to try his luck again in the afternoon.

TEN

Grissmann sat on the bench sunning himself. He had taken off his cap, closed his eyes, and turned his face toward the sun.

His hopes had been newly nourished by the coin he'd found. Somehow he saw the money as a sign of his competence. He had acted quickly, bending over before the drunken man had noticed. I took action, he thought. Acting is always better than planning. And it's possible to act entirely on one's own.

This evening he intended to steal that woman from the blind man Sonnenberg. Not an entirely decent plan perhaps, but so what! People hadn't exactly treated him decently. Besides, he was excited by the prospect of taking someone else's woman. He had no intention of staying with her. That was out of the question, since he was barely getting by himself with his few marks. Perhaps later, once he'd finally made some money. But then he would have other, prettier women.

No, this was just an escapade. An enticing escapade that seemed safe enough. Pinching a woman off a blind man couldn't be difficult or dangerous. Grissmann went on daydreaming. The sun did him good. He felt his blood warming. Sunshine, he thought, stretching comfortably, sunshine and women.

Fundholz sat down next to him. Grissmann opened his eyes and blinked at the old man. "Well, Fundholz, did you come up with anything?"

Fundholz shook his head.

Grissmann wondered at how alive the man seemed. Then he smelled the schnapps and understood the source of the old man's newfound vigor.

"Tell me, Fundholz, where exactly is the Jolly Huntsman?"

Fundholz looked at him, surprised. "Are you planning to go there? Do you have money?"

Grissmann nodded. "I want to go out, too, for once. Squatting around my place all evening gets too boring. I want to be around people again."

"There's always something going on at the Jolly Huntsman," Fundholz agreed. He stood up. "I have to get going. Come along and I'll explain where it is."

Grissmann stood up and joined the old man.

This time Tönnchen wasn't going to let himself be brushed off. He didn't want to spend the whole day sitting on a bench. He, too, wanted to move. Besides, he was afraid, because Fundholz was going away with the man who had given him the buns. Seeing both of them leave was too much for him. Fundholz growled at him in vain.

The old man debated what to do. There was no way he could take his fat companion along—maybe it would be better just not to go. Finally he had an idea. "By all means, Tönnchen, you should come along. We're all going to eat rutabagas. Each person has to eat at least four platefuls."

Tönnchen shrank back in fear. "I'm not eating any rutabagas."

"Everyone who comes along has to eat rutabagas," Fundholz declared firmly.

Grissmann grinned and nodded.

Tönnchen was torn between two strong urges. He wanted to go with Fundholz, but he didn't want to eat rutabagas. Under no circumstance did he want to eat rutabagas.

"Come on," said Grissmann. "Otherwise the rutabagas will get cold."

Tönnchen sat back down on the bench. "Tönnchen doesn't eat any rutabagas," he declared. "Tönnchen is waiting here."

Grissmann found that amusing. He could have a lot of fun with the idiot. Odd that he hadn't thought of it before. He walked alongside Fundholz, but after a few steps he turned around and shouted, triumphantly, "Rutabagas!"

Tönnchen winced and whimpered, "No, no."

Grissmann laughed and went on his way. "A genuine moron," he noted with satisfaction.

Fundholz nodded absentmindedly, his thoughts elsewhere. His forehead was wrinkled.

At some point I'd also like to get the old man riled, Grissmann thought. Pull a good one over the old scoundrel, that would be something. He wondered if he should turn around again and shout, "Rutabagas." No, better not. People might notice. Grissmann gave Fundholz a poke. "Why don't you come with me this evening to the Jolly Huntsman? I'll buy you a drink."

Fundholz wanted to decline. But the offer made him waver. "It'll be too late to get in our basement," he said pensively.

Grissmann thought it over. He very much wanted to take the old man along. Unfortunately he didn't have enough money to get him drunk. But as it was, Fundholz could talk to the blind man while he went after the woman. In his own way Grissmann was a constructive thinker. He always liked to play through the possible contingencies in advance, but since most of his plans only remained plans, all his thinking went nowhere. But this idea made perfect sense: It could only be a good thing to have the old man there that evening.

"I'll buy you two shots, and it's also entirely possible that somebody will come up with a place to kip. You can easily be back by ten. Worst case you'll have to sleep outside."

Fundholz found Grissmann's generous offer very tempting. That would mean three whole shots of schnapps, he mused. He was still owed one more today. And what did it matter if he had to sleep outside? He'd often "spent the night at Mother Green's."

"What about Tönnchen?" he asked.

"We can lock him in the basement," Grissmann suggested.

Fundholz agreed. They arranged to meet in the park at seven.

Grissmann went merrily on his way. Today he was downright happy. He hadn't felt so content and lighthearted in a long time.

Fundholz stayed where he was for a moment after the other man left. He considered which district he should go to. Finally he settled on a residential neighborhood he hadn't visited in a long time. Yes, that's always been a good location, he reassured himself, and set off.

ELEVEN

Tauentzienstrasse shakes as the giant double-decker buses rumble from one stop to the next, like houses on wheels. One streetcar follows another. They whiz past, ringing their bells, demanding the right of way as best they can amid the unbroken procession of automobiles.

At midday all the company managers—major ones as well as their minor counterparts—get in their cars and set out to eat. They are in a hurry and let that be known. They honk and toot their horns all at once, gnawing away at the pedestrians' nerves.

The stench of gasoline and exhaust fumes poisons the air.

How wonderful it is to sit cozily in an automobile. Clouds of dirty smoke come billowing out of the exhaust pipe, while you sit in front, oblivious, press your foot on the gas pedal, and rush ahead. It's only the others, the people you don't know, those of little importance, who have to breathe in the gas along with the air.

Of course filling the streets with so much smoke is forbidden—drivers have an obligation to spare the lungs of pedestrians, but they don't give that a second thought. They don't have time for second thoughts. They charge ahead, leaving the stench behind them.

My God, they think, so many things are illegal. So many regulations confining every motorist like so many fences. After all, drivers are sportsmen, too, even if only on a small scale. They also know that the restrictions hurt only if they're caught. Still, being a motorist isn't easy. You have to shell out for taxes, pay much too much for gas, and on top of everything else you have to keep your eyes peeled for every kid kicking a ball on the street.

Meanwhile the traffic cop on the corner has other worries. He's yelling at a woman who's blocking the flow of traffic. These damned pedestrians. All they do is hold things up, dithering this way and that, but of course there's hell to pay if somebody accidentally flattens one of these tiresome two-legged creatures.

The traffic light orders the cars to halt. They line up in rank and file. Finally the color changes, and like a herd of wild beasts they stampede forth. Onward! The battle cry of the metropolis rings out through the streets.

The streetcars sound their bells hysterically, while the buses emit a dull rumble, and the bicycle ringers give out a weak *trring-trring*. The cars and trucks produce a music all their own, a mix of darker and lighter tones. Onward!

Whatever other regulations might be in place, there are no restrictions on noise in Berlin. That much is clear.

On a pitiful, trampled bit of grass set in the middle of the asphalt, Frau Fliebusch sat perched on a bench and stared blankly at the traffic. Frau Fliebusch did not understand the times. Frau Fliebusch was the woman from yesterday.

Frau Fliebusch was around sixty years of age. She was not a wealthy woman, at least not anymore, and that was evident. She was dressed poorly and very much out of fashion. Her outfit would have passed for modern around the turn of the century, or perhaps ten years later. Her long skirt grazed the street and had been sweeping up the dust for years. Its gray color matched the gray of her face, and the grime that clung to it like a broad border dragged it to the ground. Her jacket came down to just above her knee. It had once boasted purple stripes, and a purple shimmer still shone through the fabric.

While the wheel of fashion had not been kind to her outfit, her hat was now once again very much in vogue. It was large and yellow and shaded Frau Fliebusch's face. A broken feather—actually all that was left was the shaft—lent a note of near frivolity. But the wearer was anything but frivolous. To call her melancholy would be an understatement.

Frau Fliebusch no longer understood the times, and that was her misfortune. Her mind was still stuck in the years before the Great War. Everything that came later, everything she found inimical—the war and the inflation and all the consequences of the war, the entire wickedness of recent times—had rushed past her like some horrible dream.

She didn't believe it. She didn't believe it was all true. That it was the sober, everyday reality. The same way that to this day she hadn't grasped that Fliebusch, Wilhelm Fliebusch, her strong, handsome Wilhelm, had fallen victim to a grenade. Or that her savings, her sixty thousand marks, had lost their value.

She knew for a fact that Wilhelm was alive; she could feel it. Because Wilhelm had never been sick. In fact her handsome Wilhelm had been extraordinarily healthy. He couldn't have been healthy one day and dead the next. That was impossible. It was only a plot against her, against Frau Fliebusch, née Kernemann.

And the fact that the sixty thousand marks that had been her dowry was suddenly worth less than a pfennig? That too was a plot against her, and she had said as much to the director of the bank.

Wilhelm was being held somewhere, but he would come back one day, and one day she would also recover her money. The whole nightmare would soon be over. It was obvious: People were making fun of her. Everyone was dreaming up mean things aimed against Frau Amalie Fliebusch and planning to carry them out. They kept trying to convince her that Germany no longer had a kaiser. She wouldn't have minded if that were the case, but of course it simply wasn't true! That was just another plot to confuse her, which was why she no longer read any newspapers: They, too, were full of lies.

It had all happened so quickly. From one day to the next, people she had known to be nice and kind had turned into schemers and villains, and Amalie Fliebusch was still wondering why. At the same time everything was as it had always been. She had gotten up around ten in the morning and at Wilhelm's behest had drunk some chocolate, so that she might have a fuller figure, when all of a sudden some people showed up—some officers, friends of her husband she'd known a long time. Then they tried to tell her that Wilhelm was dead.

Frau Fliebusch angrily banged her umbrella against the edge of the bench. She couldn't think about it without getting worked up.

At first she had fainted. Later, after she came to, she realized that it was all a lie—a stupid, mean lie. But the terrible thing was that the people kept on lying, without stopping, and somehow Wilhelm had to be in league with them. She hadn't heard a single word from him! He was completely silent. Instead they sent her his uniform. She had it with her. She kept it right next to her in the small suitcase.

Wilhelm was acting very unfairly. And she was going to tell him that, too. But could anyone be mad at Wilhelm for very long? Certainly not Frau Fliebusch! She smiled, touched by the thought of him. Wilhelm was always so attentive. He never came home without bringing her something. Flowers or something sweet. Frau Fliebusch sighed. Hopefully the whole nightmare would soon be over. Hopefully Wilhelm would soon be home.

People were getting stranger and stranger. They pulled away from her like ships departing a harbor. It was hard being the only rational person in a world full of fools. But how could she possibly play along? What would Wilhelm think of her if she, too, suddenly turned into a fool?

People told her she should go to the poorhouse. But what

would Wilhelm think if his wife, the daughter of Headmaster Kernemann, listened to the fools and went to a poorhouse? No. Wilhelm would never forgive her for that, she was certain. That was something he would never forgive.

Frau Fliebusch felt hungry. It was time for her midday meal. She did receive some assistance from Fräulein Reichmann, who gave her ten marks every week.

Fräulein Reichmann used to be a nice person. A kindhearted soul, even, thought Frau Fliebusch. Despite being ten years younger than Frau Fliebusch, she had always been her best friend. But then even Fräulein Reichmann had joined the liars and maintained that her own fiancé had fallen in the war. Ostensibly she was now living off her private tutoring, or so she told Frau Fliebusch. The daughter of Director Reichmann. While every child knew that Director Reichmann was a very wealthy man. For whom ten marks a week was nothing.

It was pitiful. And it was mean of Fräulein Reichmann, when she knew very well that Wilhelm would pay back every pfennig. And what was the result? Frau Fliebusch was forced to sleep in shelters and train stations, alongside people who were utterly impossible, simply because Fräulein Reichmann was so unkind to her.

Frau Fliebusch rose from the bench, indignant as she always was when she had these thoughts. Right beside her were the two bags she dragged along wherever she went. One contained Wilhelm's uniform as well as the new top hat he'd purchased just before he had to leave, while the other was full of her own clothes.

Frau Fliebusch looked around, undecided. Where should she go?

The crazy people were now running newfangled restaurants where you could pull a roll out of a machine. You put ten pfennig in a slot and then a disk turned and you could reach in and take a roll. The things people come up with! But Frau Fliebusch was no longer surprised at anything. She divided the world into the mean acts and dirty tricks that were clearly directed at her, on the one hand, and things that were indifferent, on the other.

Frau Fliebusch made her way down Tauentzienstrasse, clutching a bag in each hand. The passersby eyed her in amazement. Many recognized her by sight.

Go on and gape, thought Frau Fliebusch. Just you go on gaping. I know how despicable you all are.

TWELVE

Tönnchen was no longer alone on his bench. The park had filled up, as numerous women with children and older men arrived to enjoy the sunshine and fresh air.

In the morning the women had to take care of the housekeeping, but after noon they were glad for a chance to sit down. They brought stockings to mend as well, so they could sun themselves and work at the same time.

The older men were mostly unemployed. In the morning, when they crawled out of their beds, they were still fresh and optimistic as they set off looking for work. But after spending the entire morning beating the pavement or heading back from the welfare office, they were more inclined to melancholy. Then they would sit in the parks and squares, trying to forget that they were unemployed. They preferred to act as if they were on vacation, as though it were a privilege to be able to sit in the sun and do nothing. How well they managed to convince themselves depended on their disposition: Some succeeded while others did not.

The man sitting next to Tönnchen had succeeded. His eyes were closed. A lazy smile spread across his broad face.

Tönnchen eyed him with interest. He couldn't tell if the man was sleeping. He suspected as much, but he would have liked to know for sure. So he contemplated how he might be able to find out. Thinking always took some effort, since it was hard for him to establish the link between thought and action. At times he probably had more far-ranging ideas, but the links between his mind and his body were defective.

Now, however, a thought did occur to him, though more out of instinct. He wanted to know if the man next to him was asleep, and he had come up with a way to find out.

Tönnchen took a pin from his lapel and tested it on his thumb. It was still sharp. Slowly, hesitantly—some vague foreboding seemed to hold him back—he moved his hand with the needle closer to the man. And then he jabbed.

The man's peaceful expression vanished at once. He jumped up. "What damned idiot just stabbed me?" Then he noticed Tönnchen, with his silly shy smile. "You, stop grinning like a nincompoop!" Then the man saw the pin that Tönnchen was still holding.

Tönnchen was surprised by how quickly the man had awoken. He was just trying to make sense of this when he felt two well-aimed, forceful blows from the same man—who in any case was now very much awake.

Tönnchen jumped up and ran off. The old man followed him with angry eyes. "Stupid dog," he grumbled. The pinprick wasn't such a big deal, but he was infuriated by this unexpected attack. He had just been basking in a blissfully forgetful condition. Grumpily he closed his eyes once again, but inside he was still cursing.

The whole thing was a mystery to Tönnchen. All he understood were the slaps. They had hurt, and his cheeks were still burning a little. But since no one showed any sign of coming after him with more beatings, he soon calmed back down. Anxiously he eyed the bench where he had been sitting. The man had again closed his eyes, but he wasn't asleep. That much was now clear to Tönnchen.

He found a different bench to sit on and watched two little girls and a boy play with marbles. They were trying to roll the marbles into a hole. The game was very exciting, and the children were completely engrossed by it. They didn't pay attention to the man on the bench.

Tönnchen was also interested in the game. Slumbering in the depths of his subconscious was a memory of himself as a child at play. He didn't really understand why they were all trying to hit the hole when there was so much room around, but he still found it interesting. Unfortunately, after a whispered huddle, the children went away. The girls had spotted Tönnchen during a break in the game and had been frightened by the grinning spectator.

Tönnchen grew restless. He had nothing to do. He didn't want to dawdle any longer on a bench. He didn't see anyone he knew, and he was worried he might get another beating. So he left the park and headed uncertainly in the direction of the vegetable shop and the basement.

There Walter Schreiber had his hands full. He was waiting on four female customers at once. He rushed from basket to basket, very focused as he went about his business.

"Two lemons, five pounds of potatoes, and one pound of onions," demanded one lady with a pronounced lisp.

Walter Schreiber gave her a quick nod, but first he finished packing up for another customer.

While he packed, he kept darting back and forth, determined not to have any customer leave his shop without buying something, and since he wanted to treat everyone fairly, it took a long time for him to finish packing up the first woman's order.

He had just handed her the package when he spotted two tattered pant legs climbing down the steps. Luckily the woman was quick to stow away her purchase; otherwise it would have surely landed on the floor.

This was all he needed. The tramps showing up just when business was at its peak.

The legs grew bigger and bigger as they climbed down, until they became a whole man—Tönnchen.

Walter Schreiber was on the point of despair.

He nodded to the lady with the lisp and confirmed her order. "One lemon, two pounds of potatoes, and five pounds of onions," he repeated distractedly, all the while keeping a wary eye on Tönnchen.

The lady looked at Schreiber reproachfully. "Two lemons, five pounds of potatoes, and one pound of onions," she corrected.

Walter Schreiber took care of her order. With nagging apprehension, he kept watching Tönnchen, who had taken a position in the shop and was in the process of sampling the prunes—the premium grade, too, as Walter Schreiber grimly observed.

He served one customer after another. His facial expression became one of menacing sweetness. From time to time, he cast a murderous glance at Tönnchen, but that had no effect. Walter Schreiber wanted to avoid a scandal, but as soon as he was alone with Tönnchen he pounced on him, brimming with anger. "Get out of here this minute. Otherwise I'm fetching the police. What the devil are you thinking?"

Tönnchen's face showed his genuine amazement. For a moment he stopped chewing. Then without thinking, he reached into the prunes and grabbed another handful.

At this point Walter Schreiber lost control. His whole worldview was shaken to the core. He grabbed the huge man by the shoulders and shook him. "You damned idiot," he screeched, "put the prunes right back where you got them!"

Cowed by this response, Tönnchen did as he was told, but Walter Schreiber refused to let go of him.

"You blasted idiot, stuffing yourself with my prunes! Prunes you can't possibly pay for since you don't have any money!"

Tönnchen grew afraid. Helplessly he stared at the vegetable seller.

Schreiber's anger broke at the inanity of this stare. It's almost as if the man doesn't know what he's doing, he thought, inwardly pardoning Tönnchen of his crime as he released his grip and let him go. "You dumb numbskull," he said, with a hint of compassion.

Tönnchen smiled impishly. He looked at the prunes, and Walter Schreiber had to laugh. Taking Tönnchen by the arm, he led him away from the enticing prunes to a different crate, which contained the lowest grade. Walter Schreiber could afford to be somewhat generous with these. He reached in and gave Tönnchen two handfuls. "But now out you go!"

Beaming with delight, Tönnchen obeyed. On the stairs he turned around once more and gave a perfectly executed bow. That must have been the way Ernst Seidel had once taken his leave before going to bed.

Shaking his head, Schreiber watched Tönnchen go. The man's a bona fide baby, he thought. Still taking the bottle, even though he's bound to be at least forty years old. Then Walter Schreiber went to his desk and opened the drawer and counted his cash. He was satisfied. Today he would buy steak again, and not just for his wife, but for himself as well. The day's take had been quite good.

Tönnchen, still chewing, headed back to the park, where he planned to wait for Fundholz.

THIRTEEN

Sonnenberg had taken up a position at the entrance to the Wittenbergplatz U-Bahn station. The newsboys were shouting out the headlines right beside him, but he wasn't listening. He stood in the sun, legs wide apart, holding out a small box of matches. A tray rested against his stomach, held in place by gaily colored bands that ran over his shoulders.

Sonnenberg did not hawk his wares. He didn't speak at all. He just stood there, rigid, holding out his box of matches. He had determined that talking didn't make much sense. By evening you were hoarse, and it didn't incline more people to buy, or to give him money without buying, which he definitely preferred. Moreover, his voice was not sufficiently smooth and ingratiating. It was too harsh, too demanding. People wanted to be charitable and generous of their own accord, instead of being told to be so. If they gave him ten pfennig, they didn't just want to help Sonnenberg, they were also investing in the feeling of being noble and generous.

Sonnenberg's face was impassive. He was listening. A man who can no longer see is primarily dependent on his ears. He has to hear the movements of the others, has to make out the individual from among the steps of the many.

Sonnenberg was waiting for his wife. He had sent her to buy him some half-moon cookies. He thoroughly enjoyed eating the large, frosted confections, which sold for five pfennig apiece. But now he was impatient. Where was she keeping herself so long?

What a tiresome woman. Leaving him to stand there while she stayed away for hours. Egoistic, that's what she was. She was probably somewhere gawking at display windows again. Sonnenberg could get furious when his wife did that. She would invariably stand a long time in front of each window and rave about what she was looking at, while he stood sightless beside her.

That was all he needed to really make matters even worse than they were. To wind up with such a woman! When he had married her, he thought he'd found someone who would devote herself to him alone, someone who would see him as an end in himself. He had dreamed that she would find work and he would no longer have to sell matches.

Instead I have to go out begging just as before, and on top of that she robs me of my money, he thought, growing angry.

At the Society for the Blind, the staff had often read aloud stories about women who helped alleviate the lot of blind people, caring for them and assisting them as needed.

He had never really believed it. People weren't angels: He knew that for sure. Nevertheless he had quietly nourished a tiny hope that his wife—whose name was Elsi—would turn out to be just such an angel.

At first it had been quite lovely. It had been a long time since he'd lived with a woman, and he had been happy to no longer be alone at night. Actually he was still glad about that. If only she wasn't so colossally dumb and narrow-minded, things wouldn't be half bad, he thought, when he heard steps approaching. The stranger came to a stop in front of him, and Sonnenberg heard coins clinking together.

Aha, he thought, this man's going to give me something. He's probably searching for the smallest coin he has. Judging from the step, he believed it had to be a man.

A coin dropped into his tray. Sonnenberg nodded and gave a slight bow.

But the man just stood there, staring at the blind man.

Ahh, thought Sonnenberg, annoyed. He expects to be entertained for his five pfennig. "Thank you, kind sir," he said. His voice sounded gruff and unkind as always.

"Soldier?" the man asked. From the tone of his voice, Sonnenberg could tell he was an officer.

"Indeed!" he confirmed.

"Western Front?" the man wanted to know.

For a moment Sonnenberg said nothing. You stupid dog, he thought. Eastern or Western Front—what difference does it make to you? I'm blind, and you're standing there staring at me.

Sonnenberg was getting worked up. I'm not some amusement in a penny arcade! I don't have to talk about my life every time somebody drops a coin! Finally he answered sullenly, "I fought at Champagne." His tone was meant to cut off all further conversation.

Nevertheless, the man asked, "Pretty savage business, wasn't it?"

Could I give the man a couple good whacks? Sonnenberg wondered. I'd really like to have a go at him. This damned piece of scum, he has both eyes in his head and here he wants to get me to say a few words of appreciation. "Go buy a book about the war, if you want to remember. But for those measly coins you can't expect me to bust out into a cavalry march!"

His voice was shaking with suppressed rage. Why can't I see? Why for God's sake can't I see? I'd like to kill the man. His face flushed a deep red. His eyes hurt to the point of bursting. I'd like to murder the man. If only I could see just for a minute so I could break his neck.

He had reached the limit of his self-control and had the pressing need to vent his rage. "What are you still waiting for?" he snorted.

The man hadn't budged.

Sonnenberg took off his glasses. At least I can give the man a fright even if I can't do anything to him, he thought.

Sonnenberg's eyes, which were lifeless but outwardly intact—he had been blinded by a bullet to the head—were now staring at the man.

But the stranger seemed unaffected. "Listen," he said. "I'll give you a mark if you tell me when and where you were wounded. But it has to be the truth."

The man was writing a book about the Western Front and was collecting eyewitness accounts to make it especially convincing. He was taken aback by the blind man's rudeness.

I'll go mad, thought Sonnenberg. I'm definitely going to go mad. He balled his fists. The matches he was holding snapped. Snorting with rage, he let the crushed matchbox fall to the ground.

Sonnenberg had the feeling he was peering into a sea of blood. Everything was dark red. But that was probably just his imagination.

What could he do? How could he kill this man? This cruel person who was standing there, provoking him, probably grinning the whole time and making fun of him. This scoundrel, thinking he could plop down a mark to find out what it was like to be blind.

Sonnenberg had always been hot-tempered. He could get worked up to the point of passing out. That, too, was probably a result of his head wound. But he had never felt such hate, such white-hot rage.

It was as if he would lose his mind any minute. If the man said another word, Sonnenberg would pounce on him and twist his neck.

The veins on his forehead were bulging to the point of bursting. He stood there without moving, a blind man who basically needed someone to guide him, while a thousand burning hells raged inside him. The fury was tearing him apart, because he wasn't a humble blind man in distress. He was a strong man shaking the chains of his blindness so ferociously he practically throttled himself.

At that moment his helplessness, his inability to hurt any-one else, showed up with a vengeance. He raged inside, against himself, because the other person, the man with seeing eyes, was unreachable.

The man looked on in amazement as Sonnenberg became increasingly agitated. This blind man can't impress me with his eyes, he thought. He had been an officer and had seen all types of wounds, corpses of gassed men, and gassed men who were slowly turning into corpses while they spit their lungs out piece by piece.

He had been at the front and seen how healthy men could become cadavers in a matter of seconds. Cadavers horrible beyond imagining. What were two dead eyes compared to that? Not that he had a brutal streak or was somehow a bad man. He had simply become desensitized. This had happened all on its own, just as his tone of voice had emerged all on its own after a few years in the cadet corps.

He felt sorry for the blind man. It couldn't be good to stand there like that, selling matches, even if such a fate wasn't as bad for these people as it would have been for him. But comparisons were always misleading, and this particular one was completely inappropriate!

Better to move on, he decided. Anyway he wasn't going to get anything more out of the blind man. It seems he had aggravated him unintentionally. These days everyone was so sensitive. Every-one, even a blind beggar, wanted to be handled with kid gloves. The world had been turned on its head. That was the problem! But the poor devil standing here begging couldn't do a thing about that.

The officer thought for a moment, then finally tossed fifty pfennig on the blind man's tray and went on his way.

Elsi arrived at the same time. She tapped the blind man who was standing there, stiff with tension and full of explosive energy, like a grenade before it goes off.

Now he needed to discharge that energy, he had to explode, otherwise the rage would burst his skull wide open.

He spoke quietly, almost in a whisper: "You bitch, you goddamned bitch!"

He snatched at her, and before she could dodge his grasp, he had taken hold of her arm. He didn't hit her, just held her tight while he subjected her to an uninterrupted stream of nasty insults and expletives. In a quiet voice, he reviled her with every insult he knew. Then when he ran out, he invented new curses and combinations of insults and swear words. And all the while he kept squeezing her arm with superhuman strength without letting go.

She didn't cry out loud. She was too taken aback by his sudden outburst.

He squeezed all his anger into her arm, while she stood there beside him, eyes wide with pain, unable to move a muscle.

Sonnenberg was freeing himself, discharging his ire. And when his mouth stopped spewing out his rage, his hand took over. With an inner joy he crushed her flesh.

Then he came to his senses, recovering enough air to breathe and think. He released her arm.

She was reeling and still unable to speak. She couldn't utter a word. She couldn't even think.

In his usual unfriendly voice, Sonnenberg said, "See what's in the box! I'm standing here begging and letting myself get insulted, and you? You're on the prowl for men! And don't you say a word, I know it for a fact."

Frightened, she obeyed and counted the money. But she was still unable to speak. I want to get away from him, whatever it takes, I want to get away, even if it means going back on the street, she thought.

"Well?" asked Sonnenberg, a menacing growl lurking in his voice.

"Two marks twenty," she stuttered.

Sonnenberg sensed he had gone too far. She's just a poor wretch herself, he thought.

"Well, then, come along, Elsi. Let's go to the self-serve and get something to eat. You just can't always run off and leave me standing there," he said, as gently as he could.

Elsi didn't understand. He had just been so mean. So horribly mean, and now he was nice again. She looked at him without a word. Then they set off.

Elsi guided him carefully, nervously. She pulled herself together as best she could. Meanwhile the blind man was once again in a good mood.

"Two marks twenty. That's quite a bit," he acknowledged. "I have eighty pfennig in my pocket, that makes three marks. So let's eat something decent for once. You'll have to pick some hot sausage with potato salad and nice rolls for me."

They often ate at the self-serve restaurant near the Zoologischer Garten station.

In the last few years, modern self-serve restaurants had sprung up everywhere you looked. The same principle was at work as with the accounting machines: decreased demand for human labor, no more waiters, only vending machines. They were also successful because they appealed to the same instinct as the slot machines in the arcade.

The rolls sat appetizingly arrayed behind the large glass panels, tempting the buyer. They were also very cheap. Even a caviar roll cost only ten pfennig. To be sure it was salmon roe and not genuine sturgeon, and the roll was small, but the caviar—or not-caviar—rolls looked so appetizing that everyone wanted to try them once.

Sonnenberg, too, asked for a caviar roll. "Caviar for the people," he said. "Hand it over." He was in a really good mood. Elsi on the other hand still looked pale and frightened, which made her face seem even more birdlike than usual. But evidently she managed to recover, since she, too, found the rolls quite tasty, despite everything.

Nevertheless, every time he spoke, she thought, I have to get away from him, whatever it takes. She hoped the nice young man who had sat next to them on the bench would show up that evening in the Jolly Huntsman.

She wanted to leave the blind man as fast as possible. Before long he'll wind up all alone and it will serve him right: She was already enjoying the thought in advance. Then he'll realize what he had with me. Besides, a cripple like that should be glad just to be alive.

Elsi's spirit of resistance was stirring just as Sonnenberg was turning peaceful. She gave short, snippy answers to his questions. But Sonnenberg didn't take that amiss. He didn't want to take anything amiss anymore, and he resolved to be less short-tempered in the future. He often resolved to do that when he was in a good mood.

But he suspected that the rage would once again overpower him. For the time being, though, he was in good spirits, as much as he ever was. How nice it is, he told himself, that I now have a wife. Even if she's as thick in the head as Elsi.

He was after all still a man. He felt vigorous and strong. He needed a woman.

He heard her chewing next to him. With a tinge of emotion, he stroked her arm. "Today at the Jolly Huntsman you can dance, Elsi," he said magnanimously.

That was a heavy sacrifice, since he couldn't see how she was dancing. He was constantly afraid she might "stray" with one of the men who weren't blind. They were always just after one thing. He knew that much based on himself.

"I don't really care if I dance or not." Elsi took pains to sound indifferent and uninterested. "Besides, afterward you'd just raise hell again."

She was right. Usually her dancing ended with a wild scene at home. He was too jealous. She's a decent girl, he tried to tell himself, but at the moment he wasn't entirely convinced.

"No, tonight you should dance at the Jolly Huntsman," he pronounced. "Really, you should dance. Even with that Handsome Wilhelm."

They left the restaurant and crossed the street. When they reached the other side, the streetlight changed and huge trucks went rushing past.

An excited old lady came running after them, but the truck traffic blocked her way. By the time the street was clear, she had lost sight of them. They had probably turned into a side street or disappeared into the throng of pedestrians.

Frau Fliebusch stared across the street, all atwitter.

"With that Handsome Wilhelm," she had heard him say. Wilhelm, her handsome Wilhelm, was at the Jolly Huntsman. She absolutely had to go there.

She had to go there right away. Everything would be all right. She would get him back. He might have forgotten her. Of course, he had completely forgotten his Amalie, but she would remind him.

In front of the bus stop at the Zoologischer Garten, people stopped and thronged about a woman who, having set her two bags on the ground, had folded her hands and was mumbling something to herself. Then Amalie Fliebusch picked up her bags and made her way through the crowd.

She was no longer angry at them. All those who had sinned against her were forgiven. The splendid blind man had made everything right. She would reward him. He should be given a thousand marks. Now that Wilhelm was back, she would also regain her money.

But she had to act quickly. In a flurry, Amalie Fliebusch rushed back into the restaurant.

"Where is the Jolly Huntsman?" she asked a man who was eating his bean soup in a leisurely way after the morning's rush.

He gawped at the excited woman. He gave his ear a thoughtful scratch and then informed her that he had never been there, and consequently had no idea where it was. Besides, he was a stranger in town. But before he could tell her where he was from and relay the detailed circumstances of his stay in Berlin, Frau Fliebusch turned to someone else.

That man, too, didn't know the address, but he looked it up in the phone book. Then he jotted it down on a piece of paper and handed it to her.

"Here's the address, young lady."

She thanked him and left the restaurant to board a streetcar bound for the Jolly Huntsman.

Will he be glad to see his uniform? she wondered, full of anticipation, as she climbed into the tram.

FOURTEEN

Fundholz was sitting on the steps, slowly spooning food from a deep bowl resting on his knees. He had been lucky. After ringing three doorbells, he had finally reached the right people. The door had been marked by another beggar, and rightly so. Fundholz quietly thanked his predecessor who had left the mark.

They'd given him a whole bowlful of red berry compote. With milk. Fundholz enjoyed eating compote. It went down easily—he didn't have to chew—and tasted good.

Fundholz still had enough of a palate to taste what he ate. Bread was boring, especially when it was barely buttered. The schnapps he liked to drink scarcely had any flavor, just a hint of peppermint, but it did have other pleasant effects. And berry compote tasted wonderful.

He ate slowly, resolved not to gulp it down like Tönnchen. It was important to retain a memory, a pleasant aftertaste.

At last he was finished. He wiped his mouth with his hand. He let his tongue search for any remaining bits and then stood up to return the bowl. Such nice old people. They hadn't first spent a long time stupidly gaping at him, either. They both had just glanced briefly out the door, then the woman had told him to wait a moment and finally brought him the compote.

He knocked quietly on the door, since the kitchen was

located just behind it. The woman reappeared. "Well, how was it?" she asked in a friendly voice.

"Good," Fundholz thanked her. He understood how to pack the entire savory experience into this one word.

The woman handed him a packet. "Unfortunately I don't have any change. But come back tomorrow at the same time. Then I can give you some soup and a few coins." She gave him a friendly nod.

Fundholz assured her he would come back.

After the woman had closed the door, the old man stood there a moment. He carefully reread the name by the doorbell. These were decent people, he determined, very decent. Yet it was hardly a wealthy household. They had to be just office workers or minor bureaucrats.

Repeated experience had taught him that poorer people were inclined to offer more than rich ones. If they could, they almost always gave something, and they did so without showing off and without the tone of magnanimity with which people Fundholz considered to be enormously wealthy gave ten or twenty pfennig.

To be sure, the couple who had just given him compote and bread was hardly poor. Certainly not by Fundholz's standards. But he was well acquainted with the difference between being rich and having limited means. It was a strange world all right. His arms were still sore after beating the carpet at Frau von Trasse's. And all he had received for slaving away like that was three slices of bread with a bit of butter and nothing else.

He opened the package. It contained three slices of bread—covered with knackwurst.

Why was that? After all, rich people had more money than they needed to live off. Poor people had to make each mark count. But you were more likely to get fifty pfennig from a poor person than two marks from someone who was rich.

It was odd: Rich people apparently always carried small change. Small coins for the beggars. Perhaps they were afraid that a beggar could get cocky if he were given a whole mark. Rich people also generally had stricter codes of conduct for poor people, Fundholz thought. Admittedly he had once received a bill for twenty marks—that must have been three years back. For that reason he didn't want to be unfair.

But that had been a special case. The young man who'd offered it had undoubtedly been drunk. He had called him darling and held on to him. First Fundholz bought a decent meal with the money, and then he got drunk for two days after: The gift had allowed him to do proper justice to the bottle. Those had been real red-letter days. Unfortunately they had ended at the police station, but he recalled them fondly nonetheless. Still, not every day could be a holiday like that, and it was also nice to eat berry compote with milk and then receive some bread with sausage.

Fundholz went down the stairs and read the first nameplate, which had *Palmen* written in red letters on a piece of white cardboard. The name has a friendly ring, he thought, like something sunny. He rang the bell.

Some powerful strides approached. The door swung open, and a tall young man looked out. "Yes?" he asked.

Fundholz mumbled, "I wanted to ask for some small assistance."

The man looked at him. "Are you unemployed?"

Fundholz nodded sullenly.

"For a long time, right?"

"Yes," said Fundholz, with a certain tragic tone. He didn't say much, but he could make his voice tremendously expressive.

"I see," the man stated, as though reassured. "But nevertheless you are alive. So it stands to reason that you'll go on living without any assistance from me." He looked at Fundholz and laughed.

The old man was surprised. He clearly couldn't deny that he was alive. Or that he would likely go on living. In that regard the man wasn't wrong. But Fundholz wanted money, not compulsory logical reasoning. After a moment's thought, he said, "If everyone thinks that way, I'll starve to death."

"That would be a great pity," the man admitted. "A great pity. Above all for you."

He examined Fundholz from head to toe.

"No," he then declared. "It wouldn't be a pity just for you, it would be a loss for everyone."

He reached into his pocket and gave Fundholz fifty pfennig.

"But only," he laughed, "because it's in the common interest." Still laughing, he closed the door.

Fundholz had to laugh as well. "He could have given me that without the long speech," he mumbled merrily to himself.

He didn't take such things amiss. Especially if they resulted in fifty pfennig. He spit on the coin, which was supposed to bring good luck, and put it in his pocket.

"In any case my streak of bad luck seems to have broken." But then he immediately raised his forefinger and said, "Careful, Fundholz." He realized why he was saying that. One had to be careful not to jinx things.

He had almost forgotten his own first name. When he occasionally carried on conversations with himself, as he was doing now, he addressed himself only as Fundholz.

Twice on the same floor is seldom lucky, he thought, and he climbed down to the next floor. Right in front of the landing was a door with no nameplate. Nor was there any sign posted next to the door.

Aha, thought Fundholz, the people have just moved in. Maybe if I'm the first one to come begging, then they'll give something. He was practically giddy when he rang the bell.

He didn't hear any steps. There's probably no one home. I'll come back tomorrow, he decided, and started to leave. Then he heard someone opening the door. He turned around.

He stared dumbfounded at the woman who was peering out of the apartment.

She, too, appeared to have noticed something that seemed familiar. She sized him up with curiosity.

The woman was old. Her white hair was wildly unkempt. Her small eyes were firmly fixed on Fundholz. Her face was gaunt and bilious, her body haggard. She wore rings with stones that sparkled.

Fundholz suddenly turned around. As fast as he could, he bolted down the stairs.

No doubt about it—that was her! She was still alive. Annie, his former wife.

But she, too, had recognized him. She recognized him just as he was turning around. Only one person turned around that way, and that was Fundholz. He first turned his head on its own axle, and then his feet caught up.

So he's still alive, the scoundrel, she thought. He's really gone to seed. Turned into a beggar. She didn't make a move to stop him or even go after him. She closed the door. So, he's turned into a beggar, she repeated. Good for him.

Fundholz dashed away. He hadn't run so fast in years. His oversize pants flapped around his knees. "Just run, run away," he mumbled to himself, "and hope she doesn't come after me!"

Never again did he intend to visit this neighborhood. Never again! Not even for huge pots of compote. You can't allow yourself to be happy about anything. Because the minute you do, you get punished. He resolved never to be happy.

Exhausted, he came to a stop.

She wasn't following. She probably didn't even recognize him. How gaunt she had seemed. A shiver ran through him.

So Annie was still alive, and she was doing well. Naturally, Annie always did well. And she should! He no longer felt any bitterness toward her. Twenty years had passed since their divorce. And he had been begging for ten of those years.

It had been her fault. It was her fault that he was now a beggar. But Fundholz no longer bore her any hatred. He was generally incapable of hating anymore. Besides, she had become indifferent to him. Nevertheless he had received a shock. If you saw your wife for the first time in twenty years, especially if the divorce had been accompanied by such sad circumstances as it was in his case, then it was no trifling matter.

Fundholz leaned against a building. He felt nauseated. He couldn't get over how unfriendly she had looked.

But hadn't he suspected something like that this morning? You never know when a streak of bad luck might break, he had thought. Now he realized how right he had been: You have to always be careful, especially careful.

He straightened up again and looked around suspiciously. He didn't want to beg anymore today. He wanted to go back to Tönnchen. Slowly he started to move.

Once again he thought of Annie. A kind of chill ran down his spine, then he fell back into his usual indifference.

FIFTEEN

Grissmann went inside the library. He liked to read, but he did so more out of boredom than from a thirst for knowledge.

There were spacious public reading rooms, where newspapers and books were put out on display. Many people who were out of work came there, not just to pass the time but also to educate themselves, although this was not the case with Grissmann.

Grissmann had a narrow field of interest. Nor did he have any desire to expand it. Like many others forced into idleness, he wasn't interested in specialist books or political writings, but he also didn't care much for popular literature. He was, however, definitely interested in publications that, under the guise of sexual education, contained all sorts of treasures that went beyond pure enlightenment. He was not after enlightenment so much as entertainment.

The libraries, meanwhile, did not cater to such tastes. They rightly refused to install a pornographium simply to accommodate the wishes of certain readers. But Grissmann had other sources.

One day, when he had been lackadaisically reading a novel, he had found himself facing an older, evidently well-to-do gentleman, bending over a reference book of substantial proportions. Less concerned with the reference book itself, the man had displayed particular interest in a photograph he had discovered in the book. A collector had probably left it there by mistake.

When the gentleman looked up—not without a certain amused smile—he noticed Grissmann's grinning face and blushed, although just a little bit. They started a conversation and established a certain commonality of views and interests. The older gentleman was very interested in a rather esoteric type of photography, and they agreed to meet every Wednesday at four o'clock in the library.

To be sure, Grissmann didn't have any treasures of his own to offer, but he knew several like-minded men with whom he maintained a kind of exchange-and-borrow relationship. Grissmann procured and delivered the books and pictures. His commission consisted of being allowed to view and read the material himself. Precisely in this rather awkward area Grissmann, who was otherwise shy, developed a certain cheerful nonchalance. His acquaintances had much higher social standing than he did, but their shared proclivity allowed class differences to be forgotten.

These hobbyists functioned not unlike stamp collectors. Except there were obviously more stamp collectors than devotees of this particular pastime. Precisely for that reason, those who professed this inclination were bound by a special closeness.

Grissmann had arrived at the library. He looked around for his acquaintance, who was evidently not yet there. Grissmann picked up a newspaper and began to read. He wasn't interested in politics or the economy. What did it matter to him what was happening in Geneva? He couldn't see why he should read through all that. The increase in shipping quotas for the metallurgical industry also left him indifferent.

Grissmann was looking for drama. Finally he discovered something that seemed interesting. "Dreadful double murder in the USA," he was thrilled to read. A band of gangsters had attacked a man and woman in the state of Ohio.

Grissmann found the name Ohio exciting. Ohio had the

ring of adventure. That was undoubtedly the Wild West. Yes, there was always something going on in America; he would have enjoyed living in America. Germany on the other hand was behind the times. If someone here was robbed and murdered, all the newspapers immediately made such a hullabaloo. In America nobody gave two hoots about a couple of corpses. "With a pistol in your hand, you roam across the whole wide land," he rhymed, believing it to be true. How wonderful it would be if he were no longer Grissmann, the man without a job. In America he would certainly be a man with courage—after all, everyone there was courageous.

He finished reading the article. The murderers had escaped undetected. In America you usually escape undetected. Those Americans are pretty sharp folks.

He leafed some more through the paper. A man in Köpenick had shot his girlfriend because she'd been unfaithful. Grissmann understood that. He'd shoot his girlfriend, too, if she cheated on him. Unfortunately, though, he didn't have a girlfriend. But tonight I'll have one, he hoped. Sonnenberg will be astonished. "Fundholz is also stupid," Sonnenberg had said about the old man. Now he's going to find out that he's a lot stupider than Fundholz.

Grissmann was in a good mood. The prospects made him happy. A man sat down beside him. He looked up, and they exchanged smiles. It was the older gentleman.

His name was Dr. Hähnchen, and he was a newspaper editor, but Grissmann didn't know that. The older gentleman did know Grissmann's name, assuming he still remembered it, but he had never introduced himself. For his part, Grissmann hadn't even tried to learn the gentleman's name or anything more about him.

Grissmann's thinking was to a large degree shaped by reading crime thrillers. He enjoyed losing his thoughts in the world they evoked and was prone to fantasizing. In those moments, however, instead of slipping into the role of the detective, he saw himself as the lucky perpetrator. He liked devising criminal exploits and thinking up ways of carrying them out, and he did so frequently. Until now, however, he had never considered Dr. Hähnchen as a possible object of exploitation. He had merely registered that, judging from appearances, Dr. Hähnchen was a wealthy man.

Grissmann had a rather unclear idea of what it meant to be wealthy. He considered any person who was well-dressed to be rich. This somewhat superficial assessment had already caused him several disappointments. Some time ago he had been sharing a house with a man who lived very modestly, but who Grissmann suspected was very rich because he wore gaiters and a bowler. That was enough for Grissmann to deduce that the man possessed considerable capital. Then by chance he found out that the man was merely a waiter, which said more about the man's financial status, if not his character. Grissmann had been astonished to note that poor people, too, could wear gaiters. But he still considered this to be an exception that proved the rule.

Grissmann had spent the whole day thinking about ways to make money and enviously dwelling on the splendid lives people led in America. Now, looking at Hähnchen with different eyes, he was completely taken with his own cleverness.

Hähnchen didn't notice the fresh attention. He viewed Grissmann with indifference. Grissmann was a procurement agency for photos.

Earlier, Hähnchen had been the editor of a small-town newspaper—a moralistic, somewhat philistine provincial paper. But his obscure life as a small-town editor had given rise to some peculiar preferences. Now he operated only as a freelance writer for newspapers.

Apart from the fact that he was working on a book about the morality of the fourth estate, and despite the enormity of this undertaking, he still found time to devote to his old pleasures of discovering and collecting. He also believed that as a mature man who had sufficiently stood up for morality, he could afford certain, primarily aesthetic, escapades.

As they were speaking, Grissmann subjected Herr Doktor Hähnchen to a thorough visual examination. This reinforced his conclusion that the man had to be rich: A thick gold watch chain dangling from his vest lent his stomach an air of prosperity. Numerous fraternity ribbons from his student days dangled from his waist.

As Grissmann was winding up the actual exchange, he thought further about his partner's presumed circumstances. The gold chain alone was proof of a certain degree of wealth.

For his part, Dr. Hähnchen considered his business with Grissmann to be concluded. He stood up, stowed the pictures he had been given in his briefcase, and took his leave. "Until next time," he said in a friendly voice.

Grissmann stood up as well. "I'll also be going," he said, drily.

Hähnchen found this unpleasant. Hopefully he could lose Grissmann once he was outside. He didn't intend to show his solidarity with the unemployed man so far as to be seen with him on the street.

They passed through the library. Hähnchen spoke in monosyllables to make it clear to Grissmann that he wasn't interested in any further companionship. When they reached the street, he held out his hand.

Grissmann pretended not to see it. "Where are you headed?"

"To Steglitz," Hähnchen answered truthfully.

Grissmann thought for a moment. Should he risk the fare? But maybe he could make friends with the man and find out more about him. Grissmann was already planning again.

"Me, too," he said cheerfully, but he couldn't help turning red.

Hähnchen didn't notice. He was annoyed. That's what happened when you got involved with these people. Now he had to ride with this down-and-out unemployed bum. That's the way this lot always is, he thought bitterly—you reach out a little finger and right away they want your whole hand.

He was piqued by the man's pushiness, but nevertheless he was unable to summon the courage to leave him behind. These people always became unpleasant and wound up embarrassing a person in the middle of the street.

Both lost in thought, they made their way to the streetcar stop.

Hähnchen decided to get out several stops ahead of his home and go into a café. This was the best way to shake off Grissmann.

He was full of self-reproach. How could he have been so stupid as to get involved with this man? Herr Doktor Hähnchen, editor in chief, next to this out-of-work Missmann or whatever his name was. It would be awful if someone saw them. All the smut wasn't worth that.

Hähnchen was a sensitive man. A person who always worried about what others were thinking. But because he did have these peculiar proclivities, for better or worse he had to put up with any embarrassing consequences.

Grissmann wondered how he might best sound out his companion. He was so awkward—speaking did not come easily to him. He was great at planning but bad at executing. Conversation was simply beyond him.

"Decent weather," he said meaningfully.

Hähnchen did not disagree. He nodded.

Grissmann was silent for a while. "Do you also live in Steglitz?"

Hähnchen nodded, irritated. He hoped the man wouldn't discover any other commonalities. The next thing you knew, he'd be dropping by to visit. He was certainly importunate enough to do that. Looking at him from the side, Hähnchen found the man appalling—infantile and at the same time vicious.

"I live in Steglitz as well," Grissmann lied audaciously. He was amazed at his own bravery. It'll all work out, he told himself. Just keep going. "Which street do you live on?" he asked, even more boldly.

Hähnchen didn't answer. This could turn out to be a fine mess indeed. The man seemed to want to pay him a visit. Finally he cleared his throat and said, "I'm in the process of moving."

This wasn't exactly the answer Grissmann had been expecting. He was moving. Now he didn't know either the old or the new address. He looked at Hähnchen thoughtfully. "If you want to move, I might be able to be of assistance," he offered. "I'm out of work and know about house moving."

This bothered Hähnchen. He had the impression that the man was after something. Either he wanted to ask for money, or—even worse—he was going to blackmail him. Hähnchen decided to shake him off at all costs.

"That's a shame. Unfortunately I no longer need anyone. A firm is coming tomorrow to take care of things. Otherwise I'd be glad to have your help. Perhaps some other time."

The streetcar came, and both men climbed in.

"Moving is so much work," Grissmann said thoughtfully.

"You can say that again. An awful lot of work. And the things that get damaged!"

Grissmann didn't think that he had ever had anything damaged during a move. But that was probably because he didn't have anything to damage.

"That must mean a lot of work for your wife as well," Grissmann ventured, hoping to learn more about Hähnchen's personal circumstances.

Hähnchen was glad that he was succeeding in uncoupling himself from Grissmann. "Yes, my wife has an enormous amount on her plate."

Grissmann was sorry to hear that. Especially the fact that the man had a wife. It was easier to break into a bachelor's apartment.

"Are your children helping out?"

Hähnchen nearly burst out giggling. His children—that was priceless.

"Absolutely, my two sons are also helping out. That goes without saying—what else are they for?"

Grissmann concurred. "Especially when they're all grown up!"

"Indeed. The oldest is twenty-three, and Hans, the youngest, is already nineteen."

Hähnchen was starting to enjoy all the lies. He had fabricated a whole family. That was amusing. He felt the same enjoyment as a boy playing a trick on a friend.

As Hähnchen became more and more cheerful, Grissmann grew increasingly sullen. There was probably nothing to be had. Three men and a woman—it would be suicide to break in, and it made no sense to stay on the streetcar.

But he didn't get off, and instead tried to find out more. "Bad times, aren't they?"

Hähnchen laughed. "I can't complain. I'm alive and not so badly off."

If Hähnchen had shown as much imagination in his earlier editorials as he was now developing in his conversation with Grissmann, his readers would have been more pleased with him. In the small town where he lived and worked, he was notorious for his less-than-creative thinking.

"Does your work pay well?" asked Grissmann, who, having sunk his teeth in the man, did not want to let go so easily.

Hähnchen beamed. "One has what one needs," he said genteelly.

But then he felt a twinge. Who knows, the man might start begging for something. He was surprised at himself. He was usually given to complaining, which he did often and gladly. "The taxman's taking the butter off my bread," he always said.

"But I'm pretty pessimistic about the future," he mused, tempering his earlier statement. "Pretty pessimistic indeed!"

Grissmann didn't respond. He sat there, worried. The man has money like hay, he thought. But what good is it to me? Here

I'm starving and this fat cat doesn't know what to do with all his money. I wonder if he'd give me some if I asked.

Grissmann would certainly have preferred a friendly request that would bring in ten marks over a more risky venture that might yield a hundred marks. But he didn't quite dare ask. Rich people were hard-nosed, as Fundholz had drilled into him often enough. Grissmann didn't believe the man next to him would give him even a single mark voluntarily. He believed it would be easier to steal a hundred marks than to get ten by begging.

He wasn't exactly a ruthless person, but he wanted to become one. Only scoundrels are successful: That was how he saw the world. But he was too dumb and too cowardly to be a real scoundrel. He considered that to be his greatest misfortune.

He felt a vague rage welling up inside him.

Hähnchen, who was sitting next to him and feeling good about his childlike boasting, had no idea how deeply he had wounded and disappointed Grissmann.

Grissmann wondered how he might be able to get back at this collector of smutty pictures. It wasn't just the man's material success that galled him, but the man himself. He had the feeling that Hähnchen had a far worse character than his own. Because if Grissmann had money, he was convinced that he would be a good person. In any case, he would be more decent than the man sitting next to him.

He was getting more and more worked up. The injustice of his being poor and the other man being rich, as he assumed, made him bitter.

"You probably have a lot of smutty pictures hanging in the house?" he asked in a loud, cavalier voice.

Hähnchen turned bright red and wished he could shrink to the size of a fly and buzz away. But unfortunately that wasn't possible. Oh God oh God, what a disaster. The inner pain made him wince.

How embarrassing! This damned lowlife. If anyone had heard that, he might as well emigrate, take off to Australia. He would have gladly jumped off the streetcar, but it was moving at a crazy speed. He anxiously looked all around. A man was talking to a girl, all laughs and smiles. Hähnchen was sure they had heard.

Hähnchen was a provincial man. He had lived in a town where everyone poked their noses in everyone else's business—a town that didn't even need newspapers, because a certain class of elderly ladies served as a living source of news.

The lives of every prominent person—and Hähnchen counted as prominent—were under the constant control of this "public opinion." The citizens possessed a remarkable recall and carefully kept alive the memory of any wrongdoing or, alternatively, passed it on to the next generation.

In the metropolis of Berlin, Hähnchen had very much remained the small-town provincial. Whenever he went for a walk, he kept anxiously glancing around so as not to fail to doff his hat at any given moment. People from small towns who didn't carefully adhere to the traditional forms of greeting were not worthy citizens but depraved souls, at least in the eyes of the small town.

Hähnchen had always been able to hide his secret penchants. No one would have suspected that he might harbor such interests. But now this person was practically trumpeting his inner life for the entire world to hear. It was so embarrassing, so horribly embarrassing.

He looked beseechingly at Grissmann, who was taken aback at the effect of his words. "Surely you have some big books on the subject?" he innocently continued.

Hähnchen regained control of himself. "I have no idea what you mean, sir!"

The stern tone made an impression on Grissmann, but he wasn't thrown off track. "Well, well!" he said, giving his voice a tone of indignation. Going into details wasn't pleasant for him, either. But now he was determined to press on with his attack.

Hähnchen leaned forward. "Are you trying to blackmail me? There are police for that," he hissed, furious.

The threat seemed to make no impression on Grissmann, who grinned defiantly.

Hähnchen was frightened. He didn't want to let the man say another word. True, he hadn't spotted anyone he recognized in the streetcar, but he knew how quickly word got around. He pulled out his thin wallet, which had several small bills next to each other.

Hähnchen's hands were shaking a bit. He gave Grissmann ten marks.

"Now get lost. If I ever see you again it will turn out badly for you." His quiet threat sounded implausible.

But Grissmann was so surprised by his success that he wasn't thinking of further exploiting the situation. He took the money, grinned once again at Hähnchen, and left the streetcar at the next stop.

Both men sighed with relief.

Never again, thought Hähnchen. Never again get involved with those kinds of people.

He tried replacing his wallet, but it jammed against something and wouldn't quite fit in his breast pocket. Hähnchen looked to see what it was. Then he smiled contentedly. The pictures. Pictures he had no intention of ever returning to that lowlife.

Grissmann kept looking at the ten marks.

It had worked out. Everything had worked out. Courage was all it took. In that moment Grissmann firmly believed that he was a man of particularly good fortune.

He had ten marks. And it had gone so quickly. The others should also pay, he decided. Cold cash was worth more to him than all the pornographic pictures. He made up his mind to take even more money from the others.

Feeling satisfied, he went back on foot, to save on the fare. Now he had enough money for the evening.

I'm starting to become a genuine scoundrel, he thought happily.

SIXTEEN

Tönnchen sat on the bench and looked at the sun. He had his own special way of doing that. He shut his eyes but for a narrow slit, then opened his mouth wide and looked up.

He was sweating. Thick beads of sweat covered his forehead. The sun penetrated the old suit that clung tightly to his limbs, leaving little air. It was wonderful to sit there so warm and comfortable. But it was also very exhausting. He was hardly moving and nevertheless was getting hotter and hotter. He assumed that this came from the golden ball up in the sky, and now he was looking up to know for sure.

Admittedly you couldn't really look straight up; you could only secretly open your eyes a little and act as if you weren't looking there at all. Your eyes would hurt if you looked directly. In the meantime even his spine was sore from the strenuous bending backward. He had better stop. He moved his head back into its normal position and closed his mouth.

A man was standing in front of him. He had already been observing Tönnchen for several minutes. He had noticed how Tönnchen kept looking up, and at first had surmised he was observing a bird or a high-flying airplane. But he himself hadn't been able to see anything of the kind.

The man took a seat next to Tönnchen.

"Müller, Friedrich Müller," he introduced himself.

Tönnchen laughed.

Friedrich Müller took that as an invitation to speak.

"I'm also unemployed. You are unemployed, aren't you?"

Tönnchen went on smiling.

What kind of dimwit is this, Müller wondered. "Listen," he said, annoyed and almost threatening. "I'm a professional lock-smith."

Tönnchen nodded, frightened.

Friedrich Müller felt the need to unburden himself, and Tönn-chen struck him as a suitable audience.

"Have you been out of work a long time?"

Tönnchen nodded anxiously, which made Müller feel more conciliatory. The obese man seemed odd, downright doltish, but he needed people like that when he wanted to talk. Müller had little tolerance for being contradicted.

After a moment's thoughtful pause, he finally resumed. "What do you think of Ludendorff? He's right, isn't he?"

Tönnchen nodded once again.

"That's great. It's so rare to meet enlightened people! The general has it all figured out, no question about it!"

Tönnchen smiled. His smile was happy and less hesitant than usual.

The man registered that. "It's all the fault of the Freema-sons and the Jews. The Masons murdered Schiller! Goethe was a Freemason himself! They found the trace of a gunshot wound on Schiller's skull. He was murdered!"

Friedrich Müller went on, a little haltingly. But what he lacked in eloquence he made up with conviction that his cause was good.

Tönnchen didn't contradict him. How could he? This wasn't about rutabagas. It was about Ludendorff, Schiller, and Goethe. All things Tönnchen had never eaten.

"Goethe was a mean person all round. That's why he was a Freemason, too. Did you know that Goethe had an affair with a Jewish woman?"

Tönnchen nodded.

Disappointed, the man continued. "The Jews are all Freemasons! Goethe was also a Freemason, precisely because he had an affair with a Jewish woman! The Freemasons want to take over the world."

Tönnchen smiled.

"They do," said the man. "It's even in the Zionist protocols. All the Zionists are Freemasons! But Ludendorff managed to unmask them, you understand? He acted as if he, too, were for the Freemasons. But that was only an act. He saw everything, and then he unmasked them."

The man laughed, delighting in the general's cleverness.

Tönnchen, too, laughed. But only because the other man was laughing.

Tönnchen's laughter spurred the man on. "Ludendorff is a genius," he stated. "You realize he won the battle of Tannenberg." He leaned his mouth close to Tönnchen's ear. "And Hindenburg is actually a Freemason himself!" he said dramatically.

Tönnchen recoiled in shock.

"It's true," Müller declared earnestly. "That's why he acts as if he won the battle of Tannenberg. Because Ludendorff is against the Masons."

He shot Tönnchen a fierce look.

"It's no laughing matter. It's really true. I heard it myself! The Freemasons all have lodges," he said, with envy. "And what do people like us have? But that's because the Masons are Jews. The Jews have all the money. They have lodges all over the world. It's outrageous!" He shook his head.

Tönnchen nodded.

"Do you know that the Freemasons are to blame for everything?"

Tönnchen evidently didn't know that yet. He didn't smile, but stared at the other man open-mouthed.

Friedrich Müller was glad to find someone so interested. "It's like this: The Masons started the war. The World War. The

Freemasons wanted to force Germany to its knees. Because they hate Ludendorff. That's how it is. The Masons wanted to murder Ludendorff. But Ludendorff is still alive. Which is why they are starving Germany to death. But Ludendorff isn't going to starve. Ludendorff is going to show them! He's telling the world. He's written what kind of brothers these Masons really are."

These last words were filled with much hate and passion. Tönnchen winced.

"Are you a Freemason, too?" Müller asked mistrustfully. Tönnchen nodded.

Outraged, Müller stood up. He spat on the ground. "Disgusting. You should be ashamed. All Freemasons deserve to be strung up."

He gave Tönnchen a fierce stare.

Tönnchen, bewildered, nodded in agreement.

Friedrich Müller stormed away. The blatant mockery was difficult for him to bear.

But was it possible? They were everywhere, these Freemasons.

Tönnchen went back to squinting at the sun, his eyes almost completely shut, as if he weren't looking at anything at all.

Schiller, he thought, what does that taste like? He still had the sweet taste of Walter Schreiber's prunes in his mouth. Was that Schiller? He didn't know.

He sweated away and forgot about Schiller and the Freemasons.

SEVENTEEN

Fundholz had run too fast. He realized that now. He had a cramp in his side. He slowed his pace, but the cramp did not abate. He decided he had to take a break for it to get better.

Fundholz looked around. No policemen in sight. He crossed the street, stopped on the other side in front of a cinema, and examined the posters.

In one, a man who was evidently in a very bad mood stood with balled fists across from a clearly likable young gentleman with sharply creased pants. The young man's smile exuded fearlessness and independence.

Fundholz looked at the picture without much interest.

Behind the young gentleman was a young girl. She was very beautiful, with snow-white teeth and a tantalizing red mouth. She was snuggling up to the young man with the creases, seeking protection, and her hands lay gently and gracefully on his broad shoulders.

Written in bold lettering across the poster were the words *Tragic Love*. It had to be very tragic, because the man in the bad mood was holding a pistol in his hand, as Fundholz now noticed.

The old man turned away. In spite of his cramp, he kept on going. He didn't want to know anything about tragic love. All he wanted was peace.

On the other side of the cinema was another large poster

announcing the opening of a film set in the Alps: *Where the Mountains Crown the Heavens.*

Fundholz stopped again to look at the poster.

An older man in knickerbockers was pictured alongside a suntanned youth. They had linked arms and were smiling cheerfully. A blue sky shone behind them. A very special blue sky. A deep blue. The printer had surely used the bluest blue available. That's why the poster had turned out so beautiful.

The two men were standing on the top of a cliff. If they weren't standing so close together, Fundholz thought, one of them would surely fall off.

Suitable for all ages was written in white lettering.

Fundholz never went to the movies. First, because he simply couldn't afford to, and second, because he didn't want to. Fundholz was a realist. He saw life as it really was, every day, and had no interest in seeing what it might be.

In some respects, films serve as substitutes for real life, though they differ from other substitutes because they're so much more beautiful than reality. The men possess exceptional powers, and the women almost always exude exceptional charm.

There are also films that portray life without any sugarcoating. They are less common and probably less successful, since most people want to be dazzled. They enjoy seeing the triumphs and successes that are missing from their own lives—and that they would begrudge their acquaintances.

Here things are different. Here things just happen as a matter of course. Here even we would be successful if things were the way they're seen on the screen. How brave all the young men would be if they were real detectives. But unfortunately they are not. They have no reason, no occasion to be brave. And how gracious even the grouchiest bosses would be if their stenographers were as cute as the ones in the movies. How beautiful life would be in general, if everyone could be like a movie star and choose which role he wanted to play.

Fundholz didn't have any illusions. He'd rather have a single mark in cold cash than the jackpot offered by the movies. He hadn't stopped in front of the posters out of curiosity, but rather to have a justification for stopping. He didn't stick out here, as he was standing alongside a number of curious people doing the same thing.

One passerby after another stopped in front of the posters. They looked at the bewitching blue of the heavens and the two suntanned men. The female pedestrians, from sixty on down, focused exclusively on the young man. He was a very famous movie actor. A person who in the film recklessly braved all dangers. Didn't bat an eyelash if an avalanche came rushing down or if bad guys were shooting at him with their revolvers.

A man the way a man should be.

They would compare this man with their too-thin or too-fat husbands and conclude that they had been betrayed by life. The movie hero didn't have bags under his eyes, never went around in slippers, and never undid his collar while eating.

Fundholz looked at the poster. But he didn't see the hero or the man who was presumably the hero's father. Fundholz was seeing Annie. He saw her just as he had seen her minutes before. She had looked so old, horribly old and ugly.

It was hard to keep that memory at bay. He tried to ward it off, but it kept coming back. He didn't want to think about Annie. He just wanted to be left alone in peace. Nothing came from all this thinking. That much was certain. He could no longer change his life, nor did he want to. Why should he torment himself with memories? Memories that had faded and that Annie had reawakened. Why dwell on those old stories all over again? It had not been good. Not at all. Such a torrent of misfortune had poured over him, he had had to get through so much. He didn't want to remember. He didn't want to remember anything about what had once been.

The cramps had long since disappeared, but Fundholz was still standing in front of the poster. He struggled to regain his inner peace. He wanted to suppress anything called memory.

He closed his eyes. He had to distract himself by thinking of something calming.

"I'm going to have some schnapps this evening," he mumbled. "Tonight I'm going to have five shots of schnapps." The thought revived him. It had been a long time since he'd had five schnapps in a row. Beer was a luxury. Beer could be considered a treat. But schnapps was a necessity. Especially today.

Fundholz moved on. As he did, an elderly man broke away from the group of people standing there. Fundholz didn't pay him any attention, but he walked right up and accosted Fundholz. "Well, boss, how's business?" His voice sounded pleasantly calm.

Fundholz barely looked at him. "Bad," he said.

The man walked alongside him with heavy steps. "That's right, when we're young we work, and when we're old we beg," he said calmly. He was better dressed than Fundholz, which wasn't saying much. But even he was wearing an old gray suit that was worn through and shiny and full of patches.

Fundholz didn't answer. Once again he was expected to think about problems, about the how and the why. He was a beggar and didn't rack his brains as to whether it was right or not that he had to go begging.

"I don't beg," the man said. He didn't say this with the undertone that would imply "just don't think I'm like you." He was simply making a statement.

Nor did Fundholz find any arrogance in this statement. He by no means wished that everybody had to go begging. On the contrary, he had the feeling that the profession had suffered in recent years due to overcrowding. Besides, he didn't really care. As far as he was concerned, the man next to him could go begging or not.

The man went on talking, unhurriedly, weighing every word. "I'm living at my son's place and still have some pension, otherwise I'd also have to beg. Tell me, is it right when someone who's worked in a factory for twenty years is let go overnight? Meanwhile the pay in the last few years has been so lousy that nobody could save anything. What savings you did have were eaten up by inflation. Then one day you learn the factory is closing and everybody is dismissed. Except the director. The director stays. I guess he still has things to take care of. That's how it goes. We workers get the boot and the director stays. But don't think that we are going to put up with that in the long run. How can they throw out people who have worked in the same factory for twenty years? Simply because business isn't going well. As it is we don't gain anything when business is better. Certainly less than the stockholders. Why should we be the ones who suffer if something goes wrong now and then?"

Fundholz didn't answer. He couldn't change injustices, so why brood over them?

"That's all going to change. Things are going to be different. We won't always be the ones left with nothing."

"I don't know," Fundholz muttered. "We'll probably always be the ones that get swindled." He said this so quietly that the other man couldn't understand.

"You don't know?" The other man laughed. "But do you know that you're begging for a living? That you don't have anything to eat? Have you always just been a beggar?"

Fundholz shook his head.

"What did you used to do?"

Fundholz didn't answer. It doesn't make any difference what I used to do, he thought. Now I'm a beggar, and I'll keep on begging until the day I die, if they don't put me in the poorhouse.

The man walked awhile next to Fundholz without saying anything. "No offense," he then said drily. "But you're not exactly talkative."

Fundholz nodded. He wasn't talkative. He didn't seek out conversations and didn't expect much from them.

"Man, you have to wake up. Chase the moths out of your brainbox. Man, we're fighting for our children." The man was now a little more fired up.

"I don't have any," said Fundholz.

The man laughed. "So should the world always stay the same? Even if you don't have any children. Should the others always be able to do what they want with us?"

Fundholz grumbled. "I don't know."

"Well," said the man, "in that case you can't complain about being a beggar. I'm going to fight as long as I live!"

Fundholz scratched himself thoughtfully. Finally he said, "I'm not complaining."

The other man gave up. "Go on then. Just go on begging. You're a hopeless case. Looks like you need a good stomping so you wake up."

The man nodded goodbye and turned away, his boots heavy on the pavement.

Fundholz watched him go. I don't want to fight and I don't want a good stomping, he thought. I just want to be left in peace.

He passed a clock. It was already six. He had to hurry, since he wanted to go with Grissmann to the Jolly Huntsman. He quickened his pace and felt that he had once again overcome everything. Past as well as present. He had regained his peace.

When he reached the park a little before seven, Tönnchen went to meet him.

"Tönnchen is hungry," he announced.

Fundholz had to laugh. Tönnchen is hungry. There's someone who is truly lucky. He only thought about his stomach. Fundholz gave him two slices of bread, after first carefully removing the knackwurst from one. Tönnchen always received the quantity, but Fundholz saved the quality for himself.

They both ate, Fundholz slowly and deliberately, Tönnchen greedily and fast.

Tönnchen finished first. "Hungry," he explained—the word was as telling as it was succinct. First Fundholz finished eating, then they went to a pub. There each ordered a meatball with potatoes. Fundholz settled the bill, which came out to fifty pfennig.

He felt quite full. For the moment Tönnchen was also satisfied, although he couldn't take his eyes off a ham, but that was completely unattainable. Even Tönnchen wasn't so crazy as to expect ham.

Fundholz gave him a poke, and Tönnchen headed obediently to the door. Fundholz followed him, then they went to the vegetable shop.

Walter Schreiber was again counting the day's take. He was amazed to see the two so early. He had no intention of letting these tramps keep interfering with his business. But Fundholz explained that Tönnchen should go inside the basement now.

Schreiber unlocked the room. When he passed by the prunes—the third-grade variety—he reached in and gave Tönnchen a handful. He didn't understand why he did this. Apparently he had developed a soft spot for the man.

Tönnchen beamed. He stuffed the prunes inside his mouth and was finished right away. It didn't occur to him to give some to Fundholz. Nor did the old man expect that.

Both climbed down into the basement. Fundholz suddenly remembered he had forgotten to obtain blankets and straw, but in a fit of generosity Walter Schreiber allowed them both to use the wicker panniers again. So Fundholz constructed a bedstead for Tönnchen, and when he was finished, he turned and started for the door.

At first Tönnchen didn't understand. But when the door was closed, he realized that he was supposed to stay alone in the dark basement. The memory of another dark basement came flooding over him. He didn't want to stay alone!

He heard the key turn in the lock. That intensified his fear, and he charged at the door. "Tönnchen wants out!" he screamed.

They didn't answer. They wanted to leave him alone in the basement. But this being left alone was coupled with a terrible hunger. He felt that. Desperately Tönnchen pounded on the door with his weak, fat fists. He was a harmless sick person, not a raving madman. But now this terrible fear burst out of him.

The fear of starving. Walter Schreiber flung open the door. Fundholz was standing next to him. He was astounded at the racket Tönnchen could make.

Walter Schreiber snapped at the fat man. "Will you kindly calm down! My vegetable cellar isn't an insane asylum!"

Tönnchen whimpered. "Tönnchen wants out. Tönnchen doesn't want to stay alone. Tönnchen wants out."

Schreiber looked at Fundholz. "Take him with you. Who knows what mischief he'll get into if he's left alone?"

"Come on, let's go," Fundholz grumbled, and Tönnchen followed him, smiling. Everything was all good again. Only Fundholz wasn't so happy at how things had turned out. He would have to take Tönnchen to the Jolly Huntsman. Hopefully he wouldn't get hungry on the way.

They went to the park, where Grissmann, who was sitting on a bench, waved to them cheerfully. What's up with him? Fundholz wondered. The man's jolly mood struck him as strange. He wasn't used to seeing that in Grissmann. When they were standing in front of him, he held out his hand. "Watch Tönnchen for a bit," he requested. "I have to buy something."

Fundholz hurried to the bakery, which was just closing. Sullenly the saleslady let him in: She recognized the old man. Since he didn't place large orders, he should at least come punctually.

Fundholz asked for day-old rolls, but the saleslady shook her head. "Everybody wants the old rolls. But there's no way to bake them so they come out already old," she chided. So Fundholz bought four fresh rolls for Tönnchen and left.

When he came out of the bakery, he saw both of the others already standing on the other side of the street. Grissmann was evidently in a hurry to get to the Jolly Huntsman.

Tönnchen beamed when he realized the old man was coming from the bakery and immediately said, "Tönnchen is hungry."

Fundholz wrinkled his brow, annoyed. "I don't have anything for you."

But Tönnchen saw that the old man's jacket pocket was bulging. He pointed at it with his finger.

"Rutabagas," said Grissmann, grinning, but Tönnchen didn't believe it. He had seen the old man coming out of the place where the rolls came from. Those were bound to be rolls and not rutabagas.

"Let's take him to the basement," Grissmann suggested, but Fundholz explained how Tönnchen had resisted that.

"Well, so what?" Grissmann said, in a good mood. "Let him go on and rave away in the basement. The shop will be closed anyway. No one would hear it. He will ultimately calm himself down."

Fundholz grumpily shook his head. "Let's let him come with us."

Grissmann didn't object. Maybe Tönnchen would be good for some practical joke this evening. "Fine by me," he agreed. Then he wanted to know: "Is it far?"

"An hour," Fundholz explained, as they walked down the sidewalk.

Tönnchen eyed the old man's jacket pocket the way a man in love looks longingly at his bride.

EIGHTEEN

———

Frau Fliebusch was standing outside the Jolly Huntsman. Some dirty tin signs hung outside the facade of the building, advertising Schultheiss-Patzenhofer and some other brands of beer. Another sign visible in the window read *Dancing Evenings, Admission Free*, and above the entrance was written *Jolly Huntsman*. Earlier the pub had been called the Green Hunter, but the proprietor's license had been revoked, and the establishment was now registered in the name of his wife.

Herr Hagen stood at the door, taking things in.

Hagen was a stout man, with a large red face, a double chin, and red-rimmed eyes. He was not the proprietor, just the husband of the proprietor, but that amounted to the same thing. Since at this time of day he had nothing to do, he allowed himself some fresh air.

Herr Hagen was well-dressed. Seriously dressed, one might say. He wore striped trousers and a black jacket. Both looked good on him and gave him a dignified air. Unfortunately, however, he also wore yellow shoes. Strikingly yellow shoes, but he happened to like them very much.

He stood at the entrance, his feet wide apart. He had thrust out his stomach and let his head rest a little on his neck. The sun was shining on his face. He looked at Frau Fliebusch in a friendly way, albeit not without some amazement. She looked peculiar, but Hagen was without prejudice. He was used to a mixed crowd.

"Would you like a room?" he asked graciously, taking in her two bags.

The Jolly Huntsman rented rooms, although only to the female habitués. Moreover, Hagen preferred to see them utilized on an hourly basis, but it was a slow time. During the summer, the female habitués had little to do and therefore Hagen didn't mind letting his rooms out for an entire night.

Frau Fliebusch thanked him. "I don't want a room. I would like to speak to Wilhelm. I haven't seen him in twenty years," she confided to Hagen.

Hagen was surprised. "That's strange, very strange. Twenty years is a pretty long time."

Frau Fliebusch nodded sorrowfully. "An awfully long time. But now I have to speak to him right away!"

"Handsome Wilhelm doesn't come until ten," said Hagen, thinking that Wilhelm's mother was strange.

Frau Fliebusch was disappointed. But since she waited twenty years for Wilhelm, what were another couple hours?

"May I wait here?" she asked.

Hagen stepped courteously aside. "Just come on inside, Frau Winter. Come on inside."

"Fliebusch," she corrected. "Née Kernemann."

"Aha," Hagen muttered, amazed. "Well, go inside and have a seat, Frau Fliebusch."

She smiled gratefully and went past him, as Hagen stayed by the door. Son of a gun, he thought. No one knows that Wilhelm is really named Fliebusch. Everybody thinks his name is Winter. He probably got into some trouble as Fliebusch, and the police are after him. And not a single one of them has any idea that Fliebusch and Winter are one and the same.

Wilhelm is a talented man all right. He can write poetry, too. Hagen was glad that Handsome Wilhelm was a regular customer. He appreciated clever people—besides, men like that elevated the business. Guests came from all over to see the place. So, his real name is Wilhelm Fliebusch. Well, I'll act as if I don't know a thing about it, Hagen decided, and he lit another cigar.

Inside, the Jolly Huntsman was a far tidier place than the exterior suggested. Once a week, a passion for cleanliness overtook Frau Hagen. Together with her staff, she threw herself into cleaning the place. Tables and chairs were piled into mountains, floors mopped and waxed, surfaces dusted, counters scrubbed, and every object subjected to a cleaning so ruthless it either broke or submitted and became clean. Frau Fliebusch experienced the establishment just at the moment when it was at its most beautiful: after the cleaning and before the clientele.

The Jolly Huntsman primarily catered to evening guests. During the day there wasn't much to do, so only the small taproom by the entrance was open, to provide pedestrians and drivers a quick glass of beer. There were no tablecloths—that would have been too much. In the evening the atmosphere was too lively for tablecloths. Wooden tables were easier to clean.

Frau Fliebusch took a seat at one of the tables and stared ahead. She would have to wait a long time before Wilhelm arrived, but over the years she had learned how to keep herself occupied. She wondered why Wilhelm hadn't gotten in touch himself. If this splendid blind man hadn't mentioned his name, a lot more time would have passed before she found him.

Now it was clear how right she had been. Everyone had been lying to her in an ugly way. Wilhelm was alive, and everything would be set right again. But couldn't someone have told her earlier where he was to be found? There were no longer any decent people. Apart from her and Wilhelm of course. And the blind man—she counted him as an exception.

She was still excited, but she also felt fatigued. After such a long time of suffering, she was now suddenly about to have all her hopes come true, and that was exhausting. Amalie Fliebusch leaned back. She wanted to close her eyes just for a moment. But she fell asleep, smiling.

She dreamed that the bank had returned her money and that she and Wilhelm were walking along Unter den Linden. Everything was as it had been. People were walking around reasonably dressed. Not in these horrible new outfits. Amalie Fliebusch greeted this person and that. Wilhelm kept tipping his new top hat. Fräulein Reichmann rode past in an open carriage, and Frau Fliebusch smiled at her as well. They went to Café Bauer, and the old waiter with the Franz Joseph beard ushered them to a beautiful table. Wilhelm ordered: "My wife will have some Chartreuse and I'll take a whiskey soda." Wilhelm had been in England and since then always ordered whiskey. Frau Fliebusch worried it might not agree with him.

"You want something to drink?" a gruff voice asked.

Amalie Fliebusch woke up. This wasn't Café Bauer, and that was not the kind old head waiter. What was this? Gradually she regained awareness. "Chartreuse," she said, still somewhat muddled.

The man in front of her scratched himself, embarrassed. "We're sold out of that. Shall I bring you a schnapps?"

"No thank you," Frau Fliebusch said. "I'm just waiting here."

The man left, muttering something unfriendly under his breath, and Frau Fliebusch soon began to doze again.

Herr Hagen finished smoking his cigar and stepped inside his establishment. The way he moved conveyed great importance. He didn't walk like other people, simply placing one foot in front of the other. His legs possessed a special musicality. He kept them wide apart as he placed them on the floor, so that they seemed to lead a life of their own. Beyond stepping rhythmically up and down, they also moved in many other directions. When Hagen was in a good mood, as he was now, it seemed as if he wanted to toss away his legs—that was how acrobatically he flung them into the air. He took a step sideways, and his feet landed sideways on the floor. Stepping past Frau Fliebusch, he made his way through the establishment.

The main rooms—two large, spacious halls—were located

past the taproom. The larger of the two was open every evening, and from eight o'clock on, it featured music and dancing. In the back there was a smaller room, which Hagen typically rented to clubs. He had good connections to singing societies and sport clubs, which used his place for their celebrations and meetings.

Some of the putative singing societies and sport clubs were actually devoted less to recreational activities and more to matters of business. In Berlin they were known as Ringvereins, or "ring clubs," since they were connected in a ring, like a cartel. They dealt with prostitution, by imposing an indirect tax and by organizing all the pimps and with them a significant number of the prostitutes themselves. But that wasn't enough for them. Like other cartels, they wanted to obtain complete control over the trade by standardizing and stabilizing the prices. Their members enjoyed a certain degree of legal protection, since many of the groups retained their own lawyers, who, for a flat fee, defended all members against the state. This proved absolutely necessary, too, since several of the members did not content themselves with managing the working ladies but ran other operations as well. Consequently they often came into contact with the police and held their meetings exclusively in places considered "clean."

The Jolly Huntsman was a very clean establishment. Herr Hagen was far removed from any suspicion of working with the police. He was in his own way a man of honor. He had never turned anyone in. That benefited him in the eyes of his guests, as did a few minor convictions. They trusted him, and Hagen was happy they did.

The Ringvereins had certain American aspirations, but they differed significantly from American gangs. Even just outwardly, the members took pains to make a more civilized impression. To the degree it was financially possible, most dressed to convey a certain bourgeois uprightness. They preferred dark clothes, and for the festive meetings, they wore black bowlers and generally posed as serious businessmen.

Only the younger among them dressed more casually, which often provoked stern rebukes from the leaders. Just as the pre-war bordelleurs—proprietors of the "sporting houses"—had considered themselves conscientious supporters of the state, so the older dignitaries of the Ringvereins considered themselves responsible citizens and presented themselves as such. The modern pimp may have replaced the earlier bordelleur, but their views had remained the same.

And so they severely disapproved of the occasional—and unorganized—murder or break-in committed by members of the group. They did not want to be criminals. What they wanted, since the state had surrendered control of prostitution, having been powerless to stop it, was to take over the control themselves. They also believed that pimps could earn far more, and far more easily, than criminals. They were very much opposed to combining the two enterprises.

Herr Hagen was well acquainted with their aspirations and approved of them.

He, too, belonged to the older generation. He was a calm, earnest man, more interested in making money than in adventure. The younger generation of pimps was far too reckless for him. Murders and other crimes were bad for business. They drove the police wild and interfered in their enterprise.

Many of the members still had too few ladies under their wing. Further organizing was required. They had to recapture the western districts, which had recently seen an increase in clandestine, uncontrolled prostitution—as newly impoverished and unemployed women took to the streets.

That had to stop. That couldn't be tolerated in the long run. The amateurs were ruining business by charging starvation prices. They didn't want protection: They didn't intend this as a full-time profession, only as a temporary measure in times of crisis and life emergencies.

Hagen had also once served on the board of one of the associations, so he was familiar with their needs and problems. He knew that the younger members could be pretty ruthless, as they were inclined to resort to violence to drive the freelance street-walkers off their turfs. At the same time the police were intervening more and more aggressively, and the papers were constantly publishing editorials attacking the rings. The newcomers had to be won over with persuasion and mild pressure, and that was hard enough.

With these worries in mind, Hagen entered the hall. This evening he was expecting the 1929 Liederkranz, a singing society—although they intended to do more discussing and debating than singing.

Herr Hagen often took part as a kind of honorary member, and he knew how to represent his own interests. Amid the constant toasts, he drank one glass of brandy after the other and so prompted the guests to follow suit.

Today he was setting up some music stands and staff paper. The Liederkranz always made sure certain security measures were in place when they met. If the police showed up unexpectedly, they would start up a song and take their places behind the stands. Then they would sing, in four-part harmony, some beautiful and profound song about German forests and meadows. There was a piano in the hall, and everything was set up the same way as for the other singing societies. Hagen also set the club pennants on the table. These were little table flags made of green silk, each flaunting a horn of plenty wreathed in ivy.

When he was finished, he looked at the clock. It was six o'clock and time to eat. He always ate early so as not to have to be interrupted later on. He didn't exactly have much appetite, but that didn't matter. The fuller his stomach, the more he could drink in the evening.

He went to the taproom, where the strange old woman was sleeping.

"Call my wife," he ordered the man tending the buffet, who hurried off to do so.

Herr Hagen enjoyed great authority among his staff as well
as his guests. He had spent a year in prison for disorderly conduct—an argument with a guest had ended with Hagen putting
out one of the man's eyes. Consequently people always preferred
to agree with him.

His wife came running in, gasping for breath. She was around
forty and made the same mistake as many female proprietors:
She was her own best customer.

Her face was sallow from all the tavern air, and she seldom
went outside. She felt too comfortable for that. She felt too comfortable for everything. Nor did she help out anymore with serving in the pub. She preferred lying in bed and sucking on candy.
Just one day a week, she roused herself to perform exceptional
feats of cleaning, after which she spent the following six days
in bed.

She had also let her outward appearance go. Her hair was
sloppily pinned up, and a few strands were always flapping
around her face, as they were now. Hagen noted this with disapproval. It's just good she doesn't cook, he thought.

She sat down clumsily. "Who's that?" she asked, pointing at
Frau Fliebusch.

"The mother of one of my best guests," Hagen explained.

While both ate their meal, sweating and with no appetite,
he observed his wife. Beautiful she is not, he determined. One
simply doesn't get any younger. Could anyone believe that the
woman in front of him had once been a belly dancer? A slim
belly dancer, even? But she had become indolent. She should
have moved more when she was Dolores the Spaniard.

He brooded for a moment how he might prompt her to get
moving, but then he called for the account ledgers. The bookkeeping was the hardest thing about the business. Hagen kept
several books alongside each other. One was for the tax authority, and one was for himself. But he had lost track. He always
had more money in the till than he really should. On the one

hand that made him happy, but on the other he was bothered by this slippage of control.

But who was saying he shouldn't have even more money—a whole lot more? Perhaps his employees had discovered the gaps in his accounting and were robbing him.

It really was very difficult.

NINETEEN

Grissmann's legs were a little worn out. He had walked a lot that day. It was already after eight o'clock, and they had yet to reach the Jolly Huntsman.

Fundholz was a tiresome human being: No matter what Grissmann said, he only replied with "yes" or "no." Meanwhile, every few minutes, Tönnchen would glance at the old man and ask about rolls. It was unbearable. On top of everything else, the streetcars kept passing right by them. Grissmann had no desire to walk. He wanted to ride. The other two could catch up later.

"Hey, Fundholz, can't we take the streetcar? My feet are shot, and I don't want to walk so far."

"Yes. They all go there."

They had come to a streetcar stop.

"How much farther is it?" asked Grissmann.

"The next stop," said Fundholz.

"There's no sense taking the streetcar if it's just one stop," Grissmann said, annoyed, as he resumed walking.

"No, there isn't," Fundholz agreed.

They went on.

Children who were chasing each other outside the apartment buildings dashed past the three men, and a small boy ran into Tönnchen and fell down. He started bawling as he got back up, but once he was a safe distance away, he began shouting curse words at the grown-ups.

The three men didn't pay him any attention and went on their way, although from time to time Tönnchen would look back and smile at the boy, who was following them, still cursing away. The men then ran into a group of adolescents playing stickball in the street, interrupting their game. The boy, who was still howling with rage, pointed at Tönnchen—who was just turning around again—and told the teenagers that the fat man had knocked him over.

One of the teenagers was determined to avenge the offense. With his comrades in tow, he set out after the three men. With great swagger, he slapped his cap on his head at a slant and acted exactly like Frank Allan, avenger of the disinherited and hero of cheap thrillers, twenty pfennig apiece.

He caught up with the men and planted himself in front of Tönnchen, who came to a stop, scared. Fundholz did the same. Grissmann went on a few steps and then turned around, curious to see what would happen. In case it came to blows, he wanted to be just out of reach.

The adolescent, now joined by half a dozen comrades, saw that Tönnchen was frightened and felt further emboldened. Here was a chance to show his strength, to prove himself as a protector. Fundholz looked at him, full of expectation. He had missed the entire incident.

"Hey you," the teenager said in a deep voice. "You must be some kind of dimwit, eh? Knocking little kids into the dirt."

"He is a dimwit," Fundholz admitted.

Tönnchen smiled when he heard the old man's voice.

"And what's this got to do with you?" the adolescent hissed at Fundholz.

Fundholz turned unpleasant. Apart from his wife, the only thing he feared was the police. "Shut your trap, pip-squeak," he muttered. "Come on, Tönnchen."

The teenager was surprised. He had expected more respect.

"You must be some kind of dimwit, too," he repeated, fuming, as he fixed his gaze on Fundholz.

Fundholz didn't answer; he just took Tönnchen by the arm and pulled him away. He wanted his peace and quiet.

But the adolescent wasn't to be brushed aside so easily. "Listen, man, I'll smack you so hard you won't know if you're a man or a woman! Of course in your case that's already hard to tell," he said, grinning at Fundholz's skirtlike trousers.

This did not rattle Fundholz, who looked at the man-boy a long time, sizing him up. Then he made his move. With all his might, he landed a blow on the teenager's chin. It was a consummate uppercut.

The adolescent collapsed on the ground. He looked up, bewildered. His comrades, who were impressed by Fundholz's impeccable technique, roared with laughter and let the old man and Tönnchen go on their way.

The two caught up with Grissmann, leaving the teenager behind, cursing. The little boy had stopped crying. The defeat of his protector seemed to him sufficient consolation. Fundholz didn't pay the matter any more attention, and only Tönnchen turned around and smiled.

TWENTY

They had finally reached the Jolly Huntsman and went inside. Grissmann looked around with curiosity. At one table, an old woman had fallen asleep next to two travel bags. Grissmann's first thought was that he might steal them. But the woman was so poorly dressed, it was doubtful they contained anything of value. Besides, he had other aspirations for the evening.

They sat down, and Grissmann ordered: "Three schnapps."

The drinks were served. But before Tönnchen could grab his glass, Fundholz took it away and set it in front of himself. He then retrieved the rolls from his pocket and handed one to Tönnchen, who was unhappily eyeing the glass.

"He can't have any schnapps?" asked Grissmann.

"No," Fundholz ruled.

Grissmann didn't want to contradict the old man, whose showdown on the street had given him pause. Fundholz wasn't exactly strong, at least not as strong as he was, but the old beggar was clearly gutsy.

Toward evening a number of peddlers made their way to the Jolly Huntsman. Although these days they referred to themselves as traveling tradesmen, they were no different from the "old-school" peddlers. As in the past, they carried their enterprises under their arm or suspended over their front. They proffered their wares or else took a seat and quickly downed a glass of beer. Then they went on their way.

Little by little, the establishment filled up. The clientele at the Jolly Huntsman spanned a range of professions and social classes. And they came from all over. Factory workers and petty clerks with their girlfriends. Single men on the prowl and groups of young girls who had mainly come to dance.

Unemployed men came as well, to spend the whole evening with a half-pint of beer because it was too depressing for them at home, and binge drinkers who ran through an entire month's pay on a single evening if they felt weary of the world or found some other excuse.

There were also girls who came looking to turn a trick either for the whole night or just for half an hour, and later, around eleven, the finer set came from the western districts, eager to see how the common people entertained themselves.

For the time being the place was filling up with locals, who stood in the taproom waiting for the large dance hall to be opened.

At last the time came. Hagen personally opened the double doors, and the patrons streamed inside. Grissmann wanted to see what the festive venue looked like, so he stood up and joined the others, while Fundholz and Tönnchen stayed seated. Tönnchen was chewing his third bun. He had no interest in dance or music. His only concern was when he would get his hands on the fourth. Meanwhile Fundholz was finishing his second schnapps, eyes closed, delighted by the prospect of three more.

Grissmann entered the dance hall. The decor resembled that of the taproom, except that dozens of bare wooden tables were set up along the walls. Opposite the entrance, Grissmann saw a piano that halfway blocked a door, which evidently led to another room.

Herr Hagen had deliberately placed the piano there to drown out any possible noise coming from the meeting room of the

Ringverein. Very few guests realized that that space, too, was frequented, or by whom.

Grissmann sauntered through the hall, looking for Sonnenberg without success. The tables along the walls were quickly occupied, but Grissmann found a free one near the piano and sat down. The middle of the hall was kept clear for dancing, but it would be a while before the music started, so Grissmann ordered a glass of beer. He didn't miss the others. If he needed Fundholz, he would find him. For now the old man was just an added expense with no return on the investment.

The neighboring tables were mainly occupied by couples. Sizing them up, Grissmann saw many pretty girls, but unfortunately each one had an escort. Then he spotted an old man to his right. The man was sitting ramrod straight, despite the fact that he had already consumed most of his third glass of beer before Grissmann had managed half of his first. The man had flabby cheeks and looked to be melancholic. He noticed Grissmann and nodded to him as he again raised his glass to his mouth.

"Prost," said Grissmann.

The man thanked him.

Grissmann attempted to start a conversation. "How is it?" he asked.

The man shook his head. "Not good." He waved down a passing waiter. "Another glass."

"The beer here is pretty bad," he explained to Grissmann.

"I thought as much," Grissmann replied, feeling emboldened.

"Not good at all," the man repeated, shaking his head. "My name's Lindner, by the way. Court Bailiff Lindner," he said, introducing himself.

Grissmann gave a slight, practically reverential nod and answered, "Grissmann." So the man was a court bailiff—an official, a civil servant. And in Grissmann's eyes, a court bailiff was an official blessed with special powers. "Do you come here often?" he asked.

Lindner stroked his bare upper lip. "It's a fine enough place," he said condescendingly. Then he raised his glass and drained it.

Grissmann reflexively followed his gesture. "Bad times," he said.

Lindner nodded. "Hard times, but one can't lose heart. That's something I never do!"

The answer annoyed Grissmann. A court bailiff had no need to lose heart. The worse things turned out for others, the better things went for him. Grissmann had already experienced a few property seizures, and he knew that bailiffs were actively involved. "Well, you're doing all right," he said insinuatingly.

The other man shook his head. "You're mistaken. My own circumstances are rather humble."

The beer came, and Lindner took a sip. It was strange, but once again he found it wanting. The more he drank, the worse it tasted.

"Well, young man," he said encouragingly. "Isn't your lady friend coming?"

Grissmann grinned, flattered. "I'm here by myself."

The noise in the hall grew louder, and they practically had to yell. People at the neighboring tables were telling jokes, and everyone was roaring with laughter.

"Out for a little escapade, eh?" Lindner said loudly, once again stroking his missing mustache.

Grissmann went on grinning: He wasn't about to argue with that. He reveled in the feeling that he was a man out for escapades.

"I know, I know—to be young," Lindner exclaimed bitterly. "Young people, that's the life all right. At my age all that's left is beer."

Grissmann smiled regretfully.

Their conversation was over.

Lindner again directed his full attention to his beer glass. He couldn't help himself. It tasted disgusting. He ordered a schnapps to wash away the bad taste.

Grissmann ordered a large lager, and the waiter hurried off.

"Cool blond!" a man bellowed across the room. "Bring me a cool blond."

Grissmann gave a start. Didn't that unpleasant voice belong to Sonnenberg? Wasn't that the blind man shouting?

Cool blond meant the same as a cold lager and that meant a glass of pale beer, but cool. Since Sonnenberg would probably be playing with the band, Grissmann was determined to approach the woman once the music started up.

TWENTY-ONE

Fundholz ordered another schnapps. He had considered the matter. He wanted to be back at the vegetable stand on time, so he couldn't stay much longer. After all, why pay for nothing? If need be, he was even prepared to forgo another one of Grissmann's schnapps.

He hadn't drunk that much in a long time. He was already noticing the effect of the first two drinks and felt livelier and lighter than he had in ages. Three schnapps would be enough. Besides, everything in moderation.

The drinks arrived, and Fundholz paid, because it was the custom at the Jolly Huntsman for all but the regular clients to pay when served. Otherwise, during peak hours, the waiter might not be able to reach this or that guest when he wanted to settle the bill.

Fundholz knocked back the schnapps. He found it refreshing, and it gave his throat a pleasant scratch. Then he looked around. The old lady with the two travel bags was still sound asleep. Her head had dropped onto her chest, and her hat's old plume was like a spear pointing nowhere.

Another poor creature, Fundholz thought.

The noise in the hall suddenly stopped, and for a moment everything was still.

Then the piano started up, playing some modern hit that

Fundholz didn't recognize. The player's rendition was lively to
say the least—he showed little consideration for the instrument
and even less for his audience.

Fundholz had a feel for music. A certain intuitive musical
sense. He couldn't read notes, but in his past life he had often
attended concerts. It pained him to hear how forcefully the
piano player hit the wrong keys.

The old lady with the bags woke up. She lifted her head and
listened to the music, still drowsy. Then she noticed the old man.

"Is Wilhelm already here?" she asked.

Fundholz shrugged his shoulders. "I don't know any Wilhelm," he mumbled.

Tönnchen was pounding the table with his fists in time with
the music.

Frau Fliebusch started ruminating again. It probably wasn't
yet ten o'clock. So she could go back to sleep. But she was no
longer tired. Instead she surveyed the surroundings. The old
man was curiously dressed, but she didn't pay much attention to
that. She had her own concerns.

Herr Hagen came hurrying out of the large room. The Liederkranz would be there any moment. He gave Frau Fliebusch a
friendly nod and said, "Wilhelm will be here soon!"

Frau Fliebusch thanked him, smiling graciously.

Hagen recognized Fundholz by sight. Every so often the old
man would show up with the blind man Sonnenberg. Sonnenberg had become a regular. He often played his accordion, which
earned him a little money. Hagen didn't have anything against
that. Whatever Sonnenberg earned he wound up spending in the
locale.

Hagen went to the buffet and placed an order. Then he went
back to the dance hall. When he passed Fundholz, he gave a
friendly smile.

Fundholz didn't react and just took another swig of schnapps.
As he did so, Grissmann came and tapped him on the shoulder.
"Sonnenberg's here," he announced.

The old man nodded indifferently.

"Come and join me," Grissmann suggested.

Fundholz shook his head to decline.

Grissmann thought a moment. He had taken the old man along so he would keep Sonnenberg distracted.

"Sonnenberg's buying," he lied, to entice Fundholz.

"Really," Fundholz replied. His interest was somewhat piqued, but he remained seated.

"Oh come on, Fundholz. Why would you want to stay here? There's music over there and things are nice and lively. You also need to enjoy yourself once in a while."

Fundholz got up, but less because of the music or the live-liness. Why shouldn't he join in, if Sonnenberg was buying— which very rarely happened?

Tönnchen smiled at Frau Fliebusch as he left the room and followed Fundholz and Grissmann into the hall.

TWENTY-TWO

—

Sonnenberg was in a fine mood. He was happily drumming away on the table, his accordion by his side. Business had been good that afternoon: He had earned a whole mark and ninety pfennig. He had already forgotten the earlier incident.

Elsi, however, had not. She sat next to him, very much on edge. Where was the man from that morning? She kept looking for him but couldn't find him. If he didn't show up, she wouldn't have any fun the entire evening. She wanted to get away from the blind man. She wasn't pretty, and she knew it. Which was precisely why she had enjoyed meeting that nice man.

Sonnenberg was drinking his cool blond. The beer tasted wonderful. So refreshing after the long, dry day. He patted Elsi on the arm, which she reluctantly put up with. She hadn't ordered anything for herself, contenting herself with taking a swallow now and then from his glass.

"Why don't you have a Weisse with a shot of syrup?" Sonnenberg proposed generously.

Sonnenberg knew that Berliner Weisse beer cost forty pfennig at the Jolly Huntsman. But he was in a good mood and wanted to give her something.

Elsi ordered, and the beer was quickly delivered. It was served with a straw, and Elsi began sucking away with gusto.

"Let me have a swallow," the blind man asked.

She obeyed and shoved the glass over to Sonnenberg, who took a long gulp.

"Ah," he said appreciatively. "That tastes good! Poor man's champagne."

She took back the half-empty glass. That was just like him. First he ordered a Weisse for her and then drank half of it himself, spouting off as he did so. Elsi was annoyed. She cautiously resumed drinking through her straw, but her enjoyment was spoiled.

Sonnenberg wanted another beer. He simply shouted out into the hall, certain that some waiter would hear his voice. And indeed he was served right away. They knew he would make a fuss if things didn't go exactly as he wished.

Sonnenberg took up his accordion. He pulled it wide apart and squeezed it back together. It let out a loud shrill tone, then died away. The dancers, taken aback, all turned in his direction.

Sonnenberg grinned. "This thing has more lung power than three pianos at once," he asserted.

Suddenly Elsi caught sight of Grissmann. He was heading toward her table with the two men she'd seen that morning. She smiled, and he smiled back.

"Hello, Sonnenberg," said Fundholz.

"Ah my little Fundholz, come and join us," the blind man offered.

Fundholz accepted and fetched a chair. Tönnchen did the same. Only Grissmann remained standing.

"I'd like to dance," said Elsi.

Sonnenberg furrowed his brow. "All right, fine," he reluctantly allowed.

Elsi stood up and accompanied Grissmann to the dance floor.

"Who is she dancing with?" Sonnenberg wanted to know.

"With Grissmann," Fundholz said, in all innocence.

"Grissmann? Isn't that the fellow from this morning?" Sonnenberg began to get uneasy.

"That's right," said Fundholz. "The one sitting on the bench when we met."

"And who is that?" the blind man asked, mistrustfully, nodding toward where Tönnchen was sitting.

"That's Tönnchen."

"That's right," the fat man confirmed. "I'm Tönnchen."

Sonnenberg calmed down. "I heard you were deaf in one eye," he said.

Fundholz laughed. "Deaf in one eye is good. In his case you'd better say dim in both cheeks. But that doesn't matter."

Tönnchen smiled as he listened to them talk about him.

Fundholz handed him the last bun, and Tönnchen started eating right away.

"Say, Sonnenberg. I heard you were buying tonight," the old man said encouragingly.

"You heard wrong." Sonnenberg again grew nervous. Something wasn't right. There was some reason Elsi was dancing with this man. Just wait, he thought, if I get the jump on you, you'll be the worse for wear.

"What kind of fellow is he, this Grissmann?" he wanted to know.

Fundholz shook his head.

"Well?" The blind man demanded an answer. "Don't spend half a year thinking of what to say."

"I don't know him so well," Fundholz muttered.

"Can you see the two of them?"

Fundholz looked at the dance floor. Grissmann had pressed the woman close to him, very close in fact, and both were smiling at each other.

"Yes. They're dancing together," Fundholz said flatly.

Sonnenberg grew angry. "I know they're dancing! But how are they dancing? Is she grinning away at him?"

Fundholz noticed his jealousy. "They're just dancing like everybody else," he said evasively.

"What a stupid dog!" Sonnenberg spewed. "Open your eyes,

man! You still have a pair. I don't. Otherwise I'd be paying attention myself. Don't act like such an idiot, Fundholz. I want to know if she's playing around, you understand?"

"I have to go," said Fundholz. He didn't want to get mixed up in this kind of thing. Sonnenberg wasn't going to buy drinks. Grissmann had lied, probably on account of the woman. So what was he doing here? None of this concerned him.

Sonnenberg said calmly, "Why? Just when I wanted to drink a schnapps with you!" He shouted out, "Two schnapps!"

Fundholz stayed seated. He would drink the schnapps and then be on his way.

Sonnenberg took pains to contain himself. He wanted to have Fundholz by his side to keep an eye on Elsi. Somehow he had to manage to keep the old man there. If I catch hold of his hand, he thought, he won't be going anywhere this evening. That hussy Elsi will learn that Sonnenberg isn't as dumb as she thinks.

Sonnenberg set both hands down on the table in front of him. He played with the beer coaster. "That's right," he said. "Women. All they do is stir up trouble! Don't you agree, Fundholz?"

Fundholz agreed. "That's right, that's right."

Sonnenberg went on. "You work all day just for your woman, and to thank you she lets you just sit there by yourself while she goes dancing. You have no idea how much the accordion playing takes out of me." He held out his right hand. "Take a look. Nothing but calluses."

"I don't see anything," said Fundholz.

The blind man laughed. "You might not be able to see it, but you can feel it. Just run your hand across my palm, it's like leather."

The old man wasn't interested but indifferently did as Sonnenberg asked.

When he felt the old man's fingers, Sonnenberg grabbed him hard.

"Stop that nonsense," said Fundholz mildly.

Sonnenberg let out an unfriendly laugh. "Listen here, little Fundholz. You're going to tell me, now, what my wife is up to! You are going to describe exactly how those two are dancing! How this Grissmann and my wife are looking at each other! And if you don't, I'm going to flatten your hand into a pancake." The blind man was happy that he'd lured Fundholz into his trap.

For a moment Fundholz didn't reply, and then he said, still in a friendly voice, "Let go, Sonnenberg!"

Sonnenberg gave a contented laugh. "Not on your life."

Fundholz refused to be riled. But he also had no intention of being forced to do something he didn't want to do. He was no stool pigeon.

"Listen, Sonnenberg," he growled, "if you don't let go, I'm going to take this beer glass and smash it on your head."

Sonnenberg didn't seem to fear that possibility. "You wouldn't want to mistreat a poor blind man," he said, grinning.

Fundholz didn't answer. He tried to free his hand, but Sonnenberg was stronger.

The schnapps arrived.

"Come on, drink up!" Sonnenberg demanded.

They drank, each holding his glass with his left hand.

The music stopped for a moment.

Sonnenberg slammed his glass on the table. "Are they both coming here?" he asked.

Fundholz saw that the couple was still standing on the dance floor. "It looks like they're waiting for the next dance," he said.

The piano resumed playing, and the dancers began to move.

Sonnenberg was furious. "Listen, Fundholz, you're my friend! You have to help me! What am I supposed to do, blind as I am? You simply have to help me!"

Then he tried a gentler approach. He struggled to make his voice sound more pleading, but Fundholz could sense the snarling underneath.

"Take me to the dance floor, Fundholz! I want to talk to Elsi."

That's just going to wind up in a fistfight, thought Fundholz. The whole thing has nothing to do with me. "Let her dance if she wants to. You don't have to be so jealous, Sonnenberg. She's still young." He ended his long speech and emptied the rest of his schnapps.

Sonnenberg growled back, angry, "What do you know about women? You don't know a thing! But I do. First they dance and then they hop into bed with the bastards. But that's not going to happen with me! You think I want to be on my own again? All alone and blind to boot? She isn't just my wife. She is my eyes! But you don't understand that. If you had your way, old Sonnenberg would get run over by the first car that comes along! But you won't be seeing that happen. None of you! I'll show her what's what. I'll break every bone in her body. She's my wife, damn it! Divorce, my foot! She belongs to me, that's the law! I'll teach her all right! I'll take a stick to her so that she learns the lesson!"

Sonnenberg ordered two more schnapps. His face was glowing with rage. "Let her go to bed with him. Just let her go ahead. I'll knock some sense into her even if it means beating her to death. I'll knock sense into her all right! It's Sonnenberg she's married to and not some Grissmann! I'll teach her yet!"

Fundholz listened to Sonnenberg's outburst in silence.

Tönnchen was bored. Evidently nobody wanted anything from him, and besides, there wasn't anything to eat.

"Tönnchen wants to leave," he announced.

Fundholz muttered, "Just wait a minute."

TWENTY-THREE

Grissmann was not a skillful dancer. He led Elsi across the floor without saying anything, and the pair kept bumping against other couples. But what did that matter? He had a woman in his arms again.

Her figure wasn't at all as unappealing as he had first assumed: Her woolen dress was simply a poor fit. He felt her body against his own and determined she was slender. He pressed her close as they danced.

"You're strong," she said admiringly.

Grissmann was flattered and smiled. "Oh, not really."

"You are," Elsi insisted.

They danced awhile in silence.

"Nice music, isn't it," Grissmann said.

Elsi agreed.

"Isn't your husband joining in?" Grissmann wanted to know.

She shook her head. "He doesn't play until late in the evening," she said, giving the "he" an unkind emphasis.

Grissmann continued with his questions. "Does he play from where he's sitting, or does he move to the piano?"

"No, he always takes his chair and sits in the middle of the dancers."

"Do you come here often?" Grissmann wanted to know.

Elsi nodded. "Just about every evening."

Grissmann felt a little dizzy from the dancing. He was hungry. I have money, he thought, pleased. "Let's have something to eat after this dance," he suggested.

Elsi didn't have anything against the idea. He pulled her even closer and led her away from the piano, toward the exit. But the music kept going, and right when he thought the dance was over, it was really just beginning. By the time the song was finished, he was sweating.

"Shall we get something to eat?" Grissmann asked.

Elsi preferred to have another dance. She had almost forgotten about Sonnenberg. Grissmann was a very nice man, she decided. She enjoyed dancing with him.

Grissmann complied with her wish. The piano started up again, and they resumed dancing.

"Have you been married long?" Grissmann asked.

"No, thank God," she sighed.

Grissmann heard her groan. "I guess he's not up to doing much, being blind and all."

"He's not up to anything at all. And I'm not going to stick with him, either. Let him find someone else."

This gave Grissmann pause. Hopefully she doesn't think she's going to latch onto me, he thought. Because if she does, she's out of luck.

"I like you, you know!" he stated, blushing slightly.

"I like you, too!"

Elsi was pleased. She felt happy. This is a decent person, she thought. If only he wouldn't squeeze me so hard.

Grissmann grew bolder. "Shall we switch to first names?" he proposed.

Frau Sonnenberg didn't mind. "My name's Elsi."

"A pretty name," Grissmann acknowledged. "I'm Fritz."

All of a sudden Elsi felt a chill. "But Sonnenberg can't find out; he's very suspicious," she told him.

"Oh, him," Grissmann replied disparagingly. He laughed. "The man can't see, so he won't notice anything."

But Elsi was still afraid of Sonnenberg. He was sly and cunning.

Grissmann, on the other hand, was in a good mood. If you want something hard enough, it can be yours, he thought—you only have to really want it. He liked the idea of pulling one over on Sonnenberg. He glanced at the blind man, who was talking with Fundholz. He was gripping the old man's hand, and his face was bright red.

Aha, thought Grissmann: The old man's blabbing, he's a snitch. Well, let him blab. The blind man's not going to grab me like that, not in a million years. Still, it was pretty shabby of Fundholz. Grissmann had only been kind to the old man, and now he was spying for Sonnenberg. What a vile thing to do. Grissmann was outraged. I ought to report him straightaway, he thought, on account of the begging.

As a rule, Grissmann didn't have much sympathy for the police. He was afraid of them, because of the incident with the pushcart. But now he felt that they weren't vigilant enough.

"These beggars are all a bunch of lazy dogs," he said to Elsi. "They really need a good thrashing."

She nodded absentmindedly.

"People like us work when we can, but those tramps don't do anything except panhandle."

Grissmann resolved to get back at Fundholz. After all, he knew where the old man slept. One anonymous letter, and both he and the idiot would be arrested. Fundholz had mentioned how scared he was of the poorhouse. Grissmann would show him all right. What business was this of his? Fundholz was once again talking with the blind man. I'm going to write that letter this very night, Grissmann resolved.

No longer smiling, his face was now livid.

What is he so mad about? Elsi wondered. Hopefully it's not about me. "Do you like to dance?"

Grissmann nodded. "Especially with you." He laughed again.

"It can't be very nice, being married to a blind man. Sonnenberg seems pretty unpleasant."

Elsi confirmed this. "You're right. He's a nasty man. So brutal." He could feel her trembling in his arms.

Grissmann wanted to calm her down. "There's no reason to be considerate of someone who's that mean."

Elsi was in complete agreement. "There's absolutely no reason," she concurred.

Grissmann stepped on her toes and apologized.

Elsi was beaming. Whenever Sonnenberg bumped into her or stepped on her foot, he would actually yell at her: "Watch out, you dumb cow!" Grissmann was decidedly the more pleasant man.

"But it's nice that we met," he said.

"Yes it is! You're a lot kinder than Sonnenberg," she said, almost tenderly.

Now Grissmann was beaming. "Why don't you skip out on the blind man tonight?" he proposed.

Elsi had nothing against that. Nor did she want to skip out on Sonnenberg for just that evening, but she would explain that later.

The dance was over, and the piano player signaled that he wanted to take a break.

Elsi went with Grissmann to the taproom. Grissmann was amazed to see that the old lady was still sitting there. She clearly seemed to be waiting for something. Oh well, it was all the same to him. He ordered two pairs of hot links.

They sat down next to Frau Fliebusch. Grissmann once again eyed the old woman's travel bags. One of them was open, and Grissmann saw something white gleaming inside. Nothing special, he surmised. The bags were so old, there was no sense in even thinking about it. Besides, he no longer wanted to bother himself with such piddling things. Tomorrow he planned to put the squeeze on the other men. He was bound to get forty or fifty marks. Maybe even more. And then when the occasion arose, he'd pull off a big job. Something that really delivered.

For the moment, however, he was sitting next to Elsi. Apart from the strange old lady, there was no one else in the taproom. Grissmann put his arm around her shoulder, and she let that happen.

A beautiful day, this. First he had found a mark, then he made ten more, and now he had a woman.

When the sausages came, they both ate with a healthy appetite. Grissmann asked for some more rolls, just to prolong their meal. But he was soon finished. Elsi was still eating—an activity to which she devoted her entire attention. At last she had cleaned her plate. Grissmann pulled her close and kissed her. Her mouth was greasy, but that didn't bother him.

The server at the buffet grinned.

Frau Fliebusch looked at the door expectantly.

TWENTY-FOUR

Minchen Lindner leaned far back into the car's upholstery. The taxi started up and slowly accelerated. She lit a cigarette. Truth be told she didn't enjoy tobacco, but all the ladies smoked. It was the modern thing to do. She puffed away, filling the car with clouds of blue fumes.

Today she hadn't especially dressed up. She was wearing the same outfit she'd had on when she met Herr von Sulm. A simple checked calico dress. Along with a cute little hat. Both suited her splendidly, she had again concluded as she was putting on lipstick in front of the mirror. It was all the same to her if she had on a silk dress or a cotton one. But Herr von Sulm and the other elderly gentlemen expected her to look festive when they visited her in the evening.

This evening, Minchen had decided to be more modestly attired. First, because she didn't want to prompt her father to ask for even more, and second, because she planned to have fun. And that she could do only if she didn't stick out. She didn't want to come off as a spectator from the Kurfürstendamm out to see how the other half lives, but rather as an ordinary young woman who had arrived—but perhaps wouldn't leave—without a male friend.

And finally Minchen Lindner wanted a chance to say whatever

popped into her head, the way she used to talk, without any embellishments or elaborate turns of phrase. She also wished to dance the evening away with some nice young man. She was fed up with the elderly gentlemen.

The cigarette tasted horrible. She stubbed it out in the ashtray. She took her lipstick from her purse and gave her lips a quick swipe. Tonight Minchen wanted to look pretty. She began to whistle a popular tune. She had forgotten the lyrics but liked the melody, which was very sweet.

The taxicab had left the finer neighborhoods. Minchen Lindner peered out the window. The streets were crowded with working-class men and women, out for a stroll or headed to the cinema. The old gray apartment houses made her feel at home. She opened her window and leaned out.

There it was—the house she had lived in as a child after her father was sent to prison. That was now already ten years ago. Before that, she and her parents had lived in a lovely little apartment in Steglitz. I really had quite a nice life when I was young, she reflected. And of course she was still young.

Her father had once been a cheerful man. Too cheerful, as it turned out. After work they would often ride out to the Grunewald woods, where some establishments catered to picnickers with ads that read "Families! Brew your coffee here!" The Lindners made extensive use of such offerings.

Then one day the vile complaint arrived, and her father wound up in jail. He served his time, and when he was released, he just let himself go and no longer bothered with his family. In the end Minchen's mother had to throw him out.

Minchen recalled those hard times. Still half a child, she had gone to work in a factory, and later she found the job in the soap shop. When she was seventeen, her mother died, and from then on she had taken care of herself. Every now and then her father gave her a little money, when he was able, but that didn't happen very often.

Lately he'd been doing worse and worse. He wasn't earning

anything anymore. For a while he had found work as a watch-man, but too many things wound up stolen, and now no one would hire him, especially once they learned of his prior con-victions, which for a long time he had cleverly managed to hide. Right after he'd been released from prison, he had committed several small thefts, for which he'd been caught.

Minchen Lindner didn't worry herself about that. She helped him when she could, and in recent years she was always able to. Lindner didn't ask her where the money she gave him came from, nor was it any of his business, as far as she was concerned.

The taxi was getting close to the Jolly Huntsman. Minchen knocked on the window. "Stop here," she said. The driver obeyed.

Minchen climbed out and paid. She didn't want to pull up to the place in the cab, since that would be too ostentatious. She had no desire to show off, especially in front of her father.

When she reached the Jolly Huntsman, she went in and made her way to the buffet. "Is Herr Lindner here?" she asked.

Before the server could answer, Grissmann, who had been waiting with Elsi for the next dance, jumped up and asked, obligingly, "Do you mean Court Bailiff Lindner?"

Minchen nodded.

"Yes, he's here," said Grissmann. He found the girl extremely appealing. Much more so than Elsi. He was glad to be of service and hoped he might get to know her that way. He was certain that the bailiff didn't have a girlfriend. This must be his daughter or some other relative. It was Grissmann's lucky day. And he wanted to take advantage of it.

Elsi watched him in amazement. He is polite, she thought, naively—much more polite than Sonnenberg.

Minchen Lindner looked at Grissmann, sizing him up. She didn't like what she saw. His face seemed undeveloped and at the same time thuggish. "Thank you," she said. "I'll go inside and look for him."

"Should I help you?" Grissmann offered.

Minchen Lindner thanked him: "I'll find him myself. Don't bother."

Disappointed, Grissmann sat back down. This was becoming too complicated for him. He wanted to hold on to Elsi and at the same time get to know the other girl.

But he did know who her father was. At least that was some point of contact. The bailiff's daughter intrigued him. Not only because he found her attractive, but also because she was the daughter of a court bailiff. Lindner hadn't mentioned to Grissmann that he hadn't practiced his profession for the past ten years. He continued to adorn himself with his old title—a pale reflection of the respect he had once enjoyed.

Minchen Lindner started to leave the taproom and go into the main hall. But just then the music started up again. The dancing couples obscured her view, and she was unable to spot her father. "Where is he sitting?" she asked Grissmann.

Meanwhile Grissmann had stood up to dance with Elsi. He stopped. "Shall I fetch him?" he asked, pleased.

"No, that's not necessary. Just tell me which is his table, and I'll find him."

Elsi, standing next to him, was growing impatient. She tugged at his sleeve, but Grissmann didn't respond. Instead he smiled solicitously at Minchen Lindner.

This was beginning to annoy Minchen, who then asked curtly, "Do you even know where he's sitting?"

Grissmann stopped smiling and turned red. "He's next to the piano," he said sullenly, then left the taproom with Elsi.

Minchen Lindner stayed still. She watched the two of them dancing. They're well suited to each other, she thought. Then suddenly she heard a voice behind her. "What could be keeping Wilhelm? What if it's again all for nothing?" She turned around, amazed.

An old woman was evidently talking to herself. She looked very sad, and Minchen felt sorry for her. "He'll be here!" she said by way of encouragement.

Frau Fliebusch looked up. The young girl was smiling kindly at her.

"Do you think so?" she asked hopefully.

"Why shouldn't he come?"

Frau Fliebusch repeated Minchen's words. "That's right, why shouldn't he come?" Then she said, "I've waited twenty years for him!"

Minchen shook her head, astounded. "Twenty years, that's a very long time!"

"Isn't it?" said Frau Fliebusch eagerly. "But this evening I'm going to see him once again. Tonight, at last!"

"I'm really glad to hear it," said Minchen Lindner. "I'm sure that will be nice for you."

Frau Fliebusch looked at her, moved. "You are a lovely person," she exclaimed.

Minchen Lindner didn't quite understand the connection. But of course it was nicer to be deemed a lovely person than a bad one. She had the impression that the old lady wasn't entirely "right in the head." But she was harmless and more pleasant to deal with than many of her acquaintances who were absolutely normal. She gave the lady a friendly smile and then turned around to enter the dance hall.

"You are definitely a lovely person," confirmed Frau Fliebusch, inclined as ever to cling to newfound insights.

TWENTY-FIVE

Wilhelm Winter was unemployed—a situation that had far-reaching consequences for his life. He no longer received unemployment benefits, only welfare assistance, which was for people who had already exhausted their unemployment claims.

Wilhelm Winter wasn't interested in such subtle distinctions. He merely noted that on unemployment he'd been just barely able to manage, but as a welfare recipient, he no longer could.

He was twenty-six years old and didn't want to wind up like Diogenes in the barrel, especially considering he was hardly philosophically inclined. He wanted to live. He had no lofty ambitions, but he wanted to have enough to eat, to keep himself supplied with cigarettes, to have a place to sleep, and to be somewhat decently dressed.

As things were, he could have satisfied any one of these individual needs, or even two of them, and if he were abstemious enough perhaps even one more, but it was impossible to meet them all. The assistance was enough to eat and smoke or sleep and smoke, but then he couldn't think about clothes, or he'd have to forgo sleep.

Many people did everything in bits and pieces. They ate little, smoked little, slept alongside many others, and didn't buy any clothes apart from paper collars and new shoelaces. Wilhelm Winter had tried that as well. But he was too vigorous, he had too great an appetite, he liked smoking too much, he couldn't see himself sharing a garret with several others, and he wanted to be nicely dressed.

He was too much a human being and too little a statistic in a card file.

At the time there were many political parties, all of which offered excellent long-term solutions for the unemployment crisis. But their helpful solutions depended on their coming into power.

Wilhelm Winter had no desire to wait for long-term solutions. He was in more of a hurry, and so he went his own way. Moreover, he had the impression that while the parties often used the unemployed as political leverage, they had no real interest in supporting them with anything but promises. On the contrary, as undesirable as it might be, they even welcomed a surge in the unemployment rate, as this could be used to make things difficult for the ruling regime.

People have long believed in better times to come. Earlier prophets, being prudent, relocated these times to a paradise that would be entered into after death. Our modern era is more skeptical, and demands different, more down-to-earth offerings. So modern prophets have sped up the clock: According to them an earthly paradise is within sight. The age-old human pursuit of happiness is close to being realized. People just need to cooperate to attain what they are striving for, instead of relying on faith alone, although naturally faith still plays a significant role.

Wilhelm Winter, however, had no interest in hoping or believing. He wanted to experience a full life, and that was not part of the party platform. Politicians presented vague prospects, even going so far as to provide a timetable for the fulfillment of social needs. But even the most favorable prognoses had little to offer for the immediate future. Besides, the parties were not so concerned with Wilhelm Winter the man, since they were really only out to win over the masses of men just like him. And so he went his own way.

Winter's profession was that of unskilled laborer, which was to say he had no real profession. He was among the countless people who hadn't had the opportunity to learn a trade of any kind and were destined for a life of menial work. They entered the labor force with no other qualification than their bare bones, and this raw material was deployed where neither knowledge nor expertise was called for.

Unskilled laborers comprised a particular underclass among the workers, a kind of fourth-and-a-half estate. From a sociological perspective, they were in an especially unfavorable situation. They were the first to experience every fluctuation of the economy, and even when the shift was positive, they benefited the least. Both their standard of living and their education were below that of trained workmen. Their uncertain existence also made it impossible for them to develop a firm worldview or solid spiritual foundation. In contrast to the so-called working class, they did not present a cohesive, organized, coordinated whole, but rather an enormous sum of individuals who were mentally as well as economically adrift.

Unemployment hit these people especially hard. They had very little resistance to the misery that was so demoralizing. And those who lacked faith in the future or another belief system very quickly lost the ground beneath their feet. They became what were known as the "asocials."

Wilhelm Winter's domestic circumstances had not permitted him to learn a trade. His family hadn't been able to wait for him to finish an apprenticeship: They needed whatever he could earn right away. He had seven siblings, and his father earned barely enough to cover food and rent. So every member of the family had to do his part.

For Wilhelm, this meant starting as an errand boy at the age of fourteen. Then he worked as a newsboy, next as a runner for construction sites, then as a dishwasher—a profession that has been inexplicably romanticized ever since a dishwasher in

America became a millionaire—and lastly as a porter in a factory. But that was years ago.

In the meantime he had tried other means to provide for himself—by selling ice cream, shoelaces, and fountain pens—but without success. It had been impossible for him to find a steady job. Then as raw material, he ultimately became too expensive. The wage laws stipulated that older porters earn more than younger ones, and so the younger ones were hired.

He lived off welfare until he reached the end of his tether.

One day Wilhelm Winter staged a private act of defiance. He broke into a grocery store and attempted to make off with the cashbox. The venture was unsuccessful. The owner, a feeble old man for whom the cashbox was of existential significance, defended himself with more courage than Wilhelm Winter had thought possible.

As a result he was arrested.

The court acknowledged extenuating circumstances and sentenced him to a probationary period, which spared him time in prison.

However, he did spend four weeks in pretrial detention, during which time Wilhelm Winter came to realize that a single man was no match for an army of officials. He did not attempt to commit any further break-ins. And then, after some time, he was discovered. To put it more precisely: One day he met an older girl who asked him to be her friend. She gave him money, too.

So Wilhelm became a pimp, known around town as Handsome Wilhelm. He had an attractive figure and a bold countenance—although his face looked more audacious than he really was.

Soon he had many female friends, and they all gave him money. At first he found the idea of living off prostitutes disgusting. But with time and money, he came around to the idea. Suddenly he could once again keep himself supplied with cigarettes. He wore handsome suits. He never went hungry, and he had a nice room.

But he had also experienced the dark side of the profession when he contracted a disease, presumably from one of his female friends. He wound up in the hospital. It wasn't dangerous, but it wasn't very pleasant, either.

The hospital had just discharged him a few days earlier, and he had yet to resume his work. The disease had left him a lot of time for reflection and had awakened in him considerable disgust. He no longer wished to be paid to be the friend of women who belonged to anyone who paid them. He wanted to give another try at finding a job.

That morning he had cut out numerous job ads and had spent the day going from one potential employer to the next. And he had been met with the same result that job seekers so often encounter: The positions for which he might be suited were already filled. And for the ones that weren't, he wasn't qualified.

These included a married concierge, a butler who was also supposed to be a gardener and a chauffeur, and an errand boy with a starting salary of fourteen marks, which was decidedly too little for Wilhelm, and besides, the man had explained, there were enough young fellows around who'd be happy to have any work at all. Moreover, a grown man such as Wilhelm was hardly suited to be an errand boy.

For the time being, he continued to patronize the Jolly Huntsman, as if nothing had changed. But he was determined to put an end to this particular career. Today, he thought, is the last time I'm going to the meeting of the Ringverein.

In addition to all this, Wilhelm Winter possessed a particular talent, and his friends considered him especially gifted, although their own power of discernment was undoubtedly limited. It turned out that Wilhelm Winter composed poetry on the side. This filled his girlfriends with respect, and himself with pride.

Now he was standing by the side entrance to the Jolly Huntsman, which was reserved for members of the Ring. This way

Hagen ensured that his different sets of patrons didn't come into contact with each other.

Wilhelm Winter was wearing a bowler hat and a black suit that was narrow in the waist. He stepped through the broad, unlit entrance and approached the door labeled *Heinrich Hagen*. He rang the doorbell: two short and one long. Then after a pause, another short ring. Herr Hagen personally let him in.

"Hello, Wilhelm," he said, patting him on the shoulder.

"Hello, Heinrich," Winter replied—the two men were on a first-name basis.

"I have a surprise for you," said Herr Hagen. "Your mother is here! A nice lady, if also a bit quirky, wouldn't you say?"

Wilhelm brushed off Hagen's hand. "You're pulling my leg, right?"

Hagen said he wasn't. "Follow me. She's waiting for you in the front."

Handsome Wilhelm followed him, astounded. His mother? That was almost impossible. He hadn't seen his mother in years. Since his father died, she'd been living with his sister in Brandenburg. He didn't correspond with her much, either. Lately he'd occasionally sent her some money. But she didn't seem especially thrilled about that.

"Thou shalt not steal," she wrote in every other letter he received.

She had testified at the time of his trial as a character witness for her son. Since then, though, she'd been suspicious of him.

He hadn't wanted her to find out about the affair, but his lawyer had insisted. And in the end, he had been released without having to serve time.

He thought about the trial. Was she still angry? What had caused her to come here? Something bad must have happened in Brandenburg. Or else it was the same old story: She wanted to know how he was making a living. Clearly he couldn't admit to his mother that he was a pimp. He wasn't pleased she had made the trip. If she had at least written him in advance, but to surprise him here like this . . .

"So," said Hagen, pointing to Frau Fliebusch, "your mother's over there."

Frau Fliebusch had her eyes on the entrance door. When she heard voices behind her, she turned around.

Wilhelm looked at her in surprise. That wasn't his mother. Was someone making a joke at his expense?

He approached Frau Fliebusch. "Excuse me. My name is Wilhelm Winter. Are you waiting for me?"

Frau Fliebusch smiled. She still didn't understand the situation.

"No, I'm waiting for my husband. For Wilhelm Fliebusch, for Handsome Wilhelm."

Hagen stepped in. There must be some mistake, or else— and this seemed to him more likely—the woman wasn't entirely normal. "There's only one Wilhelm here. Only one Handsome Wilhelm, dear lady. And this is he." He pointed to Winter.

"This must be someone's idea of an idiotic joke," said Winter.

Everything started spinning before Frau Fliebusch's eyes. She clung tightly to the armrest. Once again she'd been deceived. Once again some vile, mean people had lied to her. Wilhelm wasn't here at all. Just some young man who was also named Wilhelm.

She started to cry. "My God, how long is it going to go on like this? They keep lying to me over and over!" The tears shot from her eyes and ran down her face.

Wilhelm felt sorry for her. "I don't know what to say," he excused himself. "I don't know anything about this."

He turned on Hagen, furious. "Why would you do some- thing this stupid, Heinrich? What's this about? Do you think I'll put up with whatever you dish out?" He looked at him, angry and ready to fight.

Hagen tried to calm him down. "I don't know any more than you do. This woman comes here and says she wants to talk to

Handsome Wilhelm. So I told her to wait. How can I know if she's your mother or not? If she says something like that . . ."

He spread his arms out, apologetically.

Wilhelm kept lashing out. "When I find out who did this, I'm going to punch him so hard he'll be spitting blood for months."

Frau Fliebusch went on crying, evidently little consoled by this prospect. What good would it do her if the blind man started spitting blood, like this unpleasant young man was saying? True, it had been a vile thing to do, but the blind man hadn't actually spoken to her directly, he'd just been talking with the woman who was with him. What good would it do her?

She wanted to have her Wilhelm back, and that was all. Once again he had vanished in the fog. Once again years might pass before she saw him. She had been so convinced she would find him today that her disappointment was boundless.

Gradually her worry again turned to anger. People were so mean, so vicious. Couldn't somebody tell her where Wilhelm really was? Surely many people knew. But they all lied.

A hope arose in her. Perhaps this man was also lying. Perhaps Wilhelm was coming this evening, and all the vile people just didn't want her to meet him. Frau Fliebusch was almost certain that was the case. After all, the blind man hadn't been able to see her. He couldn't have been lying. Her Wilhelm would still show up, she reasoned with herself. The blind man had to have been telling the truth.

Frau Fliebusch wiped the tears from her face. "You aren't Handsome Wilhelm at all. You're just another one of those who want to talk me into believing Wilhelm is dead. But I know he's alive!" She looked at Wilhelm Winter with contempt. "Go on, act as though you're surprised. I know better. I'm going to wait right here. I know that my Wilhelm is going to show up. Even if I have to wait here every day!"

Wilhelm Winter looked at her in astonishment. Her accusation struck him as so off the mark there was no point in getting angry.

Hagen on the other hand did react. "Looks like you have a screw loose," he said harshly. "And you won't be waiting here for as long as it suits you, but just as long as it suits me. So keep that in mind! Besides, I would advise you not to insult my guests!"

Minchen Lindner had been listening closely. She felt very sorry for the old lady who had called her "a lovely person." The compliment made Minchen feel somewhat obliged. The woman really did seem crazy. But that wasn't important. She wasn't harming anyone, and the fat proprietor had no reason to bark at her like that.

She walked over to the group. "There's no reason for you to blow up at her like that!" she said to Hagen.

He turned around and stared at her in amazement. "And who might this cheeky bigmouth be?" he asked.

Minchen Lindner placed her hands on her hips and gave him a scornful look. "If that's how you treat people, then everybody might as well leave, right? Because either you're running a tavern here or a Buddhist monastery! But if it's a public tavern, then the lady can stay the same as anybody else!"

Hagen had to laugh. He liked this girl. "Well, if you say so, then I guess I better listen!"

He tried to stroke her cheek, but she pulled her head away.

"You're right about that. It's best you just keep your mouth shut," Minchen said dramatically.

Wilhelm started to laugh.

Hagen was annoyed. "Listen here, you little cutie, why don't you simmer down," he demanded.

Handsome Wilhelm stepped up. "Would you like to dance, Fräulein?"

She sized him up warily and decided he was very much to her liking. Only his suit seemed a little peculiar. But that wasn't so important.

"Maybe later. First I want to make sure this business is settled."

"Come on, Heinrich," Wilhelm said, in a calming voice.

"The lady isn't doing anything. Why shouldn't she go on sitting there?"

"Fine," Hagen conceded. "I'm not a monster. Just no more insults. About being mean and so on, I'm not a mean person. I'm running a tavern and have the right to demand that my guests eat or drink something. This isn't a homeless shelter. I only let her stay because she said she was waiting for you."

Minchen Lindner was in a magnanimous mood. "Give the lady something to eat. I'll pay for it." She took a three-mark coin out of her purse and handed it to Hagen.

He gave a playful bow. "I kiss your hand, milady. This is good for three meals, and I'll add one as well, so that makes four."

Frau Fliebusch had barely followed the negotiations. But she understood that she was allowed to stay.

Minchen Lindner walked over to her and held out her hand. "Goodbye. You have four dinners paid for. Don't let yourself be duped."

Before Frau Fliebusch could thank her, she had left the room with Wilhelm.

Frau Fliebusch called out after her: "Thanks very much, dear child. I'll repay you when my husband comes back."

TWENTY-SIX

Sonnenberg's fury had intensified tremendously. One dance followed the next, and Elsi had yet to come back. She had never dared do that before. This was open revolt.

Fundholz was still sitting next to him. Sonnenberg had let go of his hand, but Fundholz stayed anyway, because there was schnapps! Lots of schnapps. Sonnenberg kept ordering more. As soon as he downed one glass, he asked for another. His fury made him thirsty. He was no longer completely sober.

Fundholz, too, was already inebriated. He just blinked away at Sonnenberg without paying any attention to all the man's angry grumbling. He actually felt happy and lighthearted. It was amazing! He hadn't felt so exhilarated in a long time. He was no longer thinking about the encounter with his wife. He was no longer drinking to settle his nerves: He was savoring the taste, and growing more cheerful with every glass.

Despite the music and the general din, Tönnchen had slumped back in his chair and fallen asleep like a tired child. He must have been having good dreams, because he was smiling even in his sleep.

As he watched him, Fundholz couldn't help feeling a twinge of emotion. What a character! Simply drifts off to sleep. In the middle of the tavern, in spite of all the noise. He admired the fat man for his ability to withdraw into himself like that.

Sonnenberg, on the other hand, was cursing louder and louder, with no consideration for the people at the nearby tables. Not that this seemed to bother anyone: Other people were just as loud.

A woman at one table kept shrieking with laughter at high volume. She was positively bursting with enthusiasm. Whenever she laughed, many others would join in—it was contagious. Only Sonnenberg found her annoying.

"Someone needs to land a beer glass on her head," he groaned. "This shrieking is unbearable! It sounds like a band saw on metal."

"Band saw is good," Fundholz said laughing.

But Fundholz's praise did nothing to lighten Sonnenberg's mood. "Can you see those two?" he asked.

Fundholz could see them. They were dancing nearby. Grissmann was pressing the woman even closer than before. But Fundholz didn't tell that to Sonnenberg. Why stir things up, he thought. He's a lot better off if he doesn't know than if I tell him. Most misfortune comes from knowing too much. What you don't know can't upset you.

"No," he lied. "I don't see them. Grissmann has some money. Maybe he offered to buy her something to eat in the taproom. He's a decent fellow, you know, this Grissmann!"

Sonnenberg sneered, "I know all about this kind of decent fellow. Your Grissmann's nothing but a filthy bastard!"

Fundholz didn't answer. He was in a good mood and had no desire to argue. What for? Everything would happen as it should. He couldn't prevent Grissmann from stealing Sonnenberg's wife.

"Oh come on, it's not all that bad," he said, and laughed again.

Sonnenberg was suspicious about the old man's repeated laughter.

"You must be drunk," he grumbled.

Fundholz didn't respond. Let Sonnenberg think he was

drunk. The main thing was that the blind man would order more schnapps.

Back when they used to go begging together, Sonnenberg had always made off with all the money Fundholz had cadged. So let him pay for once! Then maybe everything would even itself out. Maybe Annie, too, will someday have to make amends.

Fundholz slapped his hand to his mouth. "Enough of that, Fundholz!" he ordered himself out loud. He lifted his glass, peered inside, and determined there was still something left. He tilted it back. One shouldn't tempt fate, he thought. Because fate might be tempted to make matters worse. He again recalled his streak of bad luck. "You never know when it might break," he said out loud.

Sonnenberg let out an angry snarl. "What are you babbling on about? Go ahead and talk to yourself where you like, but not when I'm paying for what you're guzzling!"

Fundholz realized that Sonnenberg needed to vent his spleen. Let him go on ranting, he thought blithely. As long as he orders another drink.

But for the moment that was far from Sonnenberg's mind. "What kind of man are you anyway? You spend the whole night boozing, hardly saying a word, and when you do open your mouth, you just talk to yourself. If you weren't such a dunder-head, you'd have told me long ago where the two have gone. Instead you just sit here telling me lies. Maybe you're even help-ing the others, huh?"

Fundholz laughed. "I'm not helping anyone! This whole thing's none of my business."

He really was feeling jolly this evening, practically talkative. Once again he cautioned himself, but this time more quietly: "Better stop your crowing, Fundholz!"

Sonnenberg was annoyed at Fundholz's previous declara-tion. "If you don't want to help me, then why are you sitting here? Unbelievable!"

Fundholz sobered up a little. There probably wouldn't be

any more schnapps. That's what happens when you celebrate too soon. "All right, then I'll be leaving," he muttered.

But that was the last thing Sonnenberg wanted. "Of course you would. First you drink your fill and then you walk out on me. You're really just a mean son of a bitch. And you call yourself a friend!"

Fundholz looked at him in surprise. "So what do you want me to do? Stay or go?"

Instead of answering, Sonnenberg bellowed out to a waiter, "Four schnapps," he ordered, "and hurry up about it!"

Fundholz stayed. He didn't want to pass up his share of schnapps.

Sonnenberg called for something to smoke. A man came with cigars and cigarettes. Sonnenberg chose two cigars at fifteen pfennig apiece. One was for Fundholz.

Sonnenberg's bill now exceeded the cash he had on hand. But since he was a regular patron and as such enjoyed a certain amount of credit, that didn't matter.

Fundholz had never seen the man in such a giving mood. Sonnenberg's distress and anger were so great that he was generous out of desperation. The schnapps arrived, and they drank. Sonnenberg emptied both glasses one after the other, while Fundholz saved his second shot for later.

The liquor only exacerbated the blind man's rage. He chewed away on his cigar and finally flung it angrily on the table. Fundholz picked it up carefully and placed it in the ashtray.

"Outrageous," he yelled at Fundholz, "calling this a cigar. This is no cigar, it's a piece of rolled-up filth! Call over the scoundrel who sold these so I can give him a piece of my mind."

Fundholz thought his cigar tasted perfectly fine. He had no intention of complying with Sonnenberg's wish. He didn't want to cause a scandal.

Suddenly Sonnenberg yelled across the entire hall, "Elsi!"

Then, when no one answered, he shouted again, even more loudly, "Elsi, you damn bitch, are you coming or not? I'll break every bone in your body if you don't get your tail over here right now."

The people at the next table over laughed. The dancing couples paused for a moment. Even the piano stopped.

In the ensuing silence the blind man screamed, "Well, are you coming? Or do I have to fetch you?"

Tönnchen woke up and looked around, afraid.

Fundholz didn't like having so many curious eyes looking at him on account of the blind man. "Don't make such a racket, Sonnenberg," he said.

But the blind man didn't listen. "If she doesn't come here right this minute, she'll be sorry!"

TWENTY-SEVEN

Grissmann was still dancing with Elsi. But she thought he seemed strangely distracted.

He was thinking about the pretty girl he had just seen and comparing her with Elsi, although there really was no comparison. The court bailiff's daughter—for that's who he assumed she was—was an attractive girl. Exceptionally attractive, in fact.

As he led her clumsily across the floor, he no longer found Elsi very appealing. Her face was not attractive, he decided, especially compared to the other girl. Why didn't he have a pretty girlfriend? It seemed that the other girl didn't like him, though.

Well, he thought, she can have any type of man she chooses. Men with money. After all, everything depends on money. If he had money, then he would also have beautiful women. Ten marks was nothing to them, of course. But just wait, Grissmann thought. One day I, too, will have money, and then you'll show me a little more courtesy.

He maneuvered them closer to the piano. He wanted to see if the girl had already located the bailiff. Elsi snuggled close to him, but Grissmann didn't react. He was looking for Herr Lindner.

The bailiff had a whole row of empty beer glasses in front of him. The tavern was so busy, the waiters hadn't had a chance to clear things away.

Grissmann danced close to the bailiff's table. "Hello," he called.

Herr Lindner carefully set down his glass and looked up. "Hello," he answered, slurring his speech.

Grissmann called out to him, "Your daughter is here!"

"Minchen?" asked Lindner in return, without great interest.

So her name was Minchen.

"That's right," Grissmann confirmed.

Herr Lindner felt for his missing mustache. "She's a pretty one, isn't she?" he slurred.

Grissmann agreed. "Very pretty in fact!"

The bailiff nodded, flattered. "You should meet her, Herr . . ."

"Grissmann."

"Herr Grissmann," the bailiff repeated. He raised his glass. "Prost, young lady," he said to Elsi.

Elsi smiled back. "Prost." However, she thought Grissmann was far too interested in this girl. Sonnenberg was much more solid. But now Grissmann was once again holding her tightly.

Grissmann knew nothing about dancing. He didn't waltz so much as spin around and around. No matter what was playing, he simply pressed his partner close and turned in time to the music, or not in time. Nor was he alone in this: Nearly all the couples danced that way.

As a rule, workers do not take dance lessons. They have neither the money nor the time. And why should they? They're not interested in acting out some pantomime, and they don't have any particular desire to develop their style. They simply dance to enjoy themselves, which they do. But just like in any establishment, there were people in the Jolly Huntsman who weren't dancing only for themselves but were performing for others and wanted to be admired. For them dancing was not recreation or pleasure, but hard work. They sweated as they attempted to float across the floor. But no one paid them any attention, much to their displeasure.

On this evening at the Jolly Huntsman, it was above all the

pimps who were on display. Bored with the official meeting, they
had decided to enter the dance hall—at least the younger ones
had, since the older generation was still engaged in serious delib-
erations. They had a style of their own. They swung their hips
and danced seemingly without effort, though in fact this appar-
ent ease took quite a bit of work. But they lived off the ladies,
like butterflies off flowers, and were competing to expand their
protectorate.

There weren't many prostitutes in the Jolly Huntsman, but the
trained eyes of the pimps easily spotted them. They were generally better dressed, with higher hemlines, abundant makeup, and
additional qualities that distinguished them from the other female
guests. They appeared very easygoing, happy to give a friendly
glance to anyone they fancied. They and the pimps made up the
jeunesse dorée of the lower classes. And just like the genuine *jeunesse dorée*, they had no steady employment and simply went
through life in the same happy-go-lucky way as the golden youth
of the upper class.

As they grew older, the business became more complicated.
But for now, they were young, and life wasn't so difficult.
That was the thinking of the professionals, who had come to
terms with themselves and were content. The amateurs did not
patronize the Jolly Huntsman. The amateurs were not happy-
go-lucky. The amateurs said each time that for them it was the
last time.

Grissmann admired the various couples that floated by so
easily and elegantly. He knew what they did for a living. But it
wasn't that which bothered him. He would have engaged in the
same occupation if he could. But sadly no one wanted him.

He said to Elsi, snidely, "Look at them showing off and acting as though they were something else. The pimps!"

Elsi nodded, but suddenly Grissmann caught sight of Minchen
Lindner. She was dancing with a good-looking young man in a
black suit. Both danced well, without much effort. Grissmann
watched them with envy. This fancy man in his ridiculous

jacket had snatched the girl away from him. That was mean. He stepped on Elsi's toes, but this time he didn't apologize. He knew her well enough already, and it was no longer necessary to be overly polite, he thought.

Elsi followed his gaze. The same girl as before. She saw rage and disappointment in his face. Elsi wasn't overly endowed with intellect, but that much was clear to her. Grissmann might be nice, but he would definitely not be faithful, at least no longer than he felt he needed to be. Sonnenberg was much more decent. Yes, Sonnenberg beat her. But she was sure Sonnenberg wouldn't walk out on her. What would become of her if Grissmann just left her?

Elsi didn't want to wind up back on the streets. But she knew there was hardly any other way to earn money. She vacillated. Grissmann was a lot more pleasant than the blind man. After all, he spoke like a human being and not like some bellowing beast. But Sonnenberg had his advantages. With him, there was always something to eat, for example.

Grissmann didn't notice her shift in mood. He didn't want to be annoyed by Minchen Lindner anymore and so turned back to Elsi. "Let's go somewhere else this evening," he whispered to her. Elsi smiled, but she was no longer so certain that anything would come of that. For his part, Grissmann had decided that he didn't want to let go of what he had until he found something better.

Once again they danced past the table with the court bailiff. Something strange had taken place with Herr Lindner. He was no longer drinking and seemed to be occupied with a weighty problem. He was holding his right hand in front of his mouth and staring at the piano. As the couple danced past, he waved to them with his left hand.

Herr Lindner seemed to be choking down something. Just as the two were right next to him, it happened. The bailiff opened his mouth. "This damned awful beer," he wanted to say, but didn't get past "this damned." Then he returned to the establishment a considerable portion of the beer he had drunk. He happened to have a weak stomach.

But neither Elsi nor Grissmann cared about that, and they spun away, disgusted. It was still so early. They went on dancing, and when, a few minutes later, Grissmann looked back at Court Bailiff Lindner, a waiter was already busy wiping things up.

Herr Lindner sat on his chair, weakened. In front of him were two empty schnapps glasses. A bailiff like that must do pretty well for himself, Grissmann thought with envy.

Elsi's affection for Grissmann had peaked. At some point he's simply going to walk out on me, she told herself. Just like she had wanted to walk out on the blind man. If she hadn't been so afraid of Sonnenberg, she would have gone right back to him. Anxiously, she glanced in his direction.

Sonnenberg was smoking a cigar. The odd man who had said hello this morning was laughing, while the fat man was asleep. How could he sleep when Sonnenberg was in one of his bad moods? The blind man's fits of rage would wake an elephant, she thought. She concluded that Sonnenberg was no longer furious.

Grissmann was saying something to her, and she looked at him, but he was once again casting about for the other girl. No, he was definitely not the faithful type. He would soon walk out on her.

Suddenly she heard her name being called. That was Sonnenberg. He was shouting so loudly that for a moment everyone stopped dancing. Instinctively Elsi freed herself from Grissmann. When Sonnenberg shouted, you had to jump. That much she knew.

Grissmann looked at her, baffled. He wanted to put his arms back around her, but Sonnenberg started yelling again. Elsi left him and made her way through the crowd, without even turning to look at him. Grissmann followed her, angry. He wasn't afraid of the blind man. Just you wait, he thought. The woman must be out of her mind. First she ate her fill on his money, then she danced with him, and now she wants to leave him standing there.

"Just you wait," Grissmann grumbled. He had his rights to defend. Rights he had just acquired. And therefore he was not about to put up with something like this!

TWENTY-EIGHT

At first Minchen and Handsome Wilhelm didn't talk to each other. Each was trying to get used to the other's movements and adjusting as needed.

Minchen Lindner liked to dance, and she was glad her partner was a good dancer.

"Tell me, mister in the black suit, do you have a name?"

Minchen Lindner was not inhibited. She'd learned a lot about life, after all. She was no longer some innocent girl from the country. She was Herr von Sulm's special friend and equipped with quite a bit of life experience. She didn't attach any importance to form and enjoyed saying whatever popped into her head. That was precisely why she had come here, so she wouldn't have to speak in such high-flown gibberish.

Wilhelm was a little taken aback by the question. He was used to women courting him the way men usually court women. But Minchen's verve appealed to him. He had been particularly impressed by the scene with Hagen and the old lady. She was not at a loss for words and had a sharp tongue; that much he had already ascertained.

She didn't appear to be a lady "from the guild"—if she were, she would have been better dressed. Wilhelm was a master of his trade and knew that the right face could earn a lot of money.

Minchen Lindner had the right face, but he didn't believe that she put it to professional use.

Handsome Wilhelm introduced himself: "My name is Wilhelm Winter."

"I see," said Minchen Lindner. "So that's your name, or at least you claim it is. Because if your name really was Wilhelm Winter, the proprietor could have told that to the lady right away. But even though he knows you, he doesn't actually know your real name. Which is why there's all this confusion," she concluded astutely.

She believed her dance partner was what was known as a hard case. One of those whose work was under the table and on the sly, and whose endeavors clearly ran afoul of certain articles of the criminal code. That impressed her. Minchen Lindner had a sense of romance. The man was known as Handsome Wilhelm, but he didn't appear to be a pimp. He didn't look like one. Nor did he behave like one.

He carried himself more like a proper criminal—a brigand, a bandit—and not some lowlife pimp. Minchen had far more sympathy for proper criminals than for parasitic panderers and fancy men. Criminals were real men. They cracked safes, ransacked cash registers, and waged heroic battles against the state, which was so much stronger than they were. That said, she had no sympathy for pickpockets, since one of them had stolen her purse once. But bank robbers, those were men all right. To be a robber like that was to be a fighter, Minchen thought. A man like that had class. She hoped that the man in her arms was an honest-to-God safecracker.

She snuggled closer to him. She wanted to feel if he was carrying a revolver. But Handsome Wilhelm wasn't carrying a revolver and had never possessed one. Disappointed, Minchen again put a little distance between the two of them.

Wilhelm thought about what she had said. She was right. Did Heinrich possibly think he was a wanted man? Handsome Wilhelm was actually happy he wasn't. His own sense of romance had suffered somewhat when he was in custody. There are two sides to every story, including the life of a criminal, as he well knew.

"My name is Wilhelm Winter," he repeated, "and I've never gone by anything else."

"That's too bad," said Minchen dreamily.

"Why so?"

"I thought you might be a hard case," she openly admitted.

"You're thinking quite a bit about who I might be," said Wilhelm, flattered.

"Don't let it go to your head."

"Are you from here?" he wanted to know.

"No, I'm from there," she answered pertly.

Wilhelm laughed. "I like you. You're all right," he acknowledged.

Minchen Lindner took note. "My name is Hermine Lindner," she introduced herself.

Wilhelm Winter shook his head. "Hermine sounds too severe. You ought to go by Minchen."

Minchen Lindner beamed. "That's exactly what people call me."

Wilhelm acted jealous. "Who calls you that?"

Minchen didn't answer. She was thinking about her older gentlemen. And the thoughts were neither fond nor pleasant.

"Who calls me that? That's none of your business!" she said, instead.

This girl was a lot of fun. It was fun not having to be Handsome Wilhelm, who anyone could claim in return for a certain percentage. Now he was back to being Wilhelm Winter. Here was a girl he liked, and everything was nice and easy.

"But I'd really like to know." He laughed, and picked up the pace.

His laugh appealed to her. It was so fresh, so easygoing. Not like Herr von Sulm's old man's cackle and not awkward or doltish like some of the others. He laughed like a boy. Most definitely not a pimp. He was a worker or a clerk who'd had that odd suit made simply because he liked it.

Minchen Lindner wasn't set on bank robbers. There must be other real men out there as well. However she chose not to answer his question. Why should she lie to him? That wasn't necessary.

"You're a regular here. Am I right?"

Wilhelm confirmed this.

"In that case why don't you ask the piano player if he wouldn't just prefer to pick up an axe. That would be quicker."

"What would be quicker?" he wanted to know.

"Well," said Minchen, in a serious tone of voice, "I'm assuming the man wants to destroy the piano."

Handsome Wilhelm laughed, delighted.

Minchen Lindner suddenly remembered that she hadn't come here just to dance, but also to give her father some money. She spotted him sitting at a table, drinking alone. If I give him the money now, he'll just drink more, she considered. He isn't going anywhere, so I'll just give it to him later.

All of a sudden someone came up to Wilhelm.

"Hello, Willi," said a heavily made-up girl.

Wilhelm's face turned red. He felt ashamed in front of Minchen Lindner. The girl with the painted face was dancing with a heavyset, boorish-looking man.

"Hello, Elfriede," he replied.

They went on dancing, with Minchen poorer for the loss of an illusion. Aha, she thought—so that's what he is, after all. Generally speaking, Minchen was not inclined to prejudice, but she harbored a particular aversion to pimps. She found the idea of a man living off prostitutes contemptible.

Wilhelm sensed Minchen pulling away. He was annoyed. Why did Elfriede have to speak to him now of all times? She was probably jealous. Later he would give her a piece of his mind. But what use was that? Now Minchen Lindner was looking through him as if he wasn't there.

He tried to joke about it. "Berlin sure is small, you're always running into acquaintances when you least want to."

Minchen didn't react. She went on dancing automatically, indifferently.

Wilhelm was exasperated with her. "Do you know what I am?" he asked.

Minchen Lindner shook her head. Now he's going to try and sell me the moon, she imagined.

"I'm a pimp! A low-down common pimp!"

He let go of her. "You're shocked, right? Now you can find another partner. Because I'm sure you don't want to dance with a pimp, right?"

Minchen laughed. "Why not?"

The fact that he was so frank about his profession made him again rise in her estimation. To be sure it was hardly a splendid business, but she was impressed by the way he came out and said it.

"So why are you a pimp?" she wanted to know.

Winter became more talkative. He wanted to explain to her how everything was tied together. After all, it wasn't that he enjoyed the work: It was need that had compelled him to become what he was. "I'm unemployed," he said.

Minchen Lindner understood everything that entailed. She, too, had had a taste of that and had not been any more resilient than he had.

"So, you're unemployed," she repeated, commiserating.

Wilhelm warmed up somewhat. "But I'm looking for work. I've had enough of this, you understand? I don't enjoy it. At all."

Minchen didn't answer. She didn't enjoy her profession, either. Being a pimp was probably worse, but she was sick and tired of what she did.

"You know what?" Wilhelm said, changing the subject. "How about I show you the other room, our Liederkranz hall. You're not a snitch, are you?"

Minchen laughed. "You don't have to worry about that."

What Wilhelm had in mind went against half a dozen of the Ringverein's regulations. But he didn't care. As it was, he wanted to get out of the business. Why shouldn't he show the girl around? They danced over to the taproom, and when they reached the door, they let go of each other.

Frau Fliebusch was still eating. She seemed to have calmed down completely, and she gave the two a friendly nod.

"My husband will pay you back," she assured Minchen Lindner.

"That's not necessary," Minchen replied.

"Oh but I insist. You have to visit us sometime."

Minchen Lindner thanked her for the invitation. Crazy people should never be contradicted.

Wilhelm led her down the same corridor he had come through with Herr Hagen.

"You should feel flattered. The lady didn't invite me," he noted.

Minchen laughed. "I doubt we'll live to see the real Handsome Wilhelm return."

"I am the real one," Wilhelm said, offended.

"Now, now," she countered. "You're not exactly who you claim to be, either."

They stood by the heavy door, behind which they could hear the faint babble of deep voices.

"Now, don't say a word. It will only set them off," he whispered, and squeezed her hand. She squeezed back. She was enjoying the adventure. She was about to meet a genuine criminal gang—a real Ringverein.

Wilhelm opened the door, and they both stepped inside.

TWENTY-NINE

The music played on, and the dancing couples stopped paying attention to the shouting blind man. Most assumed he was drunk, which was hardly noteworthy in the Jolly Huntsman. It was just a little too early, though. But people are different: Some don't get drunk before midnight and others are soused substantially earlier. So the couples went on dancing.

Elsi was terribly afraid of how the blind man would react. As she made her way to his table, she kept wondering if she really shouldn't turn around. Sonnenberg was not going to let her behavior go unpunished. That much was certain. She slowed her pace.

Grissmann wanted to catch up to her, but before he could, she was already at the table. "Yes, Max?" she asked innocently.

The blind man sat up, taking notice. His face glowed with inner satisfaction. So, she had fallen in line and obeyed him, after all. Which is what she had to do, always.

"Come and sit by me," he said. His voice sounded inviting, but underneath, it was still smoldering with rage.

Elsi sat down obediently, across the table from Sonnenberg. There she could escape more easily if he started up. His calm composure struck her as unnatural. She looked up. Grissmann was standing in front of her.

"Well," he asked, "don't you want to go on dancing?"

Sonnenberg slammed his fist on the table. "Clear off, boy! Or else there'll be a thrashing! Have you lost your mind? Go on dancing? There'll be no more dancing here! Here somebody's going to get coldcocked! You got that, boy? Don't even think . . ."

Grissmann interrupted him. "Stop making such a racket! Or else I'll smack you, blind or not!"

Sonnenberg gave a start. "Because I'm blind, you think you can do what you want with my wife? Well you're mistaken!" He stood up. "I gave my eyes for you shirkers. Come on, boy, let's wrestle! Give me your chubby little hand! How about it?"

Grissmann didn't answer.

"Well?" asked Sonnenberg. "Maybe you'd rather box? You want to sneak behind me and conk me over the head from behind? Or are you scared?"

People at the nearby tables looked over, curious. The blind man had all sympathies on his side. They started calling out— the mildest shouts being "He's absolutely right!" and "Cowardly dog!"

A very brawny young man stood up and stepped over to the table. "Have a seat, blind man. If you'd like I can slap the boy around a little. Is that your son? Children need to be educated!" He reached back and was only waiting for the blind man's go-ahead to let loose.

Grissmann had imagined the whole thing differently. He had thought he would only be dealing with Sonnenberg. But now more and more people were joining in. He had no desire to get thrashed. "What's wrong, what's wrong?" he stammered sheepishly. "I was just joking."

Sonnenberg insisted on settling the matter himself. He was still a man, after all. He might not be able to see, but he could still wrestle, because then he could feel his opponent. I'll chop him into kindling, he promised himself. "Thank you, but I'll take care of my own affairs. That way I'll know things will be done right," he replied to the man. Then he turned to Grissmann.

"Come, my friend, give me your hand. Let's shake and make up!" Grissmann hesitated. He didn't trust the blind man. Sonnenberg didn't seem the least bit conciliatory, and looking at him now—the man was big and strong—Grissmann felt afraid.

Elsi sat quietly on her chair and watched. She was glad that Sonnenberg's fury had been diverted. She didn't wish anything bad for Grissmann, but better him than her.

Fundholz stood up. He tapped Sonnenberg on the shoulder, hoping to calm him down. "Let it go, Sonnenberg. Let's have another drink. Everything's all right. Grissmann didn't mean anything."

Sonnenberg brushed him away in a very calm voice. "Sit down, Fundholz. Who says I want to do anything to him? He wanted to do something to me. You heard the man. He said blind or not . . ."

Fundholz didn't trust him. He knew Sonnenberg's tricks, and he continued trying to calm him down. "Everything's all right now."

Tönnchen smiled cheerfully at the old man, who patted him on the shoulder and sat back in his chair. Today of all days, when Fundholz was feeling so happy and free of care, Sonnenberg shouldn't cause a ruckus. The old man wanted his peace and quiet.

Sonnenberg was still holding his hand out to Grissmann. "Not up for it, are you? Afraid I might do something to you?" His last words did not encourage Grissmann. The brawny young man was ready to pounce and place Grissmann's hand in Sonnenberg's. Grissmann's fear was evident to all.

"There's no weaseling out of it," said the young man. "First he mouths off and then he wants to run off! That's out of the question."

Grissmann actually was debating whether he shouldn't simply run away, and this intention must have shown in his face. But he realized that wouldn't work. Reluctantly he prepared to place his right hand in that of the blind man. With his left hand he carefully opened the knife in his pocket. Just in case, he thought.

The commotion had not gone unnoticed. Herr Hagen came up to them, accompanied by two elegant gentlemen. "And this is Sonnenberg," he said, by way of introduction. "Our accordion player. I'm sad to say he's blind," he added. It sounded like an excuse.

Everyone turned around, surprised. Only now did they notice Herr Hagen, who was winking at them, and the two well-dressed gentlemen.

"Probably more gawkers from the west come to look at our zoo," one man said in a low voice to his girlfriend.

Herr Hagen had heard the remark. Wrinkling his forehead in indignation, he said, "Anyone who doesn't like things in the Jolly Huntsman is free to leave." But the man liked things there and was silent.

The two gentlemen had understood the man's remark. They tried to erase the bad impression they seemed to have made by showing how easygoing they were. "Things are livelier out here with you boys," the younger of the two said appreciatively. He was a lawyer and believed that, thanks to his knowledge of human nature, he had found the right tone. These folks like keeping things lively, he thought. So he went on, "There's always something going on with you lot. It's downright enviable!"

The older man, a district judge from the province, who had entrusted himself to his friend's guidance, joined in: "Enviable!" But he wasn't feeling entirely comfortable. He could tell by the faces that there was tension in the air. There was evidently something going on between the burly blind man and the weak-looking fellow.

It had been a dumb idea to visit this tavern in the outskirts of town. They should have gone to the bar at the Fiametta or some other decent place. If a man has a chance to be in Berlin, there was no need to visit some criminal dive, because that's what he considered the Jolly Huntsman to be. "Enviable," he repeated.

"But I don't wish to intrude. Come on, Hans." He turned around and started to leave.

Hagen gave the other guests a menacing look, which meant, If anyone opens his mouth now, I'm going to take him by the collar and throw him out on his ear. Sonnenberg didn't see Hagen's expression, and even if he had, it's doubtful whether he would have let himself be intimidated.

"Enviable," he mimicked. "Enviable. We are enviable? What sort of fellows are you that you'd consider a blind beggar enviable?" The jurists weren't prepared for such questions, and before they could answer and before Herr Hagen could step in, Sonnenberg answered himself. "You're not men at all! Milksops, that's what you are! Enviable milksops! Save your sweet talk and stay out west in your wealthy villas. That's where the enviable ones like you belong!" Sonnenberg laughed at his own words, and now the others couldn't be stopped, either. They all started laughing at once and shouting unkind things.

Sonnenberg had spoken from his heart, which is why they were ignoring Hagen's threatening looks. They didn't care for any compliments. They didn't visit the establishments in the wealthy western districts and didn't want those patrons visiting theirs. They had forgotten about Grissmann. Their eyes were now fixed solely on the intruders, who had turned bright red.

"Excuse me," said the lawyer sharply. "What makes you think you can talk to us like that?"

Sonnenberg was quick to respond. "I'm talking exactly the way I think. Now see to it that you get out! Drive back where you came from! Drink your champagne or your raspberry liqueur, but leave us in peace."

"Ridiculous," said the district judge.

"What's ridiculous?" Sonnenberg wanted to know. "We're ridiculous, is that right? Something to laugh at? We're here so you can come and laugh at us. For you we're just a zoo, right? Or maybe a circus! You come here for a good laugh, is that it? You lily-livered milksops. I may be blind, but I can clearly see that raspberry liqueur dripping off your lips. Get lost and make it quick!"

Dr. Kummerpfennig, the lawyer, had never been so insulted in all his life. The blind man was below his station—very far below—so he couldn't demand satisfaction. But the well-known attorney who had represented Countess Leindorf in her divorce trial—worth nine million, not the countess, but her dowry—the respected Dr. Kummerpfennig who wouldn't take on a case with a retainer of less than a thousand marks, simply could not allow himself to be insulted by a beggar.

The district judge wanted to restrain his friend, but the lawyer was too deeply outraged.

"I would remind you that you have just committed libel in coincidence with threatening behavior. I will institute the proper legal proceedings to call you to account for your outrageous accusations." Dr. Kummerpfennig took out his notebook. "What's your name?" he asked Sonnenberg, who, taken by surprise, had gone silent for a moment.

"That's none of your damn business," he growled. "Are you hoping to start a lawsuit here or just jabber on like a dimwit? What is it you want here, anyway?" Sonnenberg's tone was now a little calmer.

Dr. Kummerpfennig's spirit of resistance stiffened. "I don't need to justify myself to you, sir." He was able to draw out the word *sir* like no one else. "You have grossly insulted my friend and myself in the presence of witnesses, grossly insulted us without reason! I demand to know your name and I am warning you that if necessary I will engage the help of a police official to find out."

He turned to Grissmann, who was staring at him, awestruck. "What is the man's name?"

"Sonnenberg," Grissmann said quietly.

Herr Doktor Kummerpfennig hadn't understood him clearly. "Speak up, please," he demanded.

This time Grissmann didn't answer, as the others were giving him menacing looks. He was afraid of what might happen next.

Kummerpfennig waited awhile. When Grissmann didn't speak, he said, "Fine. You haven't heard the last of this. There can't be that many blind people named Sonnberg or Sommberg."

"Sonnenberg," the judge corrected. He had paid attention earlier, when Hagen had introduced the blind man.

"So, it's Sonnenberg." Dr. Kummerpfennig corrected the name in his notebook.

Hagen was standing behind the two men, peeved. He didn't want to fall out with his patrons or with the two gentlemen. It was an unpleasant situation. His prodigious double chin was quivering from all the agitation. After all was said and done, he'd wind up having to appear in court as a witness. Hagen despised courtrooms.

Sonnenberg had been grinning as he listened to the conversation about his name. Now Hagen was saying to the younger man, "He probably didn't mean any harm."

Kummerpfennig looked at him fiercely. "Maybe to you, but it was enough for me!" he said dismissively.

"You stupid dog, you," Sonnenberg now resumed. "Are you sure you took everything down? My name is Max Sonnenberg. Profession: blind man. And you better add that I'm in possession of a certain paper. You'll know what I'm talking about. I was shot in the head, you see. I went to war so that a dumb dog like you could jabber away at me. While you were still a pip-squeak in diapers. So I can whack you behind your ears if I want, since I'm officially unsound of mind. And I have a hunting license to prove it!" Sonnenberg declared proudly and triumphantly.

The document he was referring to—known colloquially as a "hunting license"—declared the bearer to be mentally unsound in the manner covered by the famous Article 51 of the Penal Code, by which deeds committed by people of unsound mind were not considered criminal acts. Dr. Kummerpfennig especially enjoyed invoking this article at every murder trial. The fact that Sonnenberg was citing the same legal argument was embarrassing for him, very embarrassing. He looked at the judge, who was taking pains to suppress a smile. "Outrageous," said Kummer-pfennig. "But you deliberately slandered me and my friend, and then repeated the insult."

Sonnenberg kept on laughing. "So you better add: I was intoxicated. What do you think, Fundholz, are we intoxicated?"

Fundholz confirmed: "A little bit."

Now people started calling out to Dr. Kummerpfennig from all sides. "We are also intoxicated! Isn't that enviable?"

A number of couples had moved from the dance floor to join the group. They didn't realize what the fuss was about. All they knew was that the well-dressed man was causing the blind man trouble.

The situation was gradually becoming very unpleasant for Kummerpfennig. "We're not finished with this," he said. "You'll be hearing from me." But even he wasn't so convinced that would happen.

The brawny young man who had earlier wanted to punish Grissmann pushed his way forward. "You can finish things right now!"

He ostentatiously rolled up his sleeves, having long since taken off his jacket. "Why don't we just step outside?" he proposed.

Kummerpfennig's collar started feeling a little tight, and he automatically reached to adjust it. This gesture set off a roar of laughter.

Sonnenberg's voice was almost sweet: "Come on, give me your hand, let's shake and make up." He reached his hand out to where he sensed Kummerpfennig was standing.

"Yes! He should shake with the blind man! He should make up with the blind man! Don't be afraid, old Sonnenberg won't harm you," they called out from all sides.

But the lawyer was afraid, plain and simple. And that was unseemly. He was a jurist, not a boxer. For the first time in his

life, he regretted this. He wanted to get away from the entire
screaming mob. He just wanted to get away. He looked around
seeking help.

The district judge was more courageous. He raised both his
hands. "Quiet," he said. For a moment all were silent except for
the piano. "Quiet, gentlemen. We've made enough of a racket!"
He had barely spoken until then, which is why the others let him
say his piece. "I don't think there's any need to discuss this matter further. Herr Hagen"—here he turned to the proprietor, who
was eagerly rubbing his hands together—"how about a round
for the house!"

Everyone applauded enthusiastically. "Bravo! That's the first
sensible thing you've said yet!"

Sonnenberg was quiet. He had already said everything that
was on his mind. Besides, he didn't want to forget about Grissmann. Grissmann, that was the main thing. Hopefully he hadn't
run off in the meantime.

Grissmann had wanted to. Ever since he had learned about
Sonnenberg's special status, his fear had increased. But he couldn't
leave. People were crowding him in, and the brawny young man
was keeping an eye on him. I'll leave with the two gentlemen
from the west, he decided. But for the moment they weren't going
anywhere.

Herr Doktor Kummerpfennig let his friend handle the situation. He himself was feeling somewhat sheepish.

At that point Hagen returned, having placed the order. "For
the band as well, of course," he said. The band was the piano
player.

"Of course!" everyone shouted.

The guests sat back down and waited for their beer, leaving only the jurists, the blind man, Grissmann, and the brawny
young man still standing.

"Grissmann?" Sonnenberg asked. "Is Grissmann still there?"

The young man affirmed. "If you mean this one," he said,

grabbing Grissmann by the arm, "your friend from earlier, he's still here! We can settle with him later." He led the reluctant man two tables away. "Sit down," he commanded.

Sonnenberg sat down as well. "Save Grissmann for me," he said.

The young man called back, "You can count on it! I'll serve him to you later."

Grissmann didn't know what he should do. Anxiously he looked at the two jurists. But they were happy to have escaped from harm's way, and besides, they had absolutely no desire to get further involved in the blind man's affairs. They deliberately averted their eyes. Grissmann was afraid of Sonnenberg, but he also feared the young man. He frantically clutched at his pocketknife. It was his last resort, if all else failed.

The young man spoke to him. "I am a waiter, and you are a swine. You wanted to pinch the blind man's woman." When Grissmann started to object, he said, "Keep your mouth shut and let smarter people speak."

He had heard Sonnenberg shouting and was convinced the blind man was in the right. Being blind was bad enough, without someone trying to cheat you. The waiter was happy to stand up for a good cause and had the muscles to do so. There were few things he liked better than a proper fistfight. He worked as a waiter in a pretty wild establishment and had some experience dealing with bad people who didn't want to pay their bill or otherwise needed to be taken to task. This was his day off, and he could think of nothing better than if it ended with a real "smoker" rather than settling down quietly. Grissmann needed to pay up, and the waiter was going to make sure of it.

The beer arrived, and everyone drank.

"To the health of our noble benefactor," Fundholz called out gleefully. He had immediately grabbed Tönnchen's beer as well. Later he would buy him something to eat. After all, he had some money left that evening, thanks to Sonnenberg.

Everyone joined in: "Long live the enviable ones!"

The district judge thanked them, smiling. For his part, Dr. Kummerpfennig wasn't to be outdone. "Another round!" he ordered.

"Bravo, boy!" squawked a woman, her voice husky from the alcohol. Everyone laughed, more good-naturedly than before.

Dr. Kummerpfennig turned red, but he didn't say anything. I'm above this, he told himself.

Grissmann suddenly had a hysterical fit of rage. "Sonnenberg, you swine!"

The young man slapped him across the mouth. "Your turn is coming. Don't be impatient."

Everyone looked in astonishment at Grissmann, who was sitting on his chair, his face contorted with rage. Only Sonnenberg didn't react, but sat calmly at his table. He knew for certain he had Grissmann now. His rage had gone from hot to cold, but it had not diminished.

"Grissmann needs to pay up," he said quietly. It almost sounded indifferent.

Fundholz heard something about paying. He started thinking. Because he was no longer entirely sober, he thought out loud. "Pay? You always have to pay. Now and then you think you've been given something for free. But sooner or later you always have to pay. Every joy in life, everything—you have to pay for! Time and time again, in the end you have to pay, and it all costs too much. And in the end nothing is worth the price. Everything is too expensive! Every minute of joy winds up costing hours!"

He stopped speaking and finished his beer, lost in profound thoughts.

Sonnenberg snapped at him. "What's all this claptrap you're spouting? The minute you open your mouth out comes this nonsense!" He laughed angrily. "You think I've ever been happy I had to pay with my eyes? Never. I've always had it rotten!"

Fundholz shrugged. "I don't know," he said. He was tired. It was high time to go to sleep. Why was he still sitting here? Just because of the schnapps Sonnenberg was buying, and because of the free beer.

"I'll have to pay for it in the end, after all," he mumbled.

Sonnenberg pounded the table. "Now shut your mouth!"

Fundholz obeyed.

THIRTY

Not all the members of the 1929 Liederkranz attended the meeting. Many were indisposed, while others only came to festivities. Herr Sommer, the acting chairman, strongly disapproved of this. He was a well-nourished, spry fifty-year-old. He stood erect at the podium, a man with much life experience and a deep knowledge of the profession, which in recent years had developed from humble beginnings into such a fine organization. Sommer was very much of the old school. In his youth he had been a fairground wrestler, and he still boasted considerable physical strength.

Sommer was wearing a green sash. Everybody was wearing one. They were members of the Liederkranz and did not want to forgo the privileges that entitled them to. Green always elevated things. The bands of heavy silk lent something festive, conveyed a dignified atmosphere. The members of the Ringverein deemed themselves upright citizens and wanted to show that. Above all they wanted to show that to the police. For who would dare arrest a member of a singing club who was properly attired in a black suit adorned with a green sash and who in the event of a raid had taken his proper place behind a music stand? No one who appreciated upstanding citizens! And it was a known fact that the police considered themselves to be very upstanding.

Sommer was speaking seriously, responsibly, his words hardly distinguishable from the responsibly minded words typically offered by all manner of chairmen. "Where will it lead," he asked, troubled, "if we neglect the serious, substantive work on behalf of our organization? It will end in our dissolution, in the downfall of our organization!"

Herr Sommer tapped his beer glass and raised his voice. "We are not a pleasure club! We are an association that still has a great deal to accomplish!"

This appeal to duty roused one staid, older gentleman. "Bravo," he called out, before he dozed off again.

"Make no mistake about it," declared Herr Sommer, "there are things that need fixing. Dues are not being paid on time! Our Ringverein is not being sufficiently supported. Gentlemen . . ."

At this moment the door opened, and Handsome Wilhelm stepped inside, followed by Minchen Lindner. Wilhelm wasn't being impolite by not letting her in first: He simply thought it wise to get a glimpse of the proceedings.

A storm of protest erupted. Everyone jumped from their seat. The bylaws prohibited ladies from entering.

They shouted wildly in all directions until Sommer yelled, "Quiet!"

"My lady," he said, earnestly, as he quieted the shouting. "My lady, this is a gentlemen's association! I can't imagine what Wilhelm is thinking. Ladies are forbidden to enter!"

He gave Handsome Wilhelm a withering glance.

"The bylaws of the 1929 Liederkranz require the lady to leave at once!"

Herr Sommer looked around for Hagen but didn't find him. He wanted to give the proprietor a serious warning. Their Ringverein would go elsewhere if this ever happened again. It was only because Hagen paid Sommer a certain percentage that they didn't leave at once.

Wilhelm started to say something, but Sommer stopped him with a peremptory gesture of his wrestler's hand, then started yelling fiercely.

"The bylaws also state that any member who admits a lady

or for that matter brings any outsider will be expelled!" His voice sounded tortured, like an animal in distress. "Gentlemen! Gentlemen! We are not a pleasure club! This is not some widow's ball! We are the 1929 Liederkranz and all we want to do is sing and take care of our business!"

"Hear, hear!" the others called out their approval. "We are a Liederkranz and not a widow's ball!"

Herr Sommer was still staving off Wilhelm with his hand. "The chair hereby resolves to issue member Wilhelm Winter a stern warning. Any repeat infraction will result in his expulsion."

"Kick him out now!" called out some of the younger pimps, eager to seize the opportunity to rid themselves of competition.

"Quiet," Herr Sommer commanded in a powerful voice. "Quiet I say!"

Everyone stopped shouting, and Herr Sommer went on. As always on special occasions, he unconsciously imitated the voice of the judge who had once sentenced him to three years of prison. The judge had had such a mellifluous voice that Sommer had inadvertently accepted the verdict—merely on account of the beautiful sound. It was such a wonderful mix of dusty files and objectivity.

"The chair further wishes to communicate our displeasure to the proprietor Herr Heinrich Hagen. It is our wish to be left completely undisturbed. Singing requires peace and quiet! Music can only thrive if the musicians have complete quiet."

Herr Sommer staunchly upheld the fiction of the singing club to all outsiders.

Minchen Lindner laughed, in spite of Sommer's glances directed at her. "But I love music," she said.

"Then go to the picture show and listen all you want," Herr Sommer suggested. "We only play music for invited guests. Besides, tonight we are here to take care of accounting. You understand? Bookkeeping! In other words, strictly an internal matter. But you are hereby officially invited to our hundredth anniversary celebration!"

Everyone laughed. Sommer was great, he should definitely stay on. A model chairman.

"And when is that?" asked Minchen innocently.

"In the year two thousand twenty-nine," Sommer proclaimed solemnly.

"Aren't you going to celebrate your fiftieth?" Minchen wanted to know. "Then I could at least send my youngest grandson!"

Sommer grinned. "No decisions have been made regarding the fiftieth anniversary. In any case we will keep you informed."

Minchen curtsied to thank him. "That's very nice of you," she said. "I'll be sure to let you know which cemetery I'm buried in."

One of the younger pimps chimed in: "Don't let anything stand in your way. I highly recommend Weissensee. I live right nearby!"

"That's very considerate of you," Minchen thanked him, "but I'd prefer to sleep alone in my grave!"

There was no stopping the cheers among the pimps. "Spot on she is! Just right!" they called out. "She should stay."

As an experienced chairman, Herr Sommer always complied with the majority, particularly when he shared their opinion, as he did today. "Just a moment, madam," he said, then turned to the others. "Let us vote on the resolution to let the lady stay. Whoever is against, leave the room."

No one left.

"In which case our official meeting is hereby recessed until such time as we are shed of the fair lady."

Minchen thanked him. "Of course if you like I can leave right away!"

Sommer left the podium, feeling good about how he had managed the official business. Now he shifted to the social part of the evening, where he was very much in his element.

"My lady," he said, looking at her yearningly, "a person would have to have a dustbin instead of a heart if he were to wish to be shed of you. We are warmhearted people. We beg you to stay." He gently pulled her farther into the room and led her to a nearby seat.

Everyone roared enthusiastically.

"Sommer!" someone called out.

"Yes?" he asked, alert.

"Sommer, you belong in a cabaret!"

Sommer wanted to know why.

"It's obvious," the others called out. "You're a real bundle of laughs!"

Sommer smiled humbly. He stepped over to one of the younger members seated next to Minchen, grabbed him carefully by the lapel, and hoisted him out of his chair. "Find another one, Erne. I can't do any more walking, my legs hurt." The member complied.

Wilhelm had laughed as he listened to Sommer's speech. Everything had gone as he had thought it would. He knew Sommer, after all. He picked up another chair and placed it between Minchen and the chairman. "Prior rights," he said, by way of excuse.

Minchen Lindner protested. "That's a good one. I've known him all of ten minutes and he's already making some claim about prior rights."

Wilhelm contradicted: "It's been at least half an hour."

Sommer banged on the table. "This isn't a love nest, you two, but the 1929 Liederkranz. So perhaps wait with your declarations and don't make me jealous."

"Let's sing something," someone suggested.

Sommer stood up. "Gentlemen, gentlemen, there's nothing like being in good spirits." With some ceremony he surveyed the room. "Let us sing the beautiful song 'Im Grunewald ist Holzauktion.' All those opposed, keep your mouth shut."

No one was opposed. They all stood up, as if on cue, and began singing the popular folk song. After the first verse, everyone looked at Sommer.

He finished the song by himself. "Yes, those were good times, back then I was a real powerhouse, I weighed two hundred pounds," he said when he was through. He sounded melancholic.

Wilhelm stood up. "Chairman Sommer," he called out loudly. "Gentlemen. For today's celebration and in honor of our worthy guest, allow me to present to you my latest lyrical endeavor. I would like to point out that I'll be singing, in case that might go unnoticed in all the excitement."

Everyone looked at him respectfully. Wilhelm's way with words was almost as good as Sommer's. Many were convinced that he, too, should someday lead the Ringverein.

Wilhelm began his performance, which he accompanied by telling glances at Minchen, who listened intently.

> *I am always with you,*
> *yes it is true:*
> *always with you*
> *is loyal Lou.*
> *The days come and pass away*
> *and still, darling, I say*
> *each and every day*
> *these words of dismay:*
> *"Why out of all places*
> *am I in Berlin?*
> *Why out of all places*
> *is she in Stettin?"*
> *I write her every day*
> *and tell her of my pain.*
> *She answers every day*
> *but never boards the train.*
> *She writes lovely letters*
> *asks why I call at night*
> *very long letters*
> *she's not sleeping right.*
> *"Why out of all places*

am I in Berlin?
Why out of all places
is she in Stettin?"
I'm robbed of my sleep
my yearning's so deep
I'm drinking no more
for my heart is so sore!
I am always with you,
yes it is true:
always with you—
your loyal Lou.

Everyone applauded.

Only Sommer said, rather callously, "Hearing you sing is enough to make my hair stand on end. Your baritone sounds like the toilet in my old apartment. Thank God I moved out!"

But his comment was drowned out by the storm of questions addressed to Wilhelm.

"Did you compose that yourself?"

"Is there a way to get a copy?"

Finally one of the older men said, "Don't be so full of yourself. What kind of nonsense is that? It's ridiculous. The man's name is Wilhelm, and all of a sudden he's calling himself Lou. And I know Stettin. What a dreary place. There's absolutely nothing going on there!"

Wilhelm responded energetically. "Good God! Are you all so stupid? I don't have any girl in Stettin. That's only on account of the rhyme! Don't you get it? Only on account of the rhyme!"

Sommer nodded. "I get it all right! Just don't come up with the idea of rhyming *Ringverein* with *dirty swine*. Or I'll get really nasty!"

The poet returned to his seat, and Sommer jumped up. "The chair wishes to confer upon Handsome Wilhelm a special distinction. Handsome Wilhelm is hereby appointed to the position of Club Poet. Henceforth he is to pay double dues. Long live Handsome Wilhelm!"

Everyone joined in with their approval. "Long live Handsome Wilhelm!"

Sommer plopped down heavily into his chair. "I've heard that poets like to buy a round of beer. What do you think of that, Wilhelm?"

"Good God," he grumbled. "Not only am I expected to write poems but I'm to cover the bar tab as well. You must be out of your mind!"

Minchen consoled him. "Forget it, Lou, let me help out. Gentlemen, allow me to take care of the next round!"

Sommer pretended to object. "By no means, dear lady, by no means. But if you insist. If you really want to, as you say, I won't stop you."

A young man stood up and rang for service.

Wilhelm asked for a moment's quiet. He had something more to say. "You're all talking rubbish. Try writing a poem yourself. You think you have the wits to churn out something for fifty pfennig? You'll see you don't. The only thing you're absolutely fantastic at is talking rubbish."

A few of the more serious members shrugged in indignation.

"Well, well," one of them said. "Getting a little full of yourself, are you? Looks like your own wits might be overtaxed."

Wilhelm jumped up, ready to fight. He was more than a little upset by the criticism of his poem.

The unhappy listener also jumped up, and the two men started toward each other.

Sommer decided it was time to intervene. "Attention everyone," he said. "I'd like to point out that if chair legs are used in a fight, we decline to hold the proprietor responsible, and so if any material damage should ensue, you'll have to answer to me. If however we should wind up with a corpse or two, we'll simply sing the beautiful song 'O'er All the Tree-tops Is Now

Quiet.' This is not a sport club!" he bellowed once again. "We are a singing club! We are the 1929 Liederkranz, and don't forget that, gentlemen!"

Minchen, too, had stood up. "I have no interest in fistfights. I'm leaving."

Wilhelm turned around. "You can't do that! Under no circumstances!" He then faced the unhappy listener. "Right," he said earnestly. "We'll postpone our business! I'll pound my verse into your head another time."

The man sat down. "With all due respect, nothing against your poem. It's just your big mouth. You should leave that on the peg outside along with your coat!"

Wilhelm felt somewhat vindicated and satisfied. Meanwhile the waiter arrived, and Minchen Lindner placed her order.

She hadn't had so much fun in a long time. Admittedly, a large number of the faces didn't seem the least bit pleasant. On the contrary, there were some men there who Minchen couldn't bear to look at for long without feeling a little nauseated, even if she didn't have very high expectations. But "Dictator" Sommer decidedly gave the atmosphere something conciliatory and cheerful.

"I'm enjoying myself quite a bit," she told him. "I'll happily stay awhile longer!"

Sommer moderated his tone. "We would be delighted, dear lady! We'd be delighted, just not for too long. As chair, we must ask you not to stay for too long. Better at the next ball. Yes, as chair I insist that member Wilhelm Winter accompany the lady to the next ball."

Wilhelm said quietly, "That's not going to happen, Sommer. I'm getting out!"

Sommer finished his beer.

"What do you mean you're getting out? What are you going to do?" He joked, "The chair insists the Club Poet stay in the club!"

Wilhelm smiled. "I've had it up to here, Sommer. I want to have a job again. A real job."

Sommer cleared his throat. He felt constrained in what he could say in front of Minchen Lindner. "Real jobs aren't for song-birds like us." Then he whispered, "We'll talk about this later."

Minchen had listened to Wilhelm, surprised. "Do you have something lined up?"

"Unfortunately not yet. But I'll find something."

Sommer had doubts. "With faith in God and a few filched boards you can build a shed by autumn. Just don't take too long."

The beer came. "Long life to the gracious lady," Sommer said, raising his glass.

Everyone joined in. "Long life to gracious ladies."

Minchen laughed. "Aren't you a swell bunch," she said, almost as a tribute.

"Miss, if you should ever need protection, there's a place for you in my arms!" the man from Weissensee called out.

"Shut your mouth," Wilhelm growled. He placed his arm on Minchen's shoulder. She did not object.

"After you, after you," the other man said, backing down.

Wilhelm gave him a hard look. "I'll give you a couple right in the teeth," he offered.

Sommer laid his hand on Wilhelm's arm. "Wilhelm, I think you're looking for something, you're missing something. Just say the word, and Sommer will fix you up."

But Sommer was secretly annoyed. Handsome Wilhelm was apparently looking for a fight. Sommer, on the other hand, wanted to manage the club peacefully, even if he had to force the peace. Members of the 1929 Liederkranz weren't exactly prim and proper: On the contrary, they were quite free and unre-strained. And they didn't want to be restricted in their freedom.

"Wilhelm is regressing back to being a virgin," Herr Sommer complained.

Wilhelm said nothing. He realized that it was foolish to demand that the others change their attitude. They drank their beer, and the mood again became jovial. The men at the far end of the table started discussing professional matters.

"What's Kitti up to?" one man wanted to know. "Is she still working Hallesches Tor?"

"No." The man from Weissensee laughed. "Hallesches Tor is over and done with. Nothing doing there. She's strolling around Wittenbergplatz and Tauentzienstrasse."

Sommer cleared his throat. "We are a singing club! Perhaps the gentlemen would discuss business some other time!"

Minchen laughed. "Let them go on as far as I'm concerned! I know this Kitti, too! The tall blonde, right?"

The man from Weissensee nodded, surprised. "Only now she's a brunette. Dark hair is more *moderne*. But she used to be a blonde!"

The whole group looked at Minchen Lindner with interest. So she knew Kitti, too? Generally speaking, Kitti only associated with colleagues. So this girl was in the trade herself!

Wilhelm Winter was deeply saddened. He had believed that Minchen Lindner was something else, something more respectable, not a prostitute.

"And where do you do your strolling?" Sommer wanted to know.

Minchen was slightly offended. "I don't do my strolling anywhere!" she corrected.

"Pity," Sommer lamented, but he didn't entirely believe her.

The men now assailed her with questions. Did she also know Bertha from Halensee? The one with the false teeth? They shouted out any number of names, but Minchen didn't know them. The prostitutes in Berlin numbered in the tens of thousands. How could Minchen know every one? That was impossible.

But she did know Kitti, because Kitti was somewhat famous. She was much in demand, as her earnings showed. She was the former girlfriend of a Berlin celebrity, as she mentioned to anyone who wanted to know and also to those who didn't. Kitti had striking features: big green eyes and a very small mouth.

"Kitti always brings in good business," the man from Weissensee said, in answer to the man who had first asked about Kitti.

"She constantly has clients from the province. But they pay! I wouldn't believe it myself, but I see it. She can turn a hundred marks like nothing, and in these bad times."

Sommer shook his head. "That's hard to believe. A hundred marks! I'd like to have that girl myself!" Sommer had more mature ladies who brought in less revenue.

The man from Weissensee felt personally flattered. He talked more about Kitti, and everyone, even Minchen, listened intently. Only Wilhelm was less interested. So she's no longer in the business, he thought.

In Berlin there were young women on the streets, and there were old women. Walking down Friedrichstrasse in the evening, or along the Kurfürstendamm, it seemed like the whole city was on the stroll. But that was of course inaccurate, since many were in cars.

At this hour Berlin was already in bed or just getting up. Only the ladies of the night still had business in the city. But there were so many of them. They traipsed tirelessly and hopefully from one street corner to the next. They strolled back and forth along the same path, always hoping, always waiting, and seldom in vain.

Nor was it just women. There were men, too, out on the streets. The men intended to spend money and the ladies were resolved to take it. Neither had any reason to reproach the other and hardly ever did so. But if they did then it was the men who were eager to get away, since they considered themselves something better. They were gentlemen, after all.

The gentleman has his pleasure and keeps silent. But the ladies didn't always keep silent, especially when supply was so much higher than demand.

The ladies exhibited more self-confidence than the men. The men didn't want to be seen, while the ladies cheerfully greeted their acquaintances and chatted away. The men either had a bad conscience or they didn't, but in any case they weren't interested in running into acquaintances. They wanted to take their time choosing without being seen, to the extent that that was possible. The ladies on the other hand didn't choose; they solicited.

Perhaps it would be of interest, in this era of statistics, to look at two street corners over a decade and determine how many kilometers, how many thousands of kilometers, were covered on foot between eleven in the evening and six in the morning.

Wilhelm didn't think in statistics; his thoughts were more personal. He was glad that Minchen seemed to have changed her profession. Except he had a vague fear that she was still somehow involved, despite everything. He intended to ask her about it later.

"Shall we dance?" he asked.

Minchen Lindner was happy to oblige. She stood up. "Herr Sommer, gentlemen! This has been a feast!"

"The pleasure was all mine," said Herr Sommer. "Entirely my pleasure! I hope we will see each other again soon, dear lady!"

"Who knows," said Minchen Lindner.

Then they went out.

THIRTY-ONE

Frau Fliebusch had finished her dinner.

She had been hungry, very hungry in fact! She didn't exactly live lavishly off the ten marks that Fräulein Reichmann gave her. She could rarely enjoy a warm meal. The rolls she bought from the vending machines were hardly satisfying. To be sure, they filled the stomach and tickled the palate, and they temporarily evoked the illusion of being sated, but as the sole source of nourishment, they were decidedly not enough.

The stomach is a vigorous worker. A worker with neither soul nor understanding. It doesn't ask where food comes from or how it arrives. The stomach simply demands! Ruthlessly and ferociously! Hope and faith are beautiful things, but sadly confined to the spirit. The stomach relinquishes hope and is incapable of faith. All it wants is food, nothing else. The lack of sustenance, the searing sensation of hunger, is more powerful than a beautiful soul.

Hunger is the best cook, people say. But not only is it the best cook; hunger is also a splendid tranquilizer. People who haven't eaten for weeks are generally prepared to yield and admit the error of their ways. Opinions and ideas become pale specters if they can't be fed. A lack of nourishment rules out any display of strength.

People die, and their loss makes us feel as though we, too,

are on the brink of ruin. But one thing that doesn't perish from grief is the stomach. It shows up promptly and conscientiously and even induces committed suicides to set aside the rope and dig into a steak. The terror of the belly can compete with any other. Even Niobe would need to eat just to be able to keep on weeping.

Frau Fliebusch ate, and she did so with relish. Her tears kept coming, but tears cannot sate hunger, as even she knew. She was a vital, vigorous woman. Her body was stronger than her confused mind, which is why she kept eating instead of collapsing lifeless onto the ground as she should have.

The food tasted good. It had been such a long time since she'd had a warm meal. It was just a little too salty, but that could have been the tears. Frau Fliebusch stopped crying; her body said, "You can always cry later. It's harder to find something warm to eat." Her poor addled mind couldn't argue with that, so it kept silent. Meanwhile, her body was happy to eat the food that no longer seemed so salty. It tasted better and better.

"We still have three meals left," her stomach chuckled. Wilhelm will come yet, her soul consoled her. That's the way life is. Even poets wear woolen socks in winter. Aesthetic types can't escape the need to groom themselves, and even the most refined people snore when they sleep. Frau Fliebusch was no exception. The mind can take a break, but not the body, as long as a person is alive. She was still alive, and her body had no thought of dying. It wanted to live, to keep on living as long as possible. Now it was sated, so it stepped back, letting her mind and spirit return, which they did.

Fliebusch, she thought. Wilhelm Fliebusch. Why can't I find you? Why aren't you coming? Why do I have to search for you? That's not nice of you. Surely you can feel me searching for you, surely you can sense how much I need you.

The young girl who had earlier come to her aid passed by, along with the young man who had acted as if he too were Handsome Wilhelm. Frau Fliebusch wanted to thank her, above all for the food, but the young girl kept going. Frau Fliebusch watched her until she had shut the door. Young people, she thought, so happy and carefree, they have it good, they do.

Once upon a time she, too, had been young, eighteen years old. Back then she had met the law clerk Wilhelm Fliebusch. Handsome Wilhelm, the handsomest man in town. And among all the society girls, this handsome Wilhelm had chosen her to be his wife. Frau Fliebusch now relived each stage of her courtship and love.

She had never known financial worries. Her father had been a headmaster. He had earned what they needed, and money was never discussed. Amalie Kernemann was a well-brought-up young lady. First it had been important to get good grades at school, and later to find the right husband. And she had found him. A man like Wilhelm was certainly one of a kind. They had spent many happy years together.

How had it actually all come about? Everything went so quickly. All of a sudden life was in a state of flux. Everything had happened in rapid succession. Frau Fliebusch could no longer discern the events so clearly, no longer see the connections. She could reconstruct single moments without difficulty, but she was unable to place them in their larger context.

Music floated in from the hall next door, and feet were shuffling across the floor. People were dancing, she noted. Once upon a time she, too, had danced. And she danced well, according to Herr Fliebusch. She wanted to see it all again for herself, so she stood up.

A waiter came rushing out of the dance hall. He was carrying a glass of beer on a large tray. He placed it on her table and started to leave.

"Is that for me?" Amalie asked, amazed.

"Round for the house," he said obscurely, and raced off.

Frau Fliebusch sat back down. A round for the house? What was that? She drank a sip, but it tasted too bitter, so she stood back up.

All of a sudden she again felt disturbed. Where is Wilhelm? Where can he be? He has to come! Didn't someone say that? Yes—it was the blind man from earlier. The blind man! If she didn't find Wilhelm, at least she would find the blind man. He would know where Wilhelm was. He would surely tell her. She had to look for the blind man, and she had to look for Wilhelm! Or if she found Wilhelm, she wouldn't have to look for the blind man. But she had to do something! She didn't have time. She had to find her husband. Right away!

With hurried steps, Frau Fliebusch made her way through the big double doors.

THIRTY-TWO

———

The district judge was now enjoying the affair. Kummerpfennig had embarrassed himself, he thought. The lawyer had wanted to show him Berlin and wound up offending people right and left. Kummerpfennig should be glad that he'd had him by his side. In the future, I'll take charge, he decided, and then drank his beer. It tasted very good, and he was a connoisseur.

In the small town where he lived, he knew all the places with decent beer. Any pub or tavern that didn't tap a fresh barrel every day was worthless. Beer wasn't allowed to come into contact with air. At least that was the opinion of the judge, whom his friends considered the undisputed authority in all questions regarding beer.

"This is excellent," he praised. "The proper temperature and the exact right amount of oxygen."

Herr Hagen beamed. "The fact is I just bought a new device to control the oxygenation," he confided.

The judge wanted to hear more, and Herr Hagen explained the novelty. "Why don't you come with me and have a look yourself?" he finally suggested.

Suddenly Herr Doktor Kummerpfennig, too, was an enthusiastic expert. "Gladly," he said. "I'm also extremely interested."

The district judge chuckled and said politely to the group, "Well then, goodbye all around!"

"Go jump in a lake and stay there," Sonnenberg growled.

But he was shouted down. "How about another round, o enviable one?"

The district judged waved them off. After all, he didn't intend to finance the entire establishment. "Another time," he called out cheerfully, and the two jurists followed Herr Hagen to inspect the new beer draft machine.

The piano played a spirited march. The player was expressing his thanks for the beer and assumed the two men were officers.

Sonnenberg turned to Fundholz. "Are they gone?"

Fundholz set his glass down and stated truthfully, "Yes they are."

The blind man grinned. "So now it's time to deal with Grissmann!"

Elsi had regained some courage. She felt sorry for Grissmann: He had actually been nice to her. She placed her hand on Sonnenberg's shoulder. "Oh Max, just leave him alone, all right?"

Furious, the blind man shook her off. "You shut your mouth! I'll deal with you later! Be glad you listened when I called, or else things would be even worse for you. You and I will talk later! Just don't go thinking you can pull that off again!"

Elsi was frightened into silence, and Fundholz came to her aid. He also tried to keep Sonnenberg away from Grissmann.

"Leave him alone, Sonnenberg! That won't lead to anything. Grissmann isn't a bad guy. Let him go."

"So maybe now the idiot has something to say as well?" Sonnenberg asked, looking at Tönnchen. "Or maybe all of you will just keep your traps shut. This is my mess and nobody else's, and I'm going to clean it up all by myself!"

The brawny young man stood up from his table. Grissmann did the same. He scarcely felt afraid anymore, since he had the knife. I'll show them all right, and they'll regret it, he thought.

Sonnenberg now assumed the same stance he'd taken before the two men had arrived. "Let's go, Grissmann! Come here!"

Grissmann stepped closer to him. His right hand dangled limply by his side, while he kept his left hand in his pocket. The knife blade wasn't long, just eight centimeters, but he felt it gave him the advantage.

"Give me your hand," Sonnenberg demanded.

Grissmann's arm stiffened. His hand balled up into a fist.

"Well, come on!"

Sonnenberg's whole body was trembling with rage and agitation. He'd soon get his hands on this Grissmann. He was actually quivering with expectation. Let him feel the consequences. Let him taste what it means to try and pinch a blind man's wife!

It was no longer solely about Grissmann and Elsi; it was about the fact that Sonnenberg was blind and everyone else could see. It was about the fact that he had been wronged by life. No, not by life—by people. He had been forced to sacrifice his eyes. The others, the cowardly dogs, still had theirs! The others were better off—they could see. But he? He was forced to bear every indignity. He was blind, and he had to beg.

Begging when you could see, that was nothing. Nothing at all. But to be blind and have to live off charity! The slave of those who could see! Dependent on the friendly help and kindness of strangers.

Sonnenberg didn't want any help. He wanted to help himself and wasn't able to. He would have accepted any other misfortune. He could have been deaf or crippled or ill. Just not blind! Shackled as he was by his blindness, he was still strong, and his strength was straining against his chains. Grissmann, he thought, Grissmann, I'm going to tear you to pieces, I'm going to stomp you into the ground, you miserable louse, you swine with two eyes! I have a large account to settle, and you have to pay up!

Sonnenberg was gnashing his teeth with fury. "Let's go!" he roared.

So the man didn't want to? Was he backing out? Had the others reconsidered? Maybe they wanted to let Grissmann turn tail and run? Everything was possible, everybody was against him! The ones who can see stick together against the ones who can't! Of course, that's exactly what it was, they were afraid he might do something to Grissmann.

Then suddenly, finally, he felt a hand. "It's me," said Fundholz cheerfully.

Sonnenberg shook his hand off with contempt. "What are you up to now?"

Fundholz had shoved himself between Grissmann and Sonnenberg. He was no longer sober, which explained why he was willing to get involved.

"Ach, Sonnenberg," he said. "Why don't we simply drink the beer they've brought?"

Sonnenberg was irritated. The others laughed. The judge's round of drinks had just been delivered.

"Lay off with the beer and leave me alone!" Sonnenberg growled.

Once again he stretched out his hand expectantly. He felt something cool. It was a beer glass. Angrily he quaffed the beer.

Grissmann stood rooted in front of Sonnenberg. Fundholz generously offered him Tönnchen's glass. Grissmann drank.

Fundholz had had enough. He didn't want any more. He was standing on the razor edge between pleasant intoxication and severe drunkenness. The jolly old man was putting the others in a good mood. They were no longer so eager for a fight and wouldn't have minded if Sonnenberg had quietly sat back down.

But that was out of the question. Sonnenberg flung the empty glass onto the floor. "Let's get on with it!"

Fundholz stepped aside, frightened. People held him back so he wouldn't intervene. Grissmann placed his glass on the table and stiffened his right arm. The brawny waiter started struggling with him, trying to force Grissmann's arm upward.

Finally the waiter grew impatient. "Either you shake hands with the blind man, or I'll knock your teeth out!"

"I'll shake all right," Grissmann said quietly. He sounded

calm, almost benign, but his eyes had narrowed to slits. Now I'll show them. Now I'll show Elsi. I'll show all of them. I'm not afraid anymore! Here I am, just me against the lot of you, but I'll deal with every one of you. Everything was so wonderfully simple. All he had to do was use the knife, give the man a proper stabbing, and every problem would be solved.

The conflict with Sonnenberg was no longer some mere scuffle: It was a matter of life and death.

Grissmann versus Sonnenberg: the unemployed man against the blind one.

Here were two men caught under the wheels of life. They were crushed and crippled, physically or mentally. But the wheels lay outside their grasp and beyond their control. Their lives were what they were, and they could do nothing to change that.

They were on the verge of exploding, but all they could do was vent their pent-up frustration. And so they exploded against each other. Each now viewed the other as his mortal enemy. And all they could do was destroy each other. They could only free themselves from the strain they bore by annihilating each other—and that freedom would last only a second.

Just as two nations suddenly attack each other for no good reason and let themselves be drawn into a war that only serves the interests of people unknown and unnamed, so, too, there are moments when people give in to their destructive drives. But nations have many heads, many minds. And their conflicting interests give rise to complications and to a general reluctance that prevents many a war. Private individuals, on the other hand, are more apt to succumb to a single dominant urge.

If two states with their countless variety of interests can clash in such a violent manner, whereby millions suddenly view other millions as monsters, how much easier is it for two people to collide? Two people, whose means of existence is so tiny, whose joy in life is so minimal that the fear of losing it is easily pushed aside by their hate.

In such moments, the last thing on their minds is the law,

just as nations don't think about how many deaths are to be expected when they declare war. Grissmann and Sonnenberg were eager to go to war. They had exhausted their patience with their existence.

As a blind man, Sonnenberg had been punished for life. There are those who submit, and there are those who never and under no circumstances will put up with what they perceive as injustice or discrimination. Sonnenberg had been punished and unjustly so. He had experienced injustice on his own body, and his faith in any sense of fairness had been shattered. He no longer had any respect for the lives of others, just as he no longer had any fear of the law. Because where had the law been when his eyesight had been taken away?

He had come to understand that while pickpockets are persecuted, warmongering is perfectly legal. If it was morally right and even commendable in wartime to blind or kill someone, why should it be unethical to destroy the man who wanted to take his wife? Private murder is a matter between two persons, or at most just a few, whose interests have come into conflict. The genuine antipathy and antagonism of the combatants sets it apart from the mass slaughter between nations.

Grissmann had concluded that to succeed in life, one had to behave like a swine. This view was incorrect only because he was incapable of behaving like a great big swine. After all, little people and great personalities are held to different standards.

Quod licet Jovi non licet bovi. In other words, Jupiter is allowed to do things that an ox is not. Grissmann was neither Jupiter nor an ox. He was a little man, and for a little man, he wanted too much. His moral code may not have been entirely wrong, but his talents were too meager, and since he was unable to compensate for his lack of intelligence through might or money, he couldn't succeed no matter how ruthlessly he behaved.

So he turned to murder.

Before, it had seemed that this particular day was proof that his worldview was correct. Everything had gone the way he thought it would. Then all of a sudden came the unexpected. Sonnenberg had called out for Elsi, and she had listened. Once again the world wanted to see Grissmann squashed. He was expected to atone for what he had just attained. Once again everything was going to roll right over him.

He was innocent, he felt, because he had the right to act as he had. In his mind, there was no doubt about it. But did it even matter who was in the right? Hadn't the streetcar company fired him even though he hadn't stolen the money?

Grissmann was a simple man. He had yet to understand how much came down to the appearance of justice, and to the power at one's disposal. His thinking was primitive and straightforward. Right or wrong is immaterial: I have the knife, and he is blind!

Sonnenberg suddenly felt Grissmann's hand. With a wild burst of laughter, he pulled his opponent even closer. "Now I've got you, boy! Now I've got you! And now you're going to pay."

He grabbed his opponent's right hand in an iron grip and at the same time tried to sling his left arm around Grissmann's neck. Grissmann struggled to free himself. His left hand was in his pocket, clamped around the knife.

The blind man wanted to put him in a headlock, which is a little like a peace treaty where one party winds up kneeling on the chest of the other. The person on top wants to maintain the status quo, while his opponent desires change. This is what leads to the next war. As a rule, whoever was down last time is now resolved to win the next round. And this leads to the war after next. The headlock is an interim solution between killing a person and letting him live. Like all compromises, it is imperfect.

Grissmann was not a man for halfway solutions, above all if they were unfavorable for him. Grissmann was for total death—of his opponent, of course. He was just looking for the right moment! So he waited a few seconds.

Knife attacks are often unsuccessful. Especially when so many neutral parties are standing by, as was the case with Sonnenberg versus Grissmann. These unbiased onlookers wait until the fight is over and then side strongly with the victor, while showing compassion for the loser. They happily offer charity to the ones who were injured and new armaments to those who weren't. Their true task is to goad the warring parties to continue fighting and, in the case of nations, ensure they are adequately supplied with weapons. Neutral parties are neither for nor against a cause: They are simply for themselves, which is all they care about. Meanwhile they always have the proper point of view, precisely because they have none at all. Whatever the outcome, they claim it was the right one. As a rule, they saw it all coming and knew it would end that way. But they only say this after the fact, because they don't wish to offend with their opinion.

It's not only nations that espouse neutrality. People do as well. Neutrality is a pleasant condition that allows one to wax moderately enthusiastic about everything at little cost. Being neutral doesn't mean being cowardly but simply being prudent. That said, even neutrality harbors certain dangers. It's easy for the neutral person to find himself seated between two opponents who then join forces against him, or else the stronger first vanquishes the weaker and then turns on the neutral party.

The man is also neutral who witnesses a marital squabble with a friendly smile on his face and winds up with a chamber pot on his head. Of course he has already violated the first role of neutrality, namely to keep far away from the battlefield.

The warring parties, Grissmann and Sonnenberg, were surrounded by numerous neutral bystanders, who were protected from attack by either, thanks to their numbers. They called out fine words of encouragement and were enjoying the diversion.

Grissmann knew they would pounce on him the minute he drew the knife. But he was not afraid. His only thought was: How do I finish him off? He wouldn't have two chances. The first stab had to strike home. The objective of every warring party is to bring down all opponents in one strike. Humans are coming closer and closer to achieving this: The development of poison gas and the deployment of airplanes have made substantial contributions in this regard. It's only a matter of time before a resourceful chemist discovers a way to make air flammable, or else poisons the atmosphere completely and for all time. Such an innovation would secure peace once and for all.

Grissmann had an easier task. He only wanted to kill one person, and that was Sonnenberg. It would have been difficult to exterminate all blind people, just as it is difficult to eliminate every citizen of a state.

To date, the World War and the Inquisition have achieved the greatest success when it comes to large-scale eradication of humanity. It is to be expected that in the coming years, we will experience entirely new episodes of annihilation.

Grissmann's opponent was blind. If Sonnenberg had been able to see, he would probably have noticed something about his adversary. People who intend to commit murder are like tautly drawn bowstrings. They are highly concentrated and very much on task. All that is human fades back, and only one thing comes to the fore: the murder they intend to commit.

Just before the act, the idea of murder takes on a life of its own. Grissmann the human stepped aside, and Grissmann the murderer took his place. Grissmann the murderer did not know fear or weakness or cowardice. Grissmann the murderer knew only this: I will kill! I will kill my opponent now! And Grissmann the murderer only asked, What is the best, the quickest way for me to kill? For the moment that and only that was important. Everything that otherwise made Grissmann who he was—his weakness, his cowardice, his puny stature—all that was forgotten.

A man who has resolved to murder, a weak man who feels exhilarated, intoxicated by the thought "I can finish him off and I will"—such a man is so far gone that nothing else matters.

Sonnenberg wasn't clear about his own intentions. He raged, he hated, and he would have murdered as well, but in his case, murder had not grown into a firm commitment. He wanted to tear Grissmann to pieces, stomp him into the ground, destroy him, but he hadn't thought through the deed itself. He had not systematically played things out in his mind, had not envisaged the how, had not envisioned every single step.

Grissmann, though, had played things out. He had already murdered Sonnenberg in theory, before his knife even touched him. His pocketknife, which cost a single mark in the one-price store, with its eight-centimeter-long blade, was only carrying out what he had long before decided. And this small item, which let the plan become deed, this item that was, objectively speaking, devoid of life, became the agent of his loathing. The knife ruled the man.

Sonnenberg raised his head. His inability to see gave him near-superhuman hearing.

In a flash, Grissmann the murderer saw his chance, and he confidently steered the arm of Grissmann the unemployed. The knife came out of the pocket, and before the bystanders could cry out, it slashed across Sonnenberg's throat. The blind man lurched and let go of Grissmann. He tried to grab his neck, but his hands seemed paralyzed. Blood came streaming from the wound. Sonnenberg's mouth gurgled something unintelligible.

For a second, the blind man stayed erect, then he suddenly collapsed. He toppled like some lifeless, inhuman thing. His head banged against the floor before someone could spring to his aid.

People cried out. Women fainted, and for a second the men were transfixed. That was murder! Cowardly, underhanded murder! Murder of a blind man!

The whole thing had ceased to be entertainment, an amusing spectacle. It had become a crime. Who was guilty?

Grissmann the unemployed man, he was the murderer!

But they had put him there. They had dragged him up to the blind man. They had set them on each other, the murderer and the victim. They had staged a cockfight and were now outraged that one of the cocks had gotten serious.

The men crouched down by Sonnenberg. He was still alive.

He needs a bandage, declared the neutral parties, who had now taken sides. The side of the weaker, the murdered, but at the same time the side of the stronger, the state that would pursue the murderer.

Cloths were pulled out of every pocket. Many were dirty or well on the way to being dirty. While the bystanders looked for more bandages, the blind man was bleeding out.

When they at last had enough material, they didn't know how to apply it. The wound was too large. His neck needed to be stitched up to stop the flow of blood. The blade had not only severed the artery; it had also injured the windpipe. They called for a doctor, but there was none present. The music was still playing. The entire incident had taken only a few seconds and had yet to be widely noticed.

A worker who had taken an emergency course with the Red Cross began tending to the blind man, but it was hopeless. He wasn't dead, but he was dying. Air was whistling from his wound. Gurgling sounds were coming from his mouth.

Fundholz stared at the dying man, wide-eyed. He still didn't grasp what was happening.

"Stop the music!" one man shouted.

The piano player stopped right away. The dancers rushed toward the crowd. Throughout the hall, guests stood up from their tables and hurried over. Something had happened. They had to see what was going on. They had to get there before the others. Once everyone started crowding around, there wouldn't be anything to see.

One old lady pushed her way through. "Wilhelm!" she called out. "Is Wilhelm here?"

She saw the blind man lying in his blood. That was the man who knew where Wilhelm was. That was the man! She looked at the people standing around, her eyes wide open. She tried to bend down over Sonnenberg, but then she fell, unconscious.

Up to then, everyone had been concerned only with the blind

man. Elsi had turned a greenish white. She was still sitting and
did not move.

Maxie, she thought. Maxie. This was the only thought she had,
this thought reduced to a single word. The word that lay behind
everything that had happened. Sonnenberg and Grissmann—her
whole life—had taken an enormous turn, and the catastrophe
had come so quickly. The strong blind man had been felled by a
pocketknife.

Frau Fliebusch was lifted and placed on a chair. A woman
held her so she wouldn't fall again. She must be the dead man's
mother, the woman thought.

Meanwhile Grissmann was bolting away, followed by two
men. Grissmann the murderer was no more. He had been left
behind at the site of the deed. What was bolting away was a
human bundle: legs, body, arms, and fear! A terrible fear! Grissmann was still desperately clinging to the knife.

THIRTY-THREE

"Minchen," said Wilhelm. "Minchen, actually the name doesn't quite fit."

Minchen Lindner didn't answer. She was thinking about the Ringverein. She had imagined everything much worse than it was. As it turned out, pimps were also people.

Pimp—the word sounded vile. Being a pimp was much worse than being a prostitute. Of that she was convinced, but she hadn't found the men there all that bad. Sommer was downright nice. How had someone put it? A real bundle of laughs.

Minchen chuckled.

"Don't you agree? I'm right, aren't I?" asked Wilhelm.

"No. Why do you think so?" Minchen Lindner wanted to know.

Wilhelm repeated himself.

"Oh," she said. "So you think my name should be Josephine?"

Wilhelm held on to her more tightly.

"No, you don't have to be called Josephine, but you have to become Minchen!"

She looked at him, baffled.

"You're clearly a poet! I've been Minchen Lindner for a good while already, and now you come and tell me I have to become Minchen. Do you think I'm some kind of larva?"

Handsome Wilhelm grinned. "Who said anything about larva? I said nothing of the kind!"

Suddenly he leaned over her and kissed her. "This is what I mean," he explained.

Minchen Lindner eyed him intently. "You're not exactly timid, are you?"

"No, I'm not!"

They went on dancing. Finally Minchen said, "In that case, it's all good."

Wilhelm had thought up a beautiful, lyrical declaration of love. But Minchen Lindner's matter-of-factness caught him off guard, so that the intended words never escaped his mouth. For a moment he didn't know what to say, but then he didn't need to say anything, since Minchen spoke up for the two of them.

"My dear sir," she said, "it's very nice that you're pulling me so close, but it doesn't agree with me. My stomach happens to be quite sensitive."

Wilhelm turned red. "You're pretty cheeky."

"Cheeky is good! Did I kiss you? Well?"

Wilhelm couldn't claim she had.

"Shouldn't we stop with the *dear sir* and just use our first names?"

"Fine by me," Minchen agreed. She believed in dealing with matters promptly. And Minchen Lindner never pretended to be anything other than what she was. Otherwise she would probably have died of starvation and her gravestone would have stated, "Here lies a virgin who died because she remained one." Which is not to say that Minchen absolutely had to do what she did, but it comes pretty close to the truth.

Minchen had always been on her own: After her father had ceased being a bailiff, he had barely concerned himself with her. Many people who are on their own join forces. It's easier that way: You sing in the Salvation Army and others sing along. You join a party that's fighting the good fight, and others fight along. Because not everyone wants to sing or fight alone. Community offers greater security, at least so people imagine.

While it's all too easy for a single, young, attractive girl to escape hunger and hardship, some would prefer to jump out the window, break into houses, or forge signatures than sell themselves. Often they lack the courage or the talent to do so—that also plays a role. Many would rather starve to death than sell themselves.

If someone hires her, then she earns something; otherwise, she doesn't, which can also happen because of lack of opportunity. Opportunity and need lead to temptation, and only someone who is able to resist not just once, but always, has the absolute right to call the others shameless.

Minchen Lindner had not resisted, and she didn't regret it too much, either. Just like those who practice any profession, she looked for and found a certain moral justification for what she did. Not only did this remove any sense of shame, it practically elevated her line of work to something commendable. Besides, she was a free spirit and less corrupted by her profession than the prevailing morality would lead one to assume. Nor was she acting now as if it were the first time she had danced with a man. She wasn't one to put on an act, either for herself or for others. She took herself seriously but didn't think she was the center of the universe.

She's a nice girl, Wilhelm once more concluded. Not someone you'd meet every day. Wilhelm wasn't exactly shy himself. He was a realist and called things by their proper names, even though he liked writing poetry. Even his compositions tended to be realistic. He preferred a narrative that was to the point, since he was essentially to the point himself. For today he had overcome any impulse to wax lyrical.

From all appearances Minchen, too, was realistically inclined, so he decided to follow suit.

"Hey," he said. "Why don't we go somewhere?"

Where they might go, he didn't have to specify, as this suggestion sufficed to express his desires.

Minchen smiled. "First I have to check on my old man."

She detached herself from his arms and asked him to wait.

"I'll be right back. Stay by the piano!"

Wilhelm wanted to know which "old man" she had to check on, and Minchen explained that she meant her father. Then she made her way past the dancing couples to Court Bailiff Lindner's table.

Lindner looked very frail. He had managed to resume drinking beer, which threatened a second catastrophe at any moment.

Some people have a remarkable ability to discipline themselves. Inveterate drinkers, for example. Their tongue decides the beer doesn't taste good, their body resists every swallow, and their stomach rebels both privately and publicly, but they heroically continue to drink. The mind conquers the body: Their determination to drink is stronger than their physical resistance.

After all, it takes a lot of effort to subdue the physical aversion that keeps coming up and to carry on drinking so as to attain the summit of absolute inebriation.

Lindner possessed this capacity to a very high degree. The quantum of beer he had consumed had been enough to cause his stomach to explode, but it was insufficient to completely numb his brain. This was the purpose of his drinking, and he mortified his own body with jesuitical cruelty to attain his goal. The noble end justified the means.

He was just finishing another glass when Minchen showed up at his table. He swigged his beer with an expression of great suffering. Minchen had seen this before. Now and then the former bailiff had fits of melancholic weltschmerz, and then he had to numb himself. Today the loss of his former glory was weighing especially heavily on him.

When Minchen sat down at his table, he gave her a melancholy look. "The beer here is pretty bad!" he declared.

"So why are you drinking it?" she wanted to know.

"I have to," he said mysteriously.

Minchen didn't want to linger there for long. "I've brought you some money."

"How much?" her father asked, as he stroked his upper lip.

The loss of his mustache was something he would never get over, even if he lived to be a hundred. A mustache like that, nursed and nurtured over the years, cultivated from a tender youthful fuzz to the stiff bristles of the mature man, in time becomes a part of one's self. It had been the bailiff's coat of arms, and its loss was like that of a knight deprived of his escutcheon.

He had long been able to grow a new mustache, and someone other than the former Bailiff Lindner would have done so. But he had been unable to get over his first attempt. The embryonic first growth, when the mustache resembled a mown wheat field, had dissuaded him from further efforts. It was gone forever!

His time of authority was past, and so was that of his whiskers. An escutcheon can be patched up, and mustaches can be returned to beauty. But a patched escutcheon and a new mustache are always incomplete.

The loss of his social standing was tied to the loss of his mustache, and a new set of whiskers could not bring it back. So why go through the distress of trying? Why subject himself to the scratchy stubble?

For that reason, Lindner had contented himself with a smooth-shaven upper lip. When according to the prison regulations they had removed his mustache, it had been more bitter for him than even the verdict that had landed him in prison, because the prison officials all boasted beautiful, mighty beards.

From time immemorial, beards have been the privilege of the higher-ups. Earlier, when a soldier was promoted, in addition to higher pay he was entitled to wear a beard. While still a private, Lindner had secretly begun maintaining a beard. This had been graciously tolerated because his superiors were pleased with him. But once he became an officer, there was no stopping the growth.

Lindner attained his goal faster than the president of the republic, who was forced to spend sorrow-filled nights struggling with a mustache trainer so his whiskers could reach the desired height. Lindner's facial hair was even faster-growing and more luxurious than His Majesty the Kaiser's. His beard was exemplary, the finest in the regiment.

But now it was all gone, and that was more shattering for Lindner than the loss of his wife, who moreover had thrown him out. He didn't speak about it. He carried his sadness quietly within himself. But the feeling of being maimed weighed upon him.

Minchen was too modern to muster any understanding of the tragedy of lost beards. She had a good understanding of herself, and that was enough for her.

She gave her father fifty marks, and Lindner nodded in appreciation. That's how it was these days. A man had to let himself be supported by his daughter!

The sergeant—for this was the position of power that the future Court Bailiff Lindner, once so high and mighty, had achieved—was now living off his daughter. Clearly the world was on the verge of bursting apart. When bailiffs sat in prison like common folk, or when they, answering the need of the times, turned to thievery, the world was ripe to explode.

Lindner did not judge himself harshly at all. He forgot that he had embezzled money and accepted bribes. He only remembered how, out of the goodness of his heart, he had been slack in his efforts to impound certain items.

For this kindness he had been severely punished. For his empathy he had been jailed. His benevolence had destroyed him. He was convinced of that. He felt sorry for himself and considered himself a victim, essentially a martyr on the altar of kindness.

Today, however, his sorrows were especially great.

They had conducted a search of his house, because he had again been suspected of theft. They hadn't found anything, and he was in fact innocent. Moreover, he was deeply moved by his own innocence. They had rummaged through everything, refusing to believe his assurances. In the process, however, his landlady had discovered that he had a criminal record and was no longer a court bailiff, and she had given him notice then and there.

He was innocent and had been evicted!

The former Court Bailiff Lindner had been sent packing by some woman as if he were an ordinary person, a common tramp! That cut him to the quick, because despite an outward severity, Lindner was a softhearted person. Softhearted and full of understanding. At least for himself.

He had to drink to forget his misfortune. And just as conscientiously as he had drilled the new recruits in the sweltering summer heat of the barrack yard, he proceeded to drink himself into oblivion.

Minchen took her leave with a cool goodbye, but Lindner did not let that get to him. That was the way of the world. She was a young thing, and he was an old, broken man. He couldn't demand understanding from her. She was an ordinary person, but he was an extraordinarily unhappy one.

Such were Lindner's thoughts as he mournfully ordered another beer.

THIRTY-FOUR

Wilhelm stood beside the piano and watched as the man pounded the keys. It must be hard to play the piano, he mused; it was bound to require a lot of expertise. The man was reading the notes, adding sound to the black dots and bar lines. He was banging it out, as they said in Berlin, with uncanny accuracy. He was banging it out, but he was doing so nicely, Wilhelm decided. That must be hard, he thought again. That was something he couldn't do. He could whistle, but only from memory, not from notes.

In school they had singing lessons. As a young boy he had sung patriotic anthems such as "Heil dir im Siegerkranz," and later "Siegreich wollen wir Frankreich schlagen." By then the war had been three-quarters lost. Later he had sung working-class songs, such as "Brüder, zur Sonne, zur Freiheit" and others, but he always sang with more conviction than musicality. Nor had the 1929 Liederkranz done much to advance his musical education.

The notation he had learned in school was long forgotten. Back then he had also been less interested in reading music than in procuring potatoes. Now he regretted that. If he understood music, he thought, he could compose hit songs.

He envied the piano player, who was hammering the keys, his face bright red. In turn the piano player envied the dancers, who didn't have to plunk away every day well into the night. He was no genius, just a working student, whose modest musical skills paid for his studies. One thing, however, he had sworn to himself: Once I finally finish my medical studies and have my own practice, I'll never touch the piano again!

The piano player was plunking away to gain his freedom. By tackling the keys, he felt he was tackling his life. While he had hardly refined his skill in these past three years, he had nonetheless completed half of his studies. He wasn't playing any better than in the beginning, but he could now play by heart. He played as mechanically as a worker on an assembly line. The music producers churned out the hits, and even as he pounded their compositions onto the piano, he was carrying out operations in his head, performing cesarean sections and craniotomies.

The piano player had an open, pleasant face. Wilhelm would have gladly struck up a conversation, but he didn't dare. If I start talking to him, he thought, he might not be able to keep playing. Wilhelm imagined that playing the piano involved a kind of clairvoyance, and that clairvoyants, fortune tellers, and spiritualists shouldn't be disturbed, or it would bring bad luck.

I'll talk to him after he's finished or else tomorrow, Wilhelm decided. Maybe together we can compose a hit. Hit songs always make money. He'd read in the paper that a popular songwriter makes more money in a single year than Mozart had in his entire life. He didn't know Mozart but assumed the man had earned quite a lot, since the article had referred to him as "the great Mozart." Great people always earn a lot: That much he knew.

Then he saw Minchen coming and put music aside for the moment. With such a pleasant person as Minchen Lindner, even Herr von Sulm forgot about his business and how it needed to be modernized. Wilhelm, however, was younger and consequently more ardent than the business magnate. He ran toward her and again embraced her.

Minchen was in a bad mood, as she always was when she'd been with her father. She found him depressing.

"Are you angry with me?" Wilhelm wanted to know.

"That, too," said Minchen, sticking to monosyllables.

"Why?"

"You talk too much."

Wilhelm wondered what she might mean by that. She must want more action on his part.

At that moment a man ran past them. A man holding a knife in his fist.

Minchen gave a cry and shrank back. Wasn't that the man who had told her that her father was here?

The man's mouth was agape, and his eyes were wide open. A terrible fear showed on his face. He was flying through the hall, pursued by two men. The dancers mistook his fear for fury, so they nervously stepped aside when they caught sight of him. The man was racing toward the door. He was panting from exertion as well as fear. Leaping more than running, he crossed the tap-room in great, light-footed bounds.

The two men chased after him, their faces contorted as they uttered unintelligible words. One of them had a knife of his own, which he opened while he was running. The entire chase flickered by in a blur.

"Stop the music!" shouted an agitated voice.

The dancing came to a halt.

"I think he's gone berserk," Minchen Lindner whispered. She was shaking and snuggled up close to Wilhelm.

He put his arms around her to protect her, but the man had already left the hall, and everyone was rushing to a group of people who were excitedly standing around something.

"That man killed somebody," said Wilhelm soberly.

"How horrible," whispered Minchen.

"He bumped somebody off, I'm sure."

"He looked so horrible! Here he's murdered someone, and

earlier he tried to get personal with me." Minchen's knee was shuddering.

So that's what a murderer looked like, a real criminal. Nothing at all heroic about him! He was undoubtedly as cowardly as he was vile.

"How can a person just kill someone?" Minchen asked, horrified.

She had even spoken with the man. True, he had been an unpleasant type, but a murderer? She had imagined a murderer entirely differently!

"Isn't it gruesome how a person can suddenly turn into a murderer? I know him! He's the one who told me where my father was sitting, and he definitely wanted to dance with me, too. He seemed just like everybody else."

"Let's see what's going on," Wilhelm suggested.

They went over to the group. The crazy old lady was seated on a chair, with someone steadying her from behind. Minchen wanted to ask her what had happened, but the woman was unconscious. Then she spotted a man lying on the floor.

Wilhelm recognized him. "That's Sonnenberg!"

Minchen couldn't see because people were blocking her view. She tried pushing past them. But suddenly she was shoved aside.

Herr Hagen was thrusting his way through the crowd. "What's going on here? Is the man dead?"

A woman screamed frantically, "He's been murdered!"

Hagen winced. "Goddammit, that's all I needed. Can't people stab themselves somewhere else?"

Then he saw Frau Fliebusch. "What does she have to do with all this? Was she hurt, too?"

"Hardly," a man muttered. "She just fainted."

Hagen nudged Handsome Wilhelm and pulled him aside.

"Listen, go next door and tell them what's going on. I have to call the police! They need to clear out now!"

Wilhelm did as he was told. "Wait for me," he said, excusing himself from Minchen, then headed to the meeting room.

Hagen meanwhile set out on the difficult path to the telephone. This was the third incident this month. Hopefully it wouldn't cost him the concession!

The man who'd been blocking Minchen's view turned to leave. He had seen enough.

Minchen now saw Sonnenberg's face. It seemed to her that his mouth was still twitching. That was too much for her nerves. She started to cry.

I have to get out of here, she thought. I can't bear to see that face anymore!

She turned away.

THIRTY-FIVE

There are very few things that are truly once in a lifetime.

But there are two events that can be experienced only once: being born and dying.

A person is born without awareness. He is alive, of course, but he isn't thinking yet or at least not yet capable of connecting impressions and thought and putting them in context. Meanwhile a person who is dying doesn't relinquish his capacity to think as long as his brain is still able to function. Such a person is therefore able to perceive his own dying. This capacity to think may last only fractions of a second or it may last much longer, and physical paralysis or loss of consciousness does not necessarily progress hand in hand with mental decline.

Sonnenberg's death came very quickly.

Nevertheless, something must have been on his mind as he was dying. He tried speaking several times, but in vain. Presumably these were words of hate that were on the tip of his tongue. While alive he had been a good hater, and it was unlikely that he had loving things to say before his death.

The people standing around had watched in horror as the dying man tried to speak. But the words that served as a bridge between his brain and the onlookers had been taken from him.

In the moment of death, Sonnenberg's face had appeared extremely disgruntled. When his muscles slackened and the twitching subsided, a further change occurred. While he was alive, his eyelids had covered his eyes, which had died years before. Now, in death, they sprang wide open. The corners of his mouth were turned down, giving his face a pained expression.

His spirit had undoubtedly passed more quickly than his body, although his actual death had only occurred just as Minchen Lindner caught sight of him.

Fundholz had witnessed every phase of Sonnenberg's dying. Purely on instinct he was not inclined to believe in a higher justice, nor did he conceive of life as something especially valuable. But even for someone who had often witnessed it, death was still startling. Provided he wasn't completely desensitized.

Fundholz may have been quite desensitized to life, but never before had he been so aware as he watched someone die. Never in his life had he experienced each stage of dying as he did with Sonnenberg. As he studied the face of the blind man, it was as if he were seeing beyond it, as if it wasn't Sonnenberg wrestling with death, but he himself.

Fundholz didn't say anything. He was unable to. But he was thinking as he had rarely ever done.

So that's how it is. A person dies, but he's still alive while he's dying. Fundholz had never thought about what might lie between life and death. You were alive, and then you weren't— that was what he'd always thought. But now he felt there was something else between those two states. Dying didn't just entail the external physical process, which left behind nonliving flesh. It was also about some driving force, a life spark that was extinguished.

And it was this act of extinguishing, this state between light and dark—at once so brief and so long—that Fundholz believed to have felt in his own body as he witnessed Sonnenberg's death.

He was an old man and therefore closer to death than young people. He had long ago accepted the idea that the day would come when he would no longer exist. So for him, Sonnenberg's dying was different from what it was for most of the people who were still standing around the blind man. For them it was a disturbing incident, but for Fundholz it meant more: He was struggling to grasp the entire concept of dying.

His was not a complex mind, which was why this experience could occupy him so completely. He did not hugely mourn Sonnenberg. But as he looked at the blind man, he trained his thoughts beyond. And as he did so, the dead man kept him firmly in his grip. Fundholz was trying to comprehend the elemental force of death, even though his brain was not equipped, or no longer equipped, to deal with such difficult thinking. So it was hard for him, and his thoughts were not pleasant. Nevertheless, he went on thinking, thinking so hard he felt his head would explode.

Tönnchen poked him. "Tönnchen wants to leave," he whined.

Fundholz turned around, as if released. The thoughts of dying had vanished. Only the thought of Sonnenberg was left. But he was able to get past that thanks to his life philosophy, which stated: The less you think about things that can't be changed, the better and easier it is to get over them.

THIRTY-SIX

Grissmann's courage had lasted only as far as his knife had reached and ended when the deed was done. After he had withdrawn the blade, he realized that he was a man who had destroyed his life. A man who was still alive but standing under the blade of the guillotine. Only after he had committed the deed did he see the consequences.

The murder was easy, but the aftermath proved difficult. Just after he pulled the knife across the blind man's throat, he felt a surge of fear that this could result in his own death. And just as he had believed he could solve all problems with a slash of his knife, now, in the wake of the deed, he believed his life lay in the swiftness of his legs.

Men who easily trample on the lives of others, who easily take another person's life, generally harbor an all-encompassing love of themselves. For them, every limb, every bone in their body is something sacred, valuable beyond measure. And what they love most is their own head.

Of course we don't always appreciate what we have until we're in danger of losing it, when what we take for granted is challenged. Grissmann's life was now being challenged.

And only now, when the deed was already done, did he recognize how enormously valuable his life still was to him. He was no longer pitted against Sonnenberg or even the guests at the Jolly Huntsman, but against all of civilized mankind. Society wanted to capture him, either to exterminate him or to render him harmless. His life lay in his legs, so he believed. And given the immediate danger, he forgot what lay beyond.

As he was fleeing through the Jolly Huntsman, the entire danger seemed to lie in his two pursuers. Faced with these two men, he hadn't given any thought to the police or other agents of society. And that was still the case, now that he had reached the street. Still running, he turned around and saw that one of his pursuers was also brandishing a knife. Grissmann's fear increased even more. He was afraid the man would kill him without further ado. From then on he only looked ahead.

I'll outrun them, he thought with steeply rising optimism. But behind him they were crying, "Murderer! Stop him!"

Grissmann winced as though he'd been whipped. His fear became more desperate. Just don't die. Survive at any cost!

If he knew that he'd just be sent to prison. But it was equally possible they'd take his head. They were bound to condemn him to death!

None of them understood him. If they catch me, I'll have to die. They can't catch me! Run, run, I have to run a lot faster! And anyone who tries to stop me will have to answer to me!

People stopped. They heard the wild shouting behind Grissmann, but they also saw the knife in his hand. No one wanted to risk his life. What were the police for?

A car caught up to Grissmann, passed him, and then braked ten meters ahead of him. The driver jumped out and ran toward him. Grissmann held up his knife, ready to defend himself. The man stepped aside and let him go.

Grissmann raced ahead. Then he felt something hit his lower back. He stumbled, fell, and dropped his knife. The man had thrown a wrench at him, and then he caught up and wanted to overpower him. But Grissmann no longer resisted.

The other pursuers came up. The driver handed Grissmann over, and they took hold of him.

"I'd like to be there when they take your head off," said one. Grissmann howled.

The men, still panting, spoke with the driver and told him what had transpired.

"Well, how about me? Do I get a reward?" he asked coolly.

He gave the men his name, and for a moment considered whether he should give Grissmann one more kick, but he didn't. He climbed back in his car and drove off. Then he immediately phoned all the papers and told them about the murder and how he had caught the murderer. Each of them promised to pay him something. Afterward he drove home, feeling quite pleased. He wouldn't have to drive his cab anymore that night. He had earned enough.

Grissmann, however, was dragged back to the Jolly Huntsman, where they intended to hand him over to the police.

THIRTY-SEVEN

Wilhelm yanked the door open. "Everybody scram!" he yelled. "Someone was just bumped off here! The police are on their way!"

Everyone jumped up, excited. Sommer immediately grasped the situation. "Quiet!" he shouted. "Whoever hasn't paid for his beer can pay me tomorrow morning. I'll pass on the money.

"Don't leave the room all at once! Exit one at a time! Winter, go outside right away and see if there's a police car in front. Everyone who's leaving the tavern, make sure you make it out of the district! They will probably conduct a raid to find the perpetrator. If anyone should get detained, remember: No statement until you've spoken with the lawyer! That especially applies to anyone the cops might be after for some outstanding business. We haven't seen a thing! We don't know anything! We are a singing club! Anyone who can't keep his mouth shut will have to answer to me!"

Wilhelm returned. "All clear," he stated.

The club members left the establishment, one by one, through Hagen's door, and vanished in the side streets. Only Wilhelm didn't leave, despite Sommer's order. He wanted to find Minchen. Sommer yelled at him in vain before leaving, as the last of the group, with a spirited swear word on his lips.

Wilhelm went back to the dance hall and found Minchen

standing in front of Frau Fliebusch, crying. The dead man had upset her, but it was less sympathy for Sonnenberg and more revulsion at what had happened, at how unromantic the crime was, since there was nothing remotely romantic about the murderer.

She could see how sordid it all was. The murderer who had rushed past her. The vile stench of cowardice that hovered over the deed.

She had seen the tall heavy man lying in front of her, the man who had been murdered by this weakling Grissmann only because he had the misfortune of being blind. Otherwise, she was convinced that the murdered man would have dealt with the murderer.

Frau Fliebusch came to. "I want to ask the blind man," she said quietly.

"He's dead," said Minchen Lindner.

Frau Fliebusch objected. "I wouldn't have expected that of you, that even you would join up with the liars. Pfui!"

Minchen Lindner tried in vain to explain that she had meant the blind man, but Frau Fliebusch wasn't listening.

"Everybody lies," she said, aggrieved. "Every single one! But that doesn't matter! I'll find him anyway! I will look for him, and I will find him," she promised. She had already forgotten about the blind man. She left the hall and turned around when she reached the door. "Wilhelm is alive," she called out in a firm voice. Then she strode through the taproom, her head high, and out onto the street.

Frau Fliebusch had recovered her battle cry and her life program. She had her mission. As long as she believed in that, she felt her life had purpose. This day and all the incidents that had interfered with her life were overcome. "Wilhelm is alive."

Handsome Wilhelm had watched the old lady's excitement and her powerful exit with amazement. Now he turned to Minchen Lindner. "You're crying," he determined. Minchen didn't answer.

"Why are you crying?" he wanted to know.

She glared at him. "I'm not crying at all," she claimed.

But she was still crying.

Wilhelm pulled her away. "Come, let's go. We can't bring the dead back to life. And we'll have trouble with the police if we stay any longer. They're bound to be here in a minute."

"You're a brute," she stated, but went with him.

When they were out on the street, Wilhelm took out his silk handkerchief and wiped her tears. She took it from him and snorted into it.

She tried to smile but was unable to. Her self-assurance, which otherwise never left her, was gone. She didn't feel on top of things at all, but rather more sniveling and sorrowful than ever before.

Wilhelm consoled her. "It's all pretty bad, but there's nothing we can do to change it."

Minchen flared up. "Pretty bad? No—it's a nasty dirty disgrace! Just think: stabbing a blind man. A blind man!"

Then they kissed.

Wilhelm spoke, almost mechanically: "Shall we get married? Then together we can be done with all the filth?"

Minchen answered, "I have seven thousand marks. We could open a grocery store."

THIRTY-EIGHT

No one concerned themselves with Elsi. Minutes had passed since the blind man had died, and Elsi was still sitting there without saying a word, staring at Sonnenberg. He was dead, that was beyond any doubt. Sonnenberg was dead. Grissmann had stabbed him.

From one minute to the next, the blind man had gone from being both her terror and her provider to a pile of unfeeling flesh. Elsi's capacity for thinking was limited, but she immediately realized the consequences of this death. If Grissmann hadn't been such a shady character, she would have left the blind man, and everything would have turned out differently. Or, if she hadn't met Grissmann at all that morning, none of this would have happened.

Certainly she bore some of the guilt. She was the cause of the disagreement, the reason for the conflict that had led to a murder. But that wasn't what was oppressing her. It was not so much Sonnenberg's death per se as the impact it would have on her life.

Once again she would have to wander the streets at night, searching for men. Men who she knew would be unfriendly and mean to her, who would treat her like some poor-quality merchandise, like some used consumer good. Whole nights strolling the streets, often in vain. With hunger in her belly and a frozen smile on her face. Everything was starting all over. Her old life was finished.

Once she had been able to choose between two men, between Grissmann and Sonnenberg, and she chose the wrong one. Sonnenberg was dead. For him, everything was finished, but she still had years ahead of her. Endless years trolling for men.

Elsi had stopped thinking about what had happened. The blind man was dead. His brutality and meanness but also his providing for her were all in the past. Ahead lay her old life, which she'd been able to escape thanks to Sonnenberg.

She had stuck with the blind man so as not to have to go back to that. She had put up with his beatings and mean tricks so as not to have to return to the streets.

Then Grissmann had appeared.

When she saw him, she had thought she might be able to improve her lot. Perhaps, she thought, there might be a better man than Sonnenberg, even for a woman like her. That had been her mistake.

She hadn't loved the blind man. She had never loved anyone. She had always been in need and had always hoped to improve her lot. Sonnenberg had been the only person who, in rare moments, had treated her like a human being. But his occasional kindness, which she had never really understood, had always been followed by even greater brutality. She had been a slave. But she was better off as Sonnenberg's slave than surviving on her own.

She had wanted to find a new master. One who wasn't so cruel, one who would beat her less. She had never even imagined that someone would truly love her: It was enough for her to be treated decently. And she had believed that Grissmann would treat her decently.

But then she'd felt this fear that Grissmann would turn out to be just as mean as Sonnenberg, or even worse, that he might abandon her. She hadn't wanted that. She would rather be beaten than have to return to the streets.

She had lost the courage to go on. The foolish hope she had placed in Grissmann had cost Elsi her last refuge. Now I have to go back to the streets, she thought, and she found this thought sadder than if a dozen people had been murdered in her presence.

Her life stretched out before her, so gray that she had no sympathy for other people's tragedies or misfortunes. For her, Sonnenberg had been valuable in one way only: as the man who had saved her from the streets. Now he could no longer do that. Sonnenberg was dead, Grissmann was being hunted, and Elsi was once again all on her own.

THIRTY-NINE

—

Fundholz saw the homicide squad car come to a halt. Now they're going to detain me, he thought. He had broken away too late, because he'd spent too much time brooding. Now they would grab him and perhaps never let him go.

The men climbed out and headed for the door. Fundholz was standing close to the entrance, riveted to the ground. He didn't dare leave. If I go, it will look suspicious, he thought, and if I stay, they will detain me.

This streak of bad luck. This disgusting streak of bad luck would now even cost him his freedom. He was again completely sober. Sonnenberg's death had been like a cold shower that released him from his alcoholic fog.

The men went past him. The first looked him briefly in the eye and asked, "Were you there? Did you see or hear anything?"

Fundholz had enough presence of mind to say, "No, we're just waiting for a friend. He went inside to fetch some cigars."

The man nodded and went on.

Fundholz poked Tönnchen who was sleepily smiling away. Both started to move. They turned into a side street, and Fundholz suddenly began running, for the second time that day, but just as quickly. Tönnchen followed, wheezing. After a while he stopped. "Tönnchen is stopping," he called out.

Fundholz turned around. "Come on," he said. "They want something from us."

The fat man smiled mischievously. "Tönnchen is hungry!"

The old man went back and grabbed him by the sleeve. "Let's go. We'll eat later."

Tönnchen obeyed.

Fundholz no longer felt any fear. He was out of reach of the police. The streak of bad luck is over, he thought. And he had actually gotten off easy.

As the two men walked next to each other, Fundholz was suddenly overcome with a feeling of joy. Perhaps it was the schnapps, or perhaps it was relief.

He pinched Tönnchen in the arm.

"The two of us," he said, nothing else.

Tönnchen smiled.

ACKNOWLEDGMENTS

This translation was greatly helped by a residency at MacDowell, for which I remain thankful.

I am especially grateful to Sara Bershtel for steering me to this project and so many others, for her keen editorial advice, and above all for her friendship.

Philip Boehm

MORE FROM THIS AUTHOR

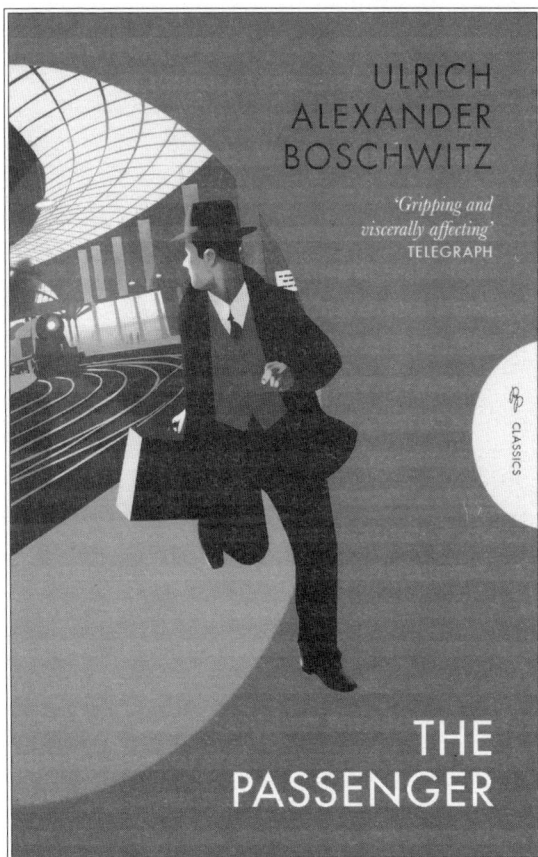

ULRICH
ALEXANDER
BOSCHWITZ

'Gripping and
viscerally affecting'
TELEGRAPH

CLASSICS

THE
PASSENGER

AVAILABLE AND COMING SOON
FROM PUSHKIN PRESS

Pushkin Press was founded in 1997, and publishes novels, essays, memoirs, children's books—everything from timeless classics to the urgent and contemporary.

Our books represent exciting, high-quality writing from around the world: we publish some of the twentieth century's most widely acclaimed, brilliant authors such as Stefan Zweig, Yasushi Inoue, Teffi, Antal Szerb, Gerard Reve and Elsa Morante, as well as compelling and award-winning contemporary writers, including Dorthe Nors, Edith Pearlman, Perumal Murugan, Ayelet Gundar-Goshen and Chigozie Obioma.

Pushkin Press publishes the world's best stories, to be read and read again. To discover more, visit www.pushkinpress.com.

THE PASSENGER
ULRICH ALEXANDER BOSCHWITZ

TENDER IS THE FLESH
NINETEEN CLAWS AND A BLACK BIRD
THE UNWORTHY
AGUSTINA BAZTERRICA

SOLENOID
MIRCEA CĂRTĂRESCU

THE WIZARD OF THE KREMLIN
GIULIANO DA EMPOLI

AT NIGHT ALL BLOOD IS BLACK
BEYOND THE DOOR OF NO RETURN
DAVID DIOP